In the midst of the cold war, the CIA's finest and most fatal female agent, Diana Riley, vanishes. Kidnapped by the KGB and taken to the backcountry of North Carolina, she and her team of unsavory partners are forced to undergo illegal experimentation.

But, when the experiments leave them horribly deformed and unable to reenter society without someone crying monster, the previously glamorous and high-maintenance spies must escape KGB captivity and avoid recapture at the hands of Nikola, a ruthless KGB agent with an intense and well-justified grudge against her former flame.

A NineStar Press Publication

Published by NineStar Press
P.O. Box 91792,
Albuquerque, New Mexico, 87199 USA.
www.ninestarpress.com

Seven-Sided Spy

ISBN: 978-1-947904-88-0

Printed in the USA
First Edition
January, 2018

Also available in eBook, ISBN: 978-1-947904-82-8

Warning: This book contains graphic violence and mentions of an eating disorder.

Seven-Sided Spy

Hannah Carmack

To Jean

Without whom they are only halves

Cast of Characters

(In Order of Appearance)

Tim Carroll, Codename: Dresden
Diana Riley, Codename: Hera
Da Vinci Moretti, Codename: Niccolò
Wesley Russ, Codename: Nikola
Rigan Hevel, Codename: Marco
Ruby Starr, Born: Robin Harrison
Roderick Walt, Codename: Gulliver
Sergei Durova, Codename: Kal

Postman

AUGUST 3, 1963 THROUGH AUGUST 30, 1963

Shortly after midnight, the mood in the Nightmare Café finally calmed down. Duke Ellington's "Warm Valley" spun out softly from a late-night telecast. Couples on the dance floor swayed and glided like figure skaters on air. Dresden sat stiffly in a red booth at the back of the place, a newspaper lay out in front of him so his watching would not look conspicuous. He admired the gentle crane of lovers' arms, the way eyes locked and spoke a language known only to two, and the faintest hint of a smile as it pulled at a woman's lips. The dancers stepped so carefully, as though nothing else in the world mattered, but Dresden's old-time fantasy cut out at the fading of piano keys and the familiar howl of Buddy Holly's voice coming from the radio as the dance floor flooded. Music like this was fine, but it did not captivate Dresden the way a ballroom waltz did. It was then that a woman's hand grazed the top of his shoulder.

"Come on, Dresden." Her voice sounded like honey, sweet and slow flowing.

He waited for the café's door to close behind her, before getting up and following her out onto the cold, barren streets of DC. He took one last glance at the dancing ensemble as he left.

Outside on 22nd Street, she waited. Her name was Hera, and she was a *goddess* amongst men. With cascading pin curls the color of wheat and full apple cheeks that dimpled when she smiled, she radiated beauty. Her laugh could steal hearts. Her talent was unmatched. But these facts made her no less parasitic to Dresden. When they were together, he did not offer any warmth or words. Instead, they waited in silence. The only acknowledgement of the other's existence came when the woman leaned back against a street-parked car and lazily held out a pack of thin cigarettes to him. Dresden considered the offer for a moment, but shook his head, deciding against it. She shrugged, lit one for herself, and continued to wait.

Finally, the man their evening hinged on showed up. He was short and scrappy-looking, with a swarthy tan and a sloppily tucked button-up. He came from the back of the café, talking to Hera and Dresden even though they were clearly out of earshot. Eventually, he got close enough that Dresden could make out what he was saying.

"And you two are just standing here like a couple of damn pariahs!" The man's face lit up brilliantly with a grin. Any tension between Dresden and Hera dispersed for the time-being.

"Are we good to go?" Hera asked. "Is everything done?"

"Good as gold, but not if you two keep skulking out here." The man turned to Dresden expectantly.

There was another lull of silence as Dresden stared back at him with a blank expression. Things were starting to get uncomfortably quiet when it dawned on him. "You have the keys, Niccolò," Dresden said. "That's why we're standing outside the car."

"Oh! Ha! Guess that means this one is on me." Niccolò snorted as he rummaged through his pants pockets, first pulling out some lint, then a bottle opener, and finally their keys. "There we go." He stepped around to the front of their car. It was a 1962 Corvair with a black exterior and cozily lined seats. "Let's book," he ordered as he slid into the driver's seat

Hera waited, not moving an inch until Dresden pushed the seat forward and crawled into the back. She never settled for anything less than shotgun.

"How did it go?" she asked as she climbed into the passenger's side.

"Well enough for the rookie team to take it back over." Niccolò turned the ignition and then pulled into the road.

"Isn't that keen." Hera sighed, obviously discontent. She rested her hand under her chin and propped her elbow up on the windowsill.

Niccolò spoke with an undeniable amount of sarcasm, "Clean-up crew not all you dreamt it to be, beautiful?"

"Don't you think it's just a little bit ironic? The CIA has only, what...six or seven female agents and one of them is stuck on cleanup. It's 1963! You think we'd be past this." Hera curved her lips into a warm smile. Niccolò and Hera shared a coy glance that was quickly cut short by Dresden.

"It is not ironic when the female agent put herself there in the first place," Dresden said.

Every muscle in Hera's face started to change.

"Honestly, I quite like it here," he added. "I was hoping we would possibly elect to extend our assignment." *Hoping* and *possibly* were added to create the illusion of choice. He had no intention of leaving the States again.

"The work may be easy, but it's unfulfilling, don't you think? We're making no difference here in DC. Your talent and fine attention to detail would be better utilized in the field." She spoke fairly, showing no sign of bias. "Besides, we're not even here on a certified assignment, Dresden. You know that."

There was a slow calmness about the exchange that set the group on edge. Niccolò tightened his grip on the steering wheel. White-knuckled, he cleared his throat. "So did you guys eat at the diner? Their pierogis were not that bad. I had this one filled with a raspberry coulis. Just heavenly. Delectable really. All that and more. The best pi—"

"Of course, I could not forget that, Hera." Dresden ignored Niccolò's plea for normalcy. "I know we are here on punishment. A punishment which was grossly short for the offense." Dresden turned his attention out the window so he didn't have to make eye contact with Hera, who was now fully turned in her seat and staring him down.

"What was that?" She offered him a chance to recant.

"Here, let me clarify," Dresden said with such a dangerous control that his voice did not once falter in staring down his superior agent. "I am talking about when you exaggerated your clearance level, took advantage of a security breach, and then pinned it on Niccolò and me. Now, to verify the aforementioned, I feel like three months' cleanup crew was a pretty lenient punishment."

"Man!" Niccolò shouted, trying to drown out the two of them. He banged his fist on the steering wheel. "Are we all still on this? Are we still arguing about whose fault the security breach was?" He sounded deceptively joyful. "Because you know what, we can put it on me and lay this whole argument to bed." Niccolò let out a wheeze of uncomfortable laughter.

"What Hera did was crooked, and she knows it." Dresden shook his head.

Niccolò cut in again, not letting Hera work a word in edgewise. "And when you steal from dukes and I lie to holy men, it's crooked, too, but we keep going. That's the job. Intelligence work relies on deception." Niccolò pulled the car over to the side of the road, sweat building up on his forehead. He leaned in close to his partners and made large exaggerated gestures with his hands. "I can't take you two aping out all the time. We are a team. An incredibly successful team, at that. Arguably one of the CIA's best teams. With one of the CIA's first and finest female agents. The breech is in the past. Let's just move on from it. I cannot handle being in the middle of you two, especially while driving!"

Dresden didn't allow an inkling of silence. "I can't see you like this, Niccolò." He turned to Hera. "Let me out. I'll walk from here."

"No, Dresden, it's fine. I'll drive us. I just want the situation here to simmer down before I start driving again, or we'll all end up in the hospital because I will have an aneurysm on the parkway, and that'd be a drag." Niccolò sassed, looking to and from his partners as though trying to solicit some kind of empathetic response, but they'd have none of it. "Anyway," Niccolò segued, "we just had a pretty golden mission back there and we did it as a *team*. We were all on board and we made something amazing happen because of it. Why don't we go back to that moment and get drinks or something? Celebrate a bit."

"I am just expressing my desire to stay in DC." Dresden unbuckled from his seat. "Hera, if you would please. I'd like to leave."

Eyes wide, Hera's glassy gaze turned to Niccolò. At first, Dresden didn't understand what was going on. Once he realized what she was doing, he was disgusted. She was waiting for permission. Like the thirty-some-year-old killer needed the go-ahead from her boyfriend-of-the-month to let him out of the car.

Dresden spoke again. "I will make you both move if I am not out of this car in the next ten seconds."

Niccolò ran his hands through his hair and relinquished with a sigh. "You may as well let him out." Niccolò dramatically collapsed onto the steering wheel. "Once he's set, he's set. That's just him. Such a Dresden thing to do. Go on. We'll see you in the morning. Same time, same place as always, right?"

Dresden smiled, although there was no warmth to it. "As always, Niccolò."

Hera opened the passenger side door, slid out, and then allowed for Dresden to step out onto the sidewalk.

As he stood there looking at her, luscious blonde curls blowing in the breeze, she spoke, "I do hope we can have peace, Dresden. Please understand that what's done is done, and all I did was the best I could. He's forgiven me. Can't you?"

"He couldn't be mad at you even if he tried," Dresden hissed.

"Because I won't let him?" Her face remained relaxed. "I am tired of having this same conversation with you, Dresden. You need to fall in line."

"I am tired of you manipulating and lying to get what you want, but it looks like we'll both have to settle for the night." Dresden gritted his teeth into a grin and then quickly turned and walked away.

As soon as he heard the Corvair pull back into traffic, it was as though a weight lifted off his shoulders and he could breathe again. He and Niccolò had been partners for five years. They'd spent those years together, successfully running missions, training new operatives, and climbing their way up the ranks. Working with Hera, nicknamed the Goddess because of her codename and notoriety, was supposed to be an honor. She was the best field operative the CIA had to offer. She had an irrefutably high success rate, but she brought an endless string of theater with her.

Dresden had to reset, switching his focus instead on the crowd of faces passing him by on the busy streets of DC's shopping district in order to avoid his own kind of aneurism. It was only after a minute had passed, that someone familiar approached. And although it took Dresden a moment to catch her attention, his face flushed red when their gazes finally locked. It was Ruth.

"Timmy," she called out, a big, toothy grin already on her face.

A wave of cool air hit him right as Ruth's voice rose above the crowd. Hearing his real name always provided him with a feeling of comfort and control. The people he hated called him Dresden. The people he loved called him Tim. He straightened up and stood still, looking for the twiggy little thing wearing some variety of in-crowd fashion.

Ruth swiftly made her way over to Tim and then greeted him with a big hug and a peck on the cheek. She was significantly shorter and a decent amount younger than he, so she stood on her tiptoes as her arms wrapped around his neck for a fleeting moment.

"How ya been, Timmy? Haven't seen ya in a few days." Her eyes sparkled.

A number of things drove Tim mad about Ruth. She had eyes that glowed with youth and hope, a laugh that filled the room with melodic dreams, and a swaying dance of a walk, but perhaps the trait he admired most was her kindness.

"Ruth," he said fondly. "I've been well enough. Things have been busy at the post office."

"I could tell." Ruth had an eager bounce about her. "I was watching when you pulled up. Was that the woman?" she whispered, her face scrunching in excitement. "The one who has been messing with your coworker's head? Because that looked like a *bad scene*."

Tim chuckled. "The very one," he answered. "But none of that. I just got my blood pressure down. How have you been, Ms. Ruth Lee? I haven't seen you around the mailboxes in a while."

"Oh, I've been staying with one my girlfriends." Ruth stiffened up. Tim could read in her body language that she was not only about to lie but lie poorly. "Just closer to work."

Tim raised an eyebrow, skeptical. "Something is troubling you."

"Ah, it's nothing really. Ronnie just hasn't written in a while and I'm worried. It's not like him to not write. So, I stay over at her place, just helps keep my head straight—" Ruth's voice dropped as her focus drifted from Tim's face to slightly over his shoulder. "That's her now, actually. She just got outouva picture and I was waitin' to walk home with her. Why don't we get together for a bite Tuesday, yeah? I can tell you everything over..." She moved her hands as though grabbing for some forgotten word. "Oh, what did you say they called fries overseas?"

"Chips," Tim mused.

Already, Ruth's thoughts seemed miles away from whatever she and her fiancé, Ronnie, had been fighting about. She waved her friend over.

"But, to answer your question, I believe we already had plans for Thursday. Would you rather we meet on Tuesday?" Tim asked.

"Oh, both." Ruth boasted. "This'll be a two-parter." She held up two fingers for emphasis. "I can just feel it. So, I'll see you Tuesday and Thursday at Dicks, yeah?"

"Sounds like a gas." Tim tilted his head just to the right enough to recapture her gaze from her friend. "I'll see you Tuesday and Thursday at Dicks. I'm heading back home now. Did you want me to grab your mail and slide it under your door?"

"Nah, it's all good. Thanks, though, Timmy. You're always thinkin' ahead." She pulled him into a hug and gave him another brief kiss on the cheek.

Tim waited for Ruth and her friend to completely vanish from his line of sight before starting toward the Upper East Side of town. He was farther from his apartment than he would have liked, but he couldn't take another minute in that car. Hera had changed Niccolò. There was no doubt about it. She'd changed everything about the dynamic of their team. It worried him, but he had to press on.

His apartment complex was only two blocks from the brightly lit and bustling historical district. Despite its promising location, the building was run-down. The basement windows were boarded up, and the call box looked like it'd taken one too many punches from a drunk's fist. There was always the smell of river water wafting on the air, and some variety of sinister character lurking around the front stoop. It wasn't much and it wasn't pretty, but their confinement to DC was only three months long. This was one of the few places that would rent for such a short lease. Occasionally Tim entertained the thought of where his partners might live. He imagined Hera living in a glamorous studio uptown with what she'd call a "posh" interior, and Niccolò living half his night in a bar and the other half in the back of the Corvair.

Inside the building's entryway, there were rows of beaten bronze mailboxes. The lighting buzzed with a fluorescent hum, and Tim thought only of going upstairs, making himself a cup of coffee, and reading. But first, he stopped at the mailboxes and unlocked one: Ruth's. He grabbed a handful of letters and flipped through them carefully, stopping only for one marked with an obnoxiously kitschy stamp and addressed with a heart. He put the rest of the mail back and then continued into the lobby's handprint-smeared elevator.

Three floors up, Tim slipped off his loafers outside his door and entered. Scattered around the room were boxes flooded with files. Decorating the walls, were scribbles of half-baked thoughts on torn page corners that were left all over like a secret code or madman's drabbles. Around the room's border, stacks of books looked dangerously close to falling. A small picture of younger, significantly happier-looking versions of Tim and Niccolò sat on the kitchen counter. Although there were plenty of places in the apartment that needed tending to, the first thing Tim did was sit down at his dining room table, which was made up of some milk crates and a piece of plywood. He smoothed out the stolen letter from his pocket and then opened it with an unmatched level of tenderness. He treated the letter as though it was a ritualistic piece of holy text.

It was addressed to Ruth, and it started *"Dearest, your silence worries me..."* the rest was all sweet nothings of reunions to be had and times long spent together. Tim read silently. An occasional smile crept on his face while going through the pages. Nothing pleased him more than the sap-laden sweetness Ruth and Ronnie shared, even if he was certain that it would have to end and he'd be the one to end it.

After a few read-throughs, he put the letter down and sat for a minute, letting all the words sink in. He then placed the love letter in a large stack of mail. Tim had been hoarding Ruth and Ronnie's exchanges for almost a month now. It was as he added the newest letter to the pile that something caught his attention from the corner of the room.

Tim jumped from his seat, sending papers from the table everywhere in the wind of motion. "Hera, have you just been sitting there?" He was more confused than upset. "How did you even get in here?"

"What did you just call me?"

The voice startled Tim. He thought it was Hera. He was positive that it had to be Hera, but this voice was not that of the goddess. This voice was husky and cold.

When she came into the light, Tim saw an operative he had never met, only heard of. She was an androgynous amazon; the corners of her face were delicately angular and framed by a short champagne-blonde pixie cut. Her eyes were that of an eagle, shrewd and prepared to strike at any moment.

"Not the goddess, but her paramour," he chided. "Nikola." Her name left his mouth as though it was a taboo word. "What are you doing here?" Tim could feel his thoughts racing from one point to another. How would a fight play out in this apartment? How many neighbors were home? Were these the types of neighbors who called cops? Could he handle the collateral damage alone? Did she have back up? He thought this all while maintaining his focus on her.

She tsk'd. "Not like you're living in Fort Knox here." No matter how much Tim tried to remain calm, it was clear that she could see his distress. "Calm down, Dresden. I'm here with a business proposal."

"A business proposal from whom?" Tim moved cautiously closer, knowing that under his couch cushions was a hunting knife, and wedged in between his collection of Brontë was a semiautomatic pistol.

"Paramour. Whom." She rolled her eyes. "Don't be so proper. I don't have the time for formalities. We still have two other agents to collect before the night is through. Short and simple? I'm with the KGB now. We want the CIA's finest thief for our own. Your options are to accept it willingly or be taken by force." Her sentences were curt.

"I can't imagine this to be true," Tim spoke uncharacteristically sweet and gave a boyish smile. "A woman of your beauty? Your stature? Your articulation? They wouldn't send someone beautiful as you here to collect a brute like me." Tim stepped closer to her, staring deep into her hazel eyes, his hand now hovering beside hers.

Her face went from calculated and aloof confidence to complete distaste. "Ah, my charm and charisma from just a second ago really convinced you, didn't it? Honestly, Dresden, we suspected you wouldn't come willingly. It's refreshing to see you're still a scumbag."

"Still into broads then?"

"Even if I wasn't, your act wouldn't have worked." She followed Tim's gaze around the room before speaking again. "Stop casing the room. We did a sweep. The overly decorated hunting knife is gone, as is your pistol. As well as the gallon of homemade napalm we found in your back room. What's the story on that?"

Tim went silent. He wanted to know how they found him. He blamed this all on Hera, of course. On his own, Tim was a spy of minor notoriety, known for his stealth and thievery, but nothing on a truly grand scale. What could he do for the KGB except provide access to her?

"I'm required to at least allow you to hear the offer before I beat you black and blue. So hurry this up."

"No, thanks." Tim smiled the same, hollow smile he'd given Hera earlier that night. "I have no interest in the KGB. I have no interest in being touted around Moscow and the Ukraine and all in its likeness, no interest in the reds, the ruskies. Unless your offer is a complete halt on the arms race and a peaceful, yet fair ending to the cold war, I suggest you look for your Judas elsewhere."

Nikola's eyes sparked with mischief. "That's all I needed to hear." She caught him off-guard with a sudden and abrupt swing at his gut, her fist driving into his diaphragm upon landing. Tim doubled over, and within seconds, Nikola was coming in for a second hit. He barely managed to dodge the blow. His entire body swayed as he attempted to regain his balance. He didn't bother mulling over options. He charged at her and sent her stumbling to the ground. She quickly rolled back to her feet and grabbed the nearest dinette chair. She swung at him. Head still spinning, he turned on his heel and let the chair crash against his back. Nikola held the remains of a chair leg. She jabbed it toward him. Tim spun around again and batted it out of her hand like a mother would a child. His face felt hot, but he was calm and focused. Taking this moment to regain his footing and his breath, he started to calculate.

"We don't have to fight," she taunted, raising her fists in front of her face. She peeked out from behind a few stray strands of hair, and in her eyes, Tim could see a dangerous playfulness.

He paused, partly considering the offer but mostly taken by her gaze. Women had always been Tim's weakness, but as soon as she showed even a hint of genuine hesitance in pulling her next punch, Tim bolted for the door. As he ran, he threw the plywood from his makeshift table up in hopes of tripping her, but she lunged over the lumber and instead tackled him from behind. She wasn't heavy enough to bring him down, so instead she wrapped her legs around his waist and locked her arm around his neck. He twisted and reached for her scalp in a controlled panic. Everything blurred as he lost oxygen. He slammed her back into the interior door of his apartment, but he could feel her grip tightening. He couldn't breathe, and he knew if he didn't think fast, he was likely to stop breathing altogether. Desperate, Tim threw himself to the ground, which gave him the chance to work his own hand in to pry her arm from around his neck. He rolled away from her and jumped to his feet, then ran for the door again. But as he touched the handle and pulled, nothing budged. Frantically, he jostled the handle, yanking it harder, but it still did not move. Something or someone was outside the door, holding it in place. Tim swung back around just in time to see Nikola climb to her feet.

Blood pumping, his head cleared. There were no more options but the fire escape. He had his target in mind and was ready to get the hell out of Dodge. He put his fists out and charged at her. She spun, dodged his strike, and drove a hand into her back holster only to come up empty-handed.

"Shit." She looked up to see Tim pointing her own gun at her. "You—" She was cut off by the crack of gunfire. It was a small pistol, but the noise filled the apartment. The bullet barely missed her. "A warning shot, swell." Nikola then swung for him. He quickly deflected and bashed her right temple with the butt of the gun. She ducked just a second too late as the grip of the gun smacked against her skull and a stream of blood started down her face. She groaned and plowed into him. She slammed her shoulder into his lower abdomen, causing him to drop the gun. As it fell, it went off, breaking through one of the poorly insulated walls.

Tim shoved Nikola off him, not bothering to swing at her. He was through fighting. He picked up the gun again and shot at her twice. She managed to stumble out of the path of the first bullet, but the second buried itself into her left arm, causing blood to fan out as it exited her flesh. She doubled over, letting out a groan. He shot again, wounding her stomach. She wailed this time. She was down for the time-being. It was enough for him.

He had her gun. She was on her way out. And more than likely, there'd be other agents coming the longer he waited. He'd rather save his energy and bullets for later. So, he made his way to his fire escape, careful to wipe off his sweaty palms before climbing out the window. He scaled the ladder as fast as he could and then landed on the pavement feet-first. Once he turned his back on the apartment complex, he booked it, and that's when he was shot.

*

Dead. It was the first thought on Tim's mind as he woke in nothingness. If he remembered correctly—and he always remembered correctly—he was definitely dead. He'd been shot, one bullet shattering a spinal column, another ricocheting its way into his chest, and another taking out his liver. That's when he hit the pavement of the alleyway outside his apartment. Of course, that didn't make sense. Since he was very much alive, conscious, and cramped in an air ventilation system.

Tim originally mistook his metallic-hell for the drawers in a morgue, but after a brief crawl in the darkness, Tim could tell this was not a simple drawer. This was a labyrinth of vents and ducts. He was on his stomach, confined and hungry but alive and feeling surprisingly well for someone who should be paralyzed.

He crawled through the vents, his movements were not aimless, but exploratory. For an easy escape, he needed to find an exterior vent. He kept going over the events of the night he died, the café, the car, Ruth, and the KGB agent. Her name had been Nikola, and although bits and pieces of the memory were fuzzy, Tim was pretty sure she had killed him, not with bullets but afterward. As he bled out on the pavement and tinges of pain sent his body seizing, he remembered her standing over him with long, graceful legs and a calmness in her eyes as she broke his neck. In fact, he was positive of it. He remembered trying to fight her off and the dirty copper taste of blood in his mouth. He tried to shove this unexplainable memory to the back of his mind and carry on.

After clambering forward for eight or nine minutes, and almost falling five feet into an underground vent shaft, Tim couldn't fight the questions and honestly, thinking about his unexplained death was easier than crawling around with no end in sight. He lay there, his face barely touching the bottom of the metal vent. He was still trying to figure out the different ways he could have survived the bullets, the injury, the pain, the bleeding, the healing. Based on how he felt, he imagined it could be months, possibly even years since he'd been shot. It was as though he'd never been injured. His back felt fine. His arm wasn't weak. But most importantly, he wasn't immobile. He lay there with just the dark as company while trying to figure out the how and the why behind the entire ordeal, but his problem-solving was interrupted by a familiar voice.

"Tim? Tim?" This sorry excuse of a whisper came from an outside vent. Someone was trying to be quiet but couldn't resist screaming out. Tim would recognize it anywhere. It was Niccolò —or Da Vinci, as Tim truly knew him. Since, apparently, codenames were no longer in use.

"Da Vinci," Tim responded. "Where are we?" Hearing his own voice was like listening to grinding metal. His throat was hoarse. Tim shuffled as fast as he could through the ventilation system toward the source of the noise. His heart pounded. He could feel it shaking his entire chest. "How did we get here?"

"We're at some kind of remote KGB facility," Da Vinci hissed into the vents, his voice painfully restrained. "I took care of the guards. Don't rush."

"So it was real." Tim spoke more to himself than to Da Vinci. "For someone who was shot five or six times, I feel fantastic."

Tim could hear a shift in Da Vinci's voice. Even though Da Vinci was a fine negotiator and a prime agent for any form of deceit, Tim knew him well enough to recognize when something was wrong.

"Yeah, they, uh, yeah. They shot me, too. Point-blank." There was still a soft laugh coming from Da Vinci, but its sadness was inescapable.

Tim's heart skipped a beat as he found himself coming upon the exterior vent. It was night, but he could still make out an incredibly roughed-up Da Vinci. He had a black eye and an abundance of bandages around his scalp. His clothes were the same as the night Tim last saw him.

"All right, Tim, I'm going to be honest with you. When you get out here, you're going to be startled, and you may even feel...well, knowing you...slightly irritated, possibly uneasy."

"It's okay to say panicked." The voice that cut in was Hera's. She was alive, but Tim couldn't see her.

"What is going on?" Tim asked. "Do you two have a way to get me out of here, or am I kicking the vent open?"

"No, it's fine. We've got it." Hera spoke again, this time she sounded closer. Abruptly, a hand grabbed the exterior vent and yanked it from the wall with little effort. The hand was pale and, based on the view Tim had, coated in some kind of thin resin that was chipping away.

Moving as fast as he could, Tim pulled himself out of the vent and into the night. Once he hit the ground, his heart stopped. Before him was Hera, still strikingly tall, still clearly pissed off, but severely deformed. Her abhorrent nature gave him pause. Despite the dark, Tim could see her every flaw. Her skin was no longer smooth and peach tinted. Instead, it was dull blue and cracked. In some places, it chipped off completely, revealing membrane and muscle underneath. Tim struggled to find the right words, or any words for that matter.

It was while gawking that Tim connected two and two. He pressed his chin to his chest and examined himself. His body shared the same blue hue as Hera's. Around his wrists, clusters of veins were visible just beneath his skin. Underneath his sleeves, the veins carried on to his arms. He shot a quick glance at Da Vinci and then Hera. They were both silent, giving him the time he needed to accept what was happening. Tim's torso was covered in bandages and something was jutting out of his chest. He yanked his shirt off and began ripping off the binding off. Tim's stomach turned. More than a quarter of his heart was outside his body. Little metal tubes curled around and protected his ventricles and aorta. At first glance, the organ appeared vulnerable being out in the open, but upon pushing against it, Tim found it hard and reinforced. Although his skin did not chip away like Hera's, there was something equally disturbing about him.

Hera glanced over to Da Vinci, but she stopped short of any utterances as Da Vinci signaled her to wait. They stood above Tim, looking down as the waves of horror and disgust and awe all came to pass.

"What the hell happened?" Tim spoke coolly, as though something very minor and slightly frustrating had just transpired. He pulled his shirt back on and then pushed himself up off the ground. He sized up the facility he'd just escaped. It was a large, looming building with a brick front. It was run of the mill, except for the fact that there was no fence bordering the building, nor walls, just trees among trees. They were surrounded by woods.

"It's a hard pill to swallow." Da Vinci's voice had a level tone to it. Tim stared at Da Vinci's bandaged and covered forehead.

"They really did shoot you point-blank," Tim said haltingly.

"Diana, too," Da Vinci added.

"Diana?" Tim shifted his attention to her.

"Diana Riley," she said coldly. She was mad, but Tim doubted he was the cause.

"Tim Carroll." He bowed his head. "Diana, goddess of the hunt. That name is much more suiting."

She pressed her lips together, giving the most smile she could in that situation.

"Any idea how they managed to pull this off? Whatever this is," Tim asked.

"A steroid unlike any other from what they've told me. Something they came up with while playing with radiation." Da Vinci started walking away from the facility, and Diana and Tim followed.

"You've talked to them?" Tim kept the suspicion out of his voice.

"I sustained significantly less injury than you. Since, ya know, bit older, bit more soft. I couldn't put up as much of a fight. I went down pretty quick, so my recovery time was a lot less. We would have escaped sooner, but you only gained consciousness a few days ago. You probably don't remember much of the conversations we've had over the last couple of days, but you still managed to find your way to the vents, according to plan." Da Vinci presented a positive spin on an all-around awful situation.

"How long have I been out?" Tim's thoughts drifted back to prearranged plans and business left unattended, of Ruth. There was a woman he'd never forget.

"At least a few weeks," Diana cut in, "but we can't let that distract us. Our main objective is to get ahold of the CIA and lay low for a while in hopes of a cure. We don't know what the KGB wanted us for, but we can't risk them finding us again."

Tim nodded in agreement, but Da Vinci abruptly stopped, looking between the two of them.

"Don't know what they wanted us for? Neither of you listened to the proposition?" Da Vinci asked.

Tim and Hera exchanged looks before shaking their heads no.

"Figures." He laughed. "You two have more in common than you'll ever let on. It was going to be a super steroid, three CIA agents, three KGB agents, greatest spy team in all of existence, super-human strength, reverse radiation, writing history and claiming notoriety." Da Vinci's eyes were huge, and he suppressed a laugh.

"Greatest spy team in history," Diana scoffed.

Da Vinci turned forward again, toward the sea of forest surrounding them. "Where the hell are we supposed to go?"

"I think the bigger question is: Where are we?" Diana's words stirred Tim's thoughts as he examined their surroundings again. Apart from the KGB facility, there was no sign of nearby society. It was an endless abyss of hills. They couldn't even be sure they were in the States. Tim was uncertain they had anywhere to go with their deformed appearance. Regardless, he chose to move along.

"We are not going to find answers here. Come on." Tim nudged his way past them and headed into the endless woods. Da Vinci laughed, impressed.

"Don't know why you are hesitating. Seems like our only option," Tim added.

"It is." Diana started walking begrudgingly.

Da Vinci hung back from the two of them for only a moment, his gaze drifting up to the stars. "We're going to be okay," he said aloud. Tim and Diana looked back at him curiously.

Tim spoke steadily. "Of course, we are, Da Vinci."

Diana hummed. "Da Vinci—and here I thought Niccolò was pompous."

NPS

SEPTEMBER 3, 1963

Only crazies and thrill-seekers would go after the goddess. That's what Marco told them. But yet, there he was, neither crazy nor thrill-seeking, riding into the misty mountains on his motorbike. It'd been only a few days since the goddess escaped from a remote KGB facility hidden in the bluffs of Bryson City, North Carolina. Marco was a freelancing agent, so when the KGB approached him and asked if he could locate her so they could bring in an extraction team, he had the luxury of saying no. In this case, he told them no, dozens of times. But the bounty on her head kept growing and the KGB were relentless in their pursuit of him. A spare million dollars didn't sound so bad after a while, so he said yes.

He was confident enough in his skills. He'd done bigger jobs. But, before he could start tracking, he needed a local to show him the area, because a local could accomplish what a map couldn't. They knew where the people were. A local could show him just how frequently traveled paths were. He couldn't risk running into a pedestrian hiker on a mission like this. Besides, he knew the goddess wouldn't be hiding just anywhere. She'd be deep in the hills and as far from the KGB as someone could get in twenty-four hours.

There were three requirements for locals on a mission: intelligence, loner status, and a willingness to walk away after the mission was complete. Smart enough to get Marco in. Unknown enough not to be missed if they vanished. And a lack of interest that ensured they wouldn't follow up after everything was said and done. However, on this specific mission, there was a fourth variable that was unavoidable: they had to be black. It had been a long time since Marco stayed stateside. In his time overseas navigating ruins and tramping around, he'd forgotten how blatantly racist and dangerous Americans were. He needed someone black like him, anyone lighter would draw unnecessary attention. This far South, a guy like him could go missing and never turn back up. He had to be careful. All tips and intel pointed to Ruby Starr.

The theory that she was just the local for the job did not dissipate when Marco finally laid eyes on a tiny girl in a horrid ensemble. She was propped up against a giant van decorated with a painted mural of the stars. She wore a gray dress accented with every color known to man and presumably two known only to galactic travelers. Her wrists were densely populated with bangles, and her outfit was topped off with a pair of hiking boots.

Marco pulled in behind her van and peeled off his helmet. His curls sprang out like coils. Ruby's attention shifted toward him. She beamed like she'd seen him before or they were old friends, meeting up after a long break. He mustered up a sad excuse for a grin in return and slid off his bike, pressed the kickstand in place, and walked toward her, scanning the road for anything suspicious.

When she smiled, two perfect, craterous dimples showed on her cheeks. "That's a smooth ride you've got there. Are you Marco?"

"I am. I'd guess you're Ruby." He extended his arm and shook her hand.

"Smooth ride and a smoother accent." She gave him a sly look. "Where are you from?"

"Brazil." Now that he was close, Marco could see that her horrid fashion sense was easily overlooked because of the dreamy look in her eyes and the cascade of waves her curls made right before they stopped at her chin. "So where do we start?"

She turned to the giant bluffs before them and then looked back at Marco. "Run it by me again. What do you want? It sounds a little ridiculous and I just want to hear you say it."

"I want to see every trailhead in this part of the park, but I don't want to hike any of the trails. I'm planning on camping here once Hazel Creek reopens and I just want to get a feel for where hikers tend to be. I don't actually want to hike all the trails. That sounds exhausting. I just want to see them."

Ruby was not the kind of local you contracted or clued in. This mission was on a need-to-know basis. So a well-crafted lie would have to do.

"That's dangerous, ya know." Ruby nudged him with her elbow. "This part of the park is closed for a reason—treacherous terrain, bear attacks, inaccessibility, dangerous happenings. Sure you can handle it?"

"Do you think I'd be here asking you for help if I thought I could do it on my own?" Marco smirked, not smugly but teasingly.

"Should have thought of that one," she whispered to herself. "You're not with a commune, right?" Her tone shifted, watching him now with a skeptical eye.

Marco was taken aback by the question and the image of him in a commune. He couldn't help but laugh. "Not my bag, why?"

"All right." Ruby's position seemed to shift from closed to open as she stepped closer to him. "Let's get shaking."

Even though she had completely ignored Marco's question, he followed her into the bluffs, tying his riding jacket around his waist as they ascended. He had no desire to walk the paths most traveled, but he needed to know them. The goddess was a tactical genius. Investigating the trails with a local was just a swift way to figure out where she wasn't, so he could start to focus on where she was.

The initial hike was steep, and Marco could easily see why this part of the national park was closed. The path was choked with leaves, fallen tree trunks were scattered around the area, and the sun was especially hateful at this angle.

"We're going to want to move fast. We've only got about six or seven hours of light left. And man, you've given me a big order to fill." Ruby reached the top of the bluff and instinctually turned around to offer her hand to him. He took it and she helped pull him up over the eroding edge. "I don't think I've ever had such an ambitious request, actually. I'd say ambitious hiker, but you don't seem to want to hike."

"Is there a lot of business around illegal tour-guiding?" He took in the view. It was nothing but treetops as far as the eye could see. The whole world looked as though it were an overgrown arboretum.

"Some here, some there, mostly black folks and communes. Can't really go through the Park Service. The visitor's center is, uh, pretty pale."

"So I heard." After one good look at her lumberous legs, he didn't doubt that Ruby was in the mountains a lot. She moved like a tank, careless, unafraid, and unstoppable. She stepped wherever she pleased.

"It's a nice way to pick up some cash. Plus, I was coming out here tonight, anyway. Your job was really good timing." Ruby grabbed hold of a tree limb and hoisted herself up and over a fallen tree trunk.

"Out *here*?" Marco repeated, slightly annoyed that he might have very well caused an unwelcomed wanderer to join him in the woods that night.

"Nah, out on Lake Fontana. It's amazing out there at night with the stars all lit up. Like the skies are above and below you." She then snapped her fingers to draw Marco's attention. "So twenty feet that way, there's a trail. About two miles down that path, there's a fork. One way'll take you all the way out to Andrew's Bald, and the other will take you deeper into the creek."

"Does this one tend to get a lot of foot traffic?"

"Not much. Since the CCC ended, this entire area has been off-limits to the public, and for the most part, they keep their distance. Too afraid of bears and stuff. Buncha babies." She guzzled water from a canteen and kept her pace strong. "If we keep heading this way, then I can show you a few more paths before we have to turn back and go to a different starting point."

"Buncha babies," Marco repeated skeptically. "Are you not afraid of bears?"

"Black bears are docile creatures." Ruby paused for a moment and then added, "Besides, I have enough bear mace on me to stop an entire horde of them if the time comes."

"What? Where? There is no way you have room for all that on you." This girl was in layers among layers of fabric and had a backpack that served more as fashion than function.

Ruby gave a single loud Ha! in return. "Nice try, but I'm not gonna tell you. That's my only line of defense in the event that you're actually a creep."

"You think I'm a creep?" He laughed.

"Nah." She turned her head just enough to peek at him. "I've picked up hitchhikers scarier than you."

Marco stopped, rebuilt his pride, and then continued on. Surely he had to look at least slightly menacing. He was fit, seemingly brooding, scarily knowledgeable, and worldly, but apparently not intimidatingly so. He thought of all this while keeping the same stoic expression on his face.

"I could scare the hell out of you," he said. "But because I'm a kind man, I will not."

"Man." She snorted, hiking forward faster. She stepped without care, her ankles teeter-tottering left and right as she took a chance on each unstable rock she trusted. "Please. Ghosts, aliens, yetis, they don't scare me. I love 'em. I'd study them if I could. I watch *The Twilight Zone* with the lights off, and that stuff's really scary."

Marco just let the thought of yetis resonate in his mind for a minute. He followed in her steps carefully to ensure he didn't injure himself. "I could tell you some things about Area 51 you wouldn't believe."

"Like what?" Ruby spun around like a snapping shark, and Marco was nearly positive she'd lose her balance and he'd have to stop her from falling down the thousand-foot elevation, but she stayed strong, no help needed. She looked at him with hope, her eyes wide and brimming with possibilities. Marco suppressed a smirk.

"Well, it starts in the ruins of Greece..." He began spinning a tale for her that reached from Greece to Roswell. It was perfect really. He'd tell a story. She'd be distracted enough not to notice him scanning the trail and jotting notes. After one story, she demanded another, not rudely, not brashly, but eagerly.

This was the kind of local Marco loved, someone with an appreciation for storytelling. However, Ruby had a bad habit of interrupting. Just as the CIA was reaching into an alien spacecraft, she'd ask what color the aliens were. Just as explorers from worlds unknown came over the hills of Tibet, she'd ask about the weather on that day in history. Luckily, Marco found her questions insightful and endearing. She was making him craft a truly fleshed-out story. He had started innocently enough, names were changed, locations moved around, and facts omitted, but the stories were mostly true, but after the first three tales, he switched completely, fabricating his stories just to see what she'd believe. He quickly learned that Ruby was not gullible. In fact, she was brilliant in something Marco had always considered a pseudoscience.

Ruby cut Marco off mid-alien attack in the Himalayan Mountains. "Okay, now that one's bull. Aliens would *never* do that."

"Do what?" *Is* this *where the line was going to be drawn?* Marco thought.

"Uh, speak English." Ruby hung her hands in midair, emphasizing the obscenity of Marco's story. "Aliens are crazy-brilliant, sentient beings. Do you really think they'd pick a language as Germanic as English?"

"You got me." He could feel the sun beating on his back. He was warm inside and out.

"I thought so. As fake as that accent of yours." She winked at him before spinning around and setting foot into a shallow stream.

"My accent isn't fake." Although the mission to find the goddess was his top priority, this was a fun detour. "I'm from Brazil."

"Sure, and aliens speak English," she replied.

Marco couldn't find it in himself to move. He stood, slightly stunned, resisting the urge to laugh. "So aliens can crash land in Greece, but I can't be Brazilian?" He poked fun at her, finally mustering up the competency to move one foot in front of the other and cross an incredibly wide stream dribbling down the side of the bluff.

"The Greece story wasn't fake, was it?"

"No, no, that one was totally true," he lied, but she looked relieved. They walked in silence for a few more minutes. The longer they hiked, the more elevation they gained. Eventually, the clouds created a fog around the two of them, but her comment was still digging at him. "But you do understand, if I can't be Brazilian, you certainly can't be a Floridian."

Ruby slipped and Marco grabbed her from behind just in time to stop her from falling face-first. Once she regained her balance, she embarrassingly pulled herself from Marco's grasp and turned around, a can of bear mace in her hand.

"What kind of accusation is that? I'm not from Florida."

Marco's heart rate spiked. Why would she lie about this? He backtracked, analyzing every interaction they'd had since first meeting. What did she have to gain from lying? Where had she pulled that bear mace from? Had she had time to put a bomb on his bike? Could she have a gun buried somewhere in her layers of scarves and dresses? If he hadn't been working for the KGB, he would have suspected the KGB. He considered the situation at hand for another second before determining that odds were she wasn't a spy, but the idea of her actually being one was now eating away at him.

"You have an accent, Ruby. There is no reason to lie." He laughed nervously. "It's not clear to other native-English speakers, but for me, it's pretty easy to hear." He braced himself in case she swung at him.

Instead, she turned and scowled. "Are you a cop?" She sounded irritated, done with whatever conversation they were having.

"No," Marco replied, falsely defensive.

"Swear so?"

"Yeah. I'm not a cop, Ruby. Stop looking at me like that."

"Not a PI, either?"

He laughed again. "Not one of those, either. What are you so worried about?"

Her face reddened with shame. "Ah, shoot, Marco, I'm sorry. It's just the motorbike, the nice leather jacket, the accent. Then you said I was from Florida like you've got some secret intel or something. I don't tell people where I'm from for a reason. You don't need to know why, just that I don't like to talk about it."

Any alarm in Marco's mind dropped. He was always so paranoid. He'd rushed to a conclusion again. She wasn't some deep-undercover spy, or a KGB cover-up, just a kid doing something illegal.

Ruby groaned loudly, irritated with herself. "Oh my god, this is so embarrassing. You're the third person I've done this too."

"It's fine. You should at least admit I'm right, though." Marco snorted, following her as they reached the last mapped-out trailhead. The sun was beginning to set and time to hunt was rapidly approaching.

"Well, you aren't. Right, I mean," she said. "This is the last crossing. There are about three smaller trails that intersect here, two to the west, one to the south. The higher up the mountain, though, the less chance you'll have of seeing other people. Like I said, there're more bears up that way and less accessible bluffs. It's dangerous up there." She traced the ground with her foot. "I feel obligated to tell you that someone like us probably shouldn't be camping out here alone at night, anyway. It may not be as bad as other places, but there's still a lot of hostility."

"Thanks, Ruby. You've got nothing to worry about. Trust that I'm capable of taking care of myself."

It was as they descended the mountain, that Marco drew her in again. "It is a shame that you're not from Florida, because one of the greatest heists I've ever seen happened there." His words peaked her interest and, he led her through yet another story. As they walked down the mountains and talked, Marco laid out a mental map of the terrain as well as his game plan for the evening ahead. The hike down felt significantly slower than the hike up, allowing Marco's anxiety to build. He decided to pass the time by telling Ruby one last story. This one about Thailand, a man called the Renegade, and an unbelievable break-in. She was listening, but her excitement and questions were gone. When they were back at Ruby's van, he felt just a hint of sadness.

"So, how much do I owe you?"

"Oh, don't worry about it," she gushed. "This was such a blast. Free of charge. And I almost maced you, ya know? Doesn't feel right, taking your money."

Marco grinned. "No, no. I insist. I have more than enough cash already."

Her smile shifted to a smirk. "Why do I feel like you're not here to camp?" she asked. "For real. Don't worry about it. This has honestly been the best hike I've had in a long time. Plus, you've basically given me enough Area 51 information that I could probably break in there myself if I tried."

"Definitely don't." Marco laughed aloud, but was gravely serious inside. "Definitely don't," he repeated, thinking of what truly was in Area 51. He dug into his back pocket and pulled out a beaten leather wallet. "Twenty?" He thumbed through the bills.

She groaned dramatically. "Marco, please don't. I just can't take your money."

"Fifty then." He shifted his gaze from his wallet to Ruby. She was heavily sighing in an overly dramatic fashion.

"I just can't accept." She put her hand to her forehead and pretended to wither. "If you really want to give me something, take me for a spin on your motorbike." She stayed in her dramatic pose, but she was now peeking over at him.

Marco laughed, deeply, happily. Ruby was a doll, a sweet and kind of weird doll but a doll nonetheless. "I can make that happen."

The next thing he knew, Ruby was holding onto him tight as they rode through the Carolina hills, the wind rushing against his face and cooling him off after a long day of hiking. Ruby squealed with excitement as the twists and turns came, the bike drifting as they flew past cascades and moss-ridden mountains. Marco grinned as he felt one of Ruby's arms tighten around him and the other release so she could cut the air against her hand.

She finally stopped screaming just in time to start bubbly laughing as they slowed and came to a stop behind her van. She was still laughing when she gave Marco back his helmet and sighed with stars in her eyes.

"That is one groovy ride you've got." She smoothed out her dress and took a moment to really hold Marco's gaze. "If you find yourself free tomorrow, a couple friends and I are going out to the Typhoon Club if you'd want to tag along."

"Thanks, Ruby. Keep it real, all right?" Marco dug into his wallet and pulled out a few bills. "And just take this, please."

She grabbed it casually, and Marco revved his bike back up, then pulled out into the road. It was when he'd traveled maybe a few yards that he faintly heard her call his name, but he continued riding. He suspected she'd looked down and realized that he'd slipped her two hundred-dollar bills in a sandwich of singles.

The fun was over and the hunt was on. Marco wasted no time getting his bike parked and hidden. He hiked back into the Hazel Creek backcountry, knowing that he was in for a long night. In his riding bag was a collection of park maps and facility blueprints the KGB had given him. He had a good hunch she was somewhere in the rhododendron marshes atop the mountain. They were dense, far from the facility, and would offer coverage from aerial searches.

Given who he was dealing with, he suspected he'd fall victim to at least one or two misdirection tactics—a false path, multiple foot trails, decoys. However, she'd be limited in resources and time. Marco hoped that maybe she'd be easier to find because of this. He was wrong. After a few hours of searching, Marco was still empty-handed, having eliminated eight false paths and nearly fallen over a trip wire. It was getting dark, not dusk but truly dark. It seemed as though the mountains now grew around him and the only sound left was the chirping wildlife of the woods.

He was exhausted and sleep tempted him, but he kept moving and marked his path along the way. He kept his head down and his footsteps quiet as he listened. There were crickets off in the distance, frogs all around him, and crackling leaves, not under the foot of a spy but the paw of a bear. All hope seemed lost until a scream cut across the woodland.

DIANA'S SCREAM REVERBERATED through the woods, echoing off tree trunks and riverbanks until there was nothing left of it but a whisper in the night's sky. Hundreds of feet below ground, at the bottom of one of the mountain's many caverns, she was sprawled out, broken, and already healing. Da Vinci and Tim stared in horror.

"Shit." Tim said, gaping as a shell reformed from membrane and her previously bashed-in face regrew into her features.

Diana forced herself off the ground, pressing her arms up and then her feet. Chips of old shell fell off her. "I survived," she groaned, rocking her head from one side to the other until it gave a satisfying crack. "Guess you were right."

This troubled Da Vinci. Before she began to climb up, Da Vinci had told her of a night terror he'd had where she'd climbed the cavern wall and fell from it. He'd seen her fall before it happened. And then, despite the warning, she had still fallen. He'd been right about an odd amount of many things since leaving the facility. Da Vinci was full of either lucky guesses or accurate intuition brought on by serious night terrors and epileptic fits.

"Catch your breath. I'll scale it." Tim took the rope from Diana and began to climb the wall, his bare feet not bloodying on the way up.

Once Tim was up, Diana followed shortly behind.

FROM THE TREE line, Marco stared in horror as a pale creature rose from what he could only assume was an underground cave. It was a man but deformed with a bulging chest growth and veiny skin. Marco's stomach churned. He stood completely still and quieted his breathing, praying he lived through this nightmare.

The goddess rose next, like the living dead. Her arm, more muscle than shell, lurched out of the cavern opening. The peachy-skinned and angelic-faced woman Marco expected to find was nowhere to be seen. She had skin so pale it was nearly translucent. Her legs and face were cracked like porcelain, and any seductive nature people had reported was replaced with a tired and defeated appearance. Marco almost didn't recognize her, but upon taking a second look at those famous curls, he clapped his hands over his mouth; his heart sped up and beat so loudly that Marco worried she might hear it.

This was the goddess. Who was with her? The KGB hadn't mentioned any other agents. He held onto the nearest tree trunk for support, no longer caring about the mission. As soon as they left the clearing, he was going to bolt. But they weren't clearing out. It seemed that they were waiting for another of their macabre party. Marco could hear this third member scaling the cavern, and once he spoke, Marco knew why he was the KGB's prime candidate, why they said there was no one else for the job. Ascending from the cavern was his mentor, Da Vinci.

Marco let out a weak moan before collapsing.

When he finally came to, he could hear Da Vinci's faint and familiar voice. "Rigan, no. No, no, what are you doing here?"

Rigan. The sound of his given name was enough to shake him from his groggy state. He opened his eyes hesitantly and found Da Vinci and the monsters around him.

"Who the hell is he?" the goddess asked.

Coming back to consciousness, Rigan managed to mutter, "Niccolò, what the hell are you doing here?"

Although nothing was said, there seemed to be as much uncertainty on Da Vinci's part as on Rigan's. "Rigan, it's fine, everyone here is on a first name basis."

"Oh, pardon me," Rigan groaned. "Da Vinci Moretti, what are you doing here?" He let his head fall back onto the grass.

Da Vinci was just sitting there stunned. Rigan was expecting a reply, but it would appear Da Vinci couldn't think coherently enough to give him one.

Tim answered for Da Vinci, "It's a long story, Rigan."

Upon hearing the familiar voice, Rigan flinched. He propped himself up on his elbows and laughed when he set his eyes on the vein-ridden one. It was Tim. "Holy shit, you look rough."

"I believe you have seen better days." Tim gave a begrudging reply.

"You know him, too?" Diana crossed her arms now.

"Yeah, he's our old partner. Codename's Marco." Tim said something else, but Rigan was too focused on Da Vinci. The old man looked rough. His beard was unruly and the bags under his eyes were dark.

Eventually, Da Vinci spoke. "Rigan, what are you doing here?"

"The KGB sent me." He answered. "They didn't say it was you, Da Vinci. You know I wouldn't have taken the job if I'd known it was you."

"Did you know it was me?" Tim grumbled. Rigan shot him a dirty look in response.

Da Vinci helped pull Rigan up to his feet and then spoke to the boy in Portuguese. "Did anyone follow you?"

"No one." Rigan grew more uneasy. He and Da Vinci rarely used Portuguese, since Rigan's was substantially better than Da Vinci's. If Da Vinci opened with it, it meant he wanted to exclude other parties from the conversation. "What have you gotten yourself into?"

Da Vinci ignored the boy's question and switched back to English. "Rigan's going to help us," he told Diana.

Well, that might be an overstatement. Rigan was all for helping Da Vinci. His partners on the other hand? He could do without them.

"I don't think so." She crossed her arms and looked at Rigan coolly, her brows pinched with skepticism. "We can't let him go back. What if the KGB find him?"

"The KGB aren't going to find him, and even if they did, Rigan's not going to sing." Da Vinci placed a hand on her shoulder. "Trust me. Let him go and get help."

Diana shook her head. She didn't need to speak for her answer to be understood. "Rigan stays with us. Letting him go is too much of a risk. If he's found out, we're found out."

Da Vinci looked disappointed, but resigned and accepting. Rigan was used to seeing him with more fire to him. It was weird to see him so compliant.

Tim, on the other hand, was full-on livid. "Why? So, we can keep walking around in the woods?" he spat. "Fuck that, Diana. Rigan is our best shot. Let him go."

"Fuck you," she snapped back.

"He's our best shot, Diana. What other options do we have?" Da Vinci pleaded.

She bit her lower lip and paused. It was clear she was thinking this through.

"Rigan is a trustworthy source," Tim added. "He's a freelancer, no alliance but himself."

She inspected Rigan, meticulously, calculatingly. "If you turn us in, know that when this is said and over, I will hunt you down and I will kill you." Diana's words left nothing open to interpretation.

"Your reputation doesn't do you justice. Christ." Rigan held back a scowl, giving Da Vinci a quick look before replying. "You've got nothing to worry about with me, goddess. I'm not turning you in. I'm getting you out of here."

Diana began to walk him through her plan. "You will leave here within the next hour and hike back down the mountain. When you get back to your car, I want you to get to the nearest phone and contact Adams at his emergency number. Do you have that?" She paused long enough to let him confirm. "Tell him Hera, Niccolò, and Dresden are trapped at our current coordinates. Tell him about the KGB kidnapping us. Do not tell him about our deformities. You've got until sunrise. If you're not back by then, we'll already be on the move."

Rigan's heart pounded as his night began to unfold in front of him. These stakes were high, but Da Vinci was worth it. He owed it to him to get him out of there. "All right. That sounds smart. Hang low. I'll come back after I talk to Adams."

Da Vinci gave Rigan a quick hug. There was something rigid about him, something Rigan couldn't ignore. It made him uneasy.

"Make sure you have your gun." It was a sudden change in topic that added to his nerves. "Don't stop until you know you're safe, Rigan."

"I'll be back," Rigan assured him before rushing back to his bike as fast as he could. Something was wrong, and it wasn't just the obvious. Da Vinci was uncomfortable, and seeing Da Vinci without a calm and cool exterior was a rare and dangerous thing. When he made it back to his bike, Rigan quickly mounted and then tore through the winds and curves of the road, not waiting for the safest phone but the closest. When he found one, just getting the coins into the payphone's pay slot was nearly impossible as his hands shook. The image of Diana with a broken arm rising from the depths of the cave was etched into his mind. The dial tone hummed and then rang.

Finally, a tired voice came up on the other end of the line. "Hello?"

"Adams. It's Marco. Hera, Niccolò, and Dresden are in trouble. They need an airlift fast."

There was a pause. The man gave a warm laugh. Something about Adams' voice had a naturally calming effect on the people around him.

"You're running around with Niccolò again?" he asked.

"That's not important."

"Suppose not," Adams groaned as he audibly crawled around his bed. "That explains the enormous bounties on their heads. All right, pen and paper in hand. What're their coordinates?"

The words were on the tip of Rigan's tongue, but before he could get them out, there was a loud clatter. He was being shot at. The first bullet cut right through the payphone, destroying its insides and ending Rigan's call. The second bullet went right for Rigan, grazing his right arm.

Across the parking lot, in the pale moonlight, Gulliver stood, Rigan's KGB contact, the man who swindled Rigan into taking this job just a few days prior. He hated that spy's crooked, thin-lipped smile.

"Marco." Gulliver's English-accented voice sounded musical, as he approached the boy, gun still in hand. "Something the matter? Realize the old man is in trouble?" His closemouthed laugh was high in pitch.

"You knew." Rigan gritted his teeth until the inside of his cheek tore open. The copper taste of blood filled his mouth.

"You were the only agent we knew who wouldn't be killed on sight once finding Hera and her teammates, and we were right, no? Pops didn't let her pull the trigger, so to speak?" He oozed a snarky confidence.

Rigan wanted to talk his way out of this before it could escalate any further. "Are we going to talk about what the hell you did to them?" his words were acidic.

"Are you referencing the pleasantly corpse-colored ones?" Gulliver replied coyly.

"You're sick."

"I'm doing the best I can." Gulliver shoved his hands in his pockets and rocked back on his heels for a moment before taking a firm stance. "So are you coming willingly?"

"I'm not a canary." Rigan sized Gulliver up. He was as tall as a tree, vision impaired, and skinny as a rail. With Rigan's muscle and agility, he would win the fight, hands down, but few physically weak agents traveled alone. Rigan scanned the tree line surrounding the area. "Where's your muscle?"

"He's around." Gulliver smiled, appearing relaxed at the thought.

Rigan contemplated running at the exact moment Gulliver jabbed out his talon-like hand to clench onto Rigan's forearm. Rigan shoved Gulliver back easily and twisted away from his grip. Then, Rigan turned on his heel, ready to run for his bike when he saw the six-foot-three-inch wall of pure Soviet strength blocking him.

"Let me leave here alive!" Rigan shouted.

"Sorry, comrade." The brute had a thick Russian accent and an unapologetic expression that read *shit happens.*

Rigan reached into his jacket for his gun, only to find that it was missing. He'd put it in the seat of his bike when he and Ruby went riding. Since finding Da Vinci, he'd been in too much of a hurry to grab it.

All he had now was a pocket knife. It'd have to do. Summoning his courage, Rigan charged at the man. Rigan was thrown back like a rag doll. He ricocheted and rolled across the asphalt. Gulliver grabbed for him, but Rigan instinctively kicked, knocking the wind from Gulliver in one hit.

Gulliver wheezed. "Kal," he called for his partner and extended his arm to help balance himself.

Rigan scrambled to his feet, knife out and ready to charge again. Kal wasn't fazed. He walked over and scooped Rigan up from the pavement, brushing off the few punches he landed.

"You should've done the job." Kal threw him to the ground.

Rigan's head bobbed and his ears rang. He wasn't made for this. He scrambled to get to his feet, but with all the soreness, he fell right back to the concrete. His tailbone seared with pain.

Kal picked him up by the collar of his shirt.

"No! Stop! Stop!" Rigan thrashed back and forth. He kicked and screamed for help. He needed to save himself and Da Vinci. That's what kept him going. The idea of repaying a debt made long ago. He pried at Kal's hand. "Let me go!"

Kal drew his fist back, preparing to hit, but released him when Rigan sank his teeth into the callused skin on Kal's hand.

Rigan dropped to the ground, the taste of Kal's and his own blood turning his stomach. He attempted to move away.

"Good try," Kal kicked.

Rigan's rib cage made a loud crunching noise when Kal's blow landed.

"Fuck!" Rigan wrapped an arm around his chest. He couldn't move.

This was how Rigan went out, crumpled on the ground, hugging himself, choking on his own blood, and listening to the sound of his bones breaking with each kick.

Human

SEPTEMBER 8, 1963

Even the lord couldn't move Da Vinci. He was a lump of a man, hunched over himself with his head buried deep in his callused hands. Since Rigan failed to return, the spies had wandered through the woods seemingly directionless, mostly moving just to avoid being caught. Yet somehow, no matter how far they traveled, they always seemed to end up back at the cavern where they'd met Rigan at nights before. Da Vinci was still holding on to the hope that Rigan would return. Diana and Tim were too wrapped up in themselves to take notice of their partner's declining morale until the time came that they needed him. They had an escape plan, and it required Da Vinci to be more than the emotionless husk he currently was.

Tim sat beside Da Vinci, staring down on a bluff steep enough to kill a man with one misstep. There were snares, vines, and an overgrowth of brush just below their dangling feet.

"Come on, Da Vinci. We have to get going. He's not coming back."

"But he's not dead." Da Vinci's words were deliberate and he believed them fully. "I know he's not." He tipped his chin up and looked out into the fog of the mountains. There was a feeling gnawing at him from the inside, tearing away at the soft, fleshy lining of his stomach. "Tim, I'm not so sure we can make it out of here alive."

That was a fast way to kill the already dying mood. "Don't say that." Tim placed a cold hand on Da Vinci's back. "Everything you have said thus far has come true, and that is one premonition we cannot afford to see through."

Da Vinci inhaled loudly and then exhaled even louder. He moved backward until his head touched the ground and his legs still hung over the bluff's edge. "Oh, Tim, it was just an expression." Da Vinci gave a breathy laugh, more wheeze than harmony. "I'm just rambling on. There must be some way out of here." On his back, Da Vinci could see Diana's legs. She was gradually making her way over to them.

"We need to get moving. If we keep standing still, we'll be caught out." Diana kneeled next to Da Vinci, twisting herself so she was able to look into his eyes. "You're our main guy here. This plan will fail without you."

Still processing her words, Da Vinci glanced at Tim, who nodded in agreement. There was an undeniable somberness taking hold of Da Vinci. Every night, he had seizures, fits of the future, fits of the past. Some things he told them, other things he didn't. Regardless, the things he saw were destroying him.

"Just another minute," Da Vinci said softly, staring through Diana rather than at her.

Diana scooped her hands under Da Vinci's shoulders and Tim joined her as they lifted him back to a seated position. "Come on, Da Vinci," she stressed. "If Rigan is alive out there somewhere, you're not going to help him from here." She smoothed his hair back, mindful of his still tightly wrapped bandages. She spoke soothingly as she and Tim helped bring him to a stand. Once Da Vinci got to his feet, the race against daylight was on.

They moved like shadows in the god-sized mountains. Diana and Tim cleared the terrain like it was their second nature, animals running through familiar territory. Da Vinci mimicked their steps, slower and less graceful in his execution. The sound of crickets died in the distance, and his nerves ate him alive. He couldn't fail them. It was up to him to get out of the mountains and get help. He was the only one who could. His malady was hideable.

But, as they came to the point in their journey where he was supposed to escape into the real world via a remote road at the back of the park, he hesitated. He couldn't imagine leaving them and going to get Adams, not with all the possible risks, not with all the possible futures.

"Are you sure about this?" Da Vinci gave Tim and Diana his full attention, watching their every move for some kind of doubt.

Diana didn't give him an answer. Instead, she asked, "What's wrong?" She cut through the casual atmosphere and raised the stakes. She ran missions all the time. It was no surprise that she knew cold feet when she saw them.

"What if they capture me?" Although all three of the spies had faced looming-death on assignments, this was different. On missions, there were teams, plans, controlled environments, and an entire intelligence agency to back them up if they needed help. It was rare for an agent to go in without their team. It was even rarer for Da Vinci to be without a team, given his small size and age. It wasn't the first time any of them had done something dangerous, but it was the first time in a very long time that they'd been this close to death. Diana softly parted her lips, but before she could whisper any sweet nothings, Tim cut in.

"Da Vinci, if you're worried, then just tell us how we escape. You can see the goddamn future, *see* how we get out of here. It will save us all a lot of time," Tim snapped.

"It doesn't work like that." Da Vinci prepared to defend himself, but Tim carried on.

"Here's what I'm worried about." Tim turned his attention to Diana. "What if they capture him and they use Rigan against him? That's what's really bothering you, isn't it, Da Vinci?" Tim swung back around to Da Vinci.

Da Vinci's anxiety was undisguised. "I can't watch that kid die, Diana." He feared the conversations inevitable lapse into silence, the judgmental stares from his partners, and the verbal lashing guaranteed to follow.

However, Diana proved to be more of a saint today than anticipated. "You won't have to." She swooped in to save him. "We'll be there. Why don't we follow you to the edge of the park? It'll be risky, but Tim's the stealthiest agent in the US. He'll be able to hide us. Once you're out of the park, you're scot-free, right?"

Despite Tim's condescending sneer, he didn't seem to object.

There was a bolster of warmness rushing over Da Vinci as he started to calm. "If I get jumped, you two have my back? I mean, we don't know where the KGB are. They may have the border surrounded."

Diana was quick to assure him yes, but Da Vinci waited until Tim gave a nod in confirmation.

"All right, let's—"

"Hello?" a voice that no one seemed to recognize cut through their conversation and all a sudden Da Vinci found himself spun around and shoved while Diana and Tim bolted. It was a girl coming over the hill. She wore a thick layered dress and lugged a backpack with her. Initially, Da Vinci ignored her and pressed on, keeping his eyes on the ground as he walked past the girl, heading for the trail, but before he could get away, she spoke to him.

"Man, you shouldn't be out here this late. It's super dangerous around here." She had a light voice that was surprisingly soothing despite its low pitch. Her eyes were wide, youthful, and a deep brown. Da Vinci had seen her before in night terrors and seizures of sentience. Starting there, he knew exactly how this night was going to go. Her name was Ruby Starr, and if Da Vinci wanted to stay alive, he'd have to kill her.

"Uh, what?" Da Vinci pretended not to have heard her.

"Are you okay?" Ruby gestured to her own forehead, then to Da Vinci's. Her right hand was firmly stuffed in her pocket. Da Vinci could only guess what weapons could lurk there.

"Oh! Yes! Certainly! I just took a fall a few days ago while hiking a trail up a ways. Just got done with a very long camping trip. I was completely immersed in nature, no gear, nothing waterproof, just me and the elements, you know? Just like Thoreau. Heading down now." Da Vinci's anxieties and panic were flushed away by a wave of falseness and professionalism. "It's pretty dark and the bear activity here is pretty awful. It may be best that you turn back around."

Ruby looked Da Vinci up and down. "The view's worth it. There'll be hundreds of comets passing over the foothills tonight. It's religious really." She politely pushed past him. "Thanks for the heads-up, though, daddy-o."

Da Vinci's heart rate calmed down for the whole five seconds between when Ruby left and his partners descended from the shadows.

"What the hell, Da Vinci? You just let her walk off?" Diana scolded. "In *no* mission environment is that how we handle outliers." She crossed her arms over her chest and her gaze drove bullets into Da Vinci.

"Come on. That was a kid. Probably a local. She's going to go watch some stupid meteor shower and probably drop acid. She's not worth our time. She probably won't even remember seeing me. Let's keep going," Da Vinci urged.

"Seeing us," Tim corrected. "She clearly saw all three of us."

"She did not." Da Vinci tried being patient. "You think she would have kept walking if she'd seen you two? Anyone in their right mind would have turned tail."

"Whether she saw all three of us or not, can you imagine the conversation she'll have back at home with her friends?" Diana paused before speaking again in a significantly more nasally tone. "You're not going to believe the cat I met out in the woods yesterday, hidden between leaves and trees like a freak of nature. He *seriously* needed a shave. And weirdest of all, he was all bandaged up to like he'd fought a bear or somethin'. It was totally groovy, but he was like, such a weirdo."

The worst part was it sounded believable. Da Vinci could feel his stomach tying into knots. "She's just a kid and a waste of time, guys."

"This isn't just about us," Diana reminded him. "If word gets out, the KGB is guaranteed to find us. Then we've handed two super agents and a man that can see the future to the ruskies. How is that for a setup for World War III?"

"Whether you want the blood of a kid or a war on your hands is up to you." Tim spoke rhetorically, of course. Da Vinci slumped his shoulders. He knew what had to be done.

"At least let me do it," Da Vinci groaned. "Kid sees either one of you two coming at her, she'll die screaming and scared." He shoved his hands deep into the pockets of his pants. "I'm good for it." He was unwavering.

"You'll find her and take care of it?" Diana asked.

She knew every sly sign of deceit and then some. There was no point in Da Vinci lying. "Yes."

Tim and Diana did the same mental acrobatics they always did, exchanging a few subtle expressions and then obviously coming to a conclusion all without including Da Vinci.

"All right," Diana said.

"I'll be back soon." Da Vinci turned and then bounded up the trail. He knew exactly where Ruby was. He'd seen it all before, but this time around, in reality, he could not afford to make the same mistakes he'd seen in his prophetic fits.

When he found her, she was standing in the middle of a marsh, off the trail about half a mile. Her eyes were closed and her face was to the sky. She looked peaceful. Something about her seemed otherworldly, so in tune with the galaxies spinning around her.

Da Vinci observed her, knowing that right then was his chance to prove that the futures he saw could be changed. He could imagine killing her so easily. He'd come from behind and smother her, hand pressing over her mouth and nose till she faded away, rendering everything Da Vinci had seen moot. But as he snuck up from behind, ready to grab her, she snapped around and maced him.

Toxic, nauseous fumes stung Da Vinci's eyes to tears. He knew it was coming. He knew she was going to snap around. He'd seen it dozens of times and still, his reaction wasn't fast enough. It was as if he was stuck, damned to destiny.

"Ruby, wait," he gasped, then hacked up phlegm and spit as he panted for fresh air.

Ruby kept her arm extended out in front of her, mace in her grip. She cupped her free hand around her mouth and nose. Her expression shifted from anger to confusion to minor suspicion all very fast.

"You know my name, but I sure as hell don't know yours." She leaned her body back, clearly ready to run if the time came.

"Da Vinci, I'm Da Vinci." His chest rattled from the coughing. "I'm a friend of Marco's. He—" Da Vinci hacked loudly. "He told me about you." Da Vinci didn't have many pieces of the past and the future, but he knew for certain that her path and Rigan's had already crossed once.

It took a while for his name to register with her. Had she forgotten him so soon? "What were you doing just now?"

She was strong, but Da Vinci's trained eye could tell she was frightened. "They want me to kill you, but I'm not going to. I can't guarantee they won't. You've got to let me get you out of here while you can still go. You can't tell anyone about them."

"Saw who?"

"Don't pretend, Ruby. I'm letting you go."

"Man, you're not making any sense."

"The longer we bicker, the..." Da Vinci heaved his way through a few mumbled words, his eyes running with water and his entire face burning from the sting of the sticky spray. The air still buzzed with the noxious toxins.

Ruby relinquished. She sighed heavily, a laugh sprinkling her groan of acceptance. "What did you take? And be real with me. If you don't tell me, I can't help you come down."

"Nothing. I didn't take anything, Ruby." Da Vinci let out a distressed squawk. "Promise me you didn't see them." He struggled to stop the coughing. "Then again, I guess, why would you still have come up here if you saw them? You would have run." Da Vinci made the conversation one-sided as he finally broke through his muddled thoughts. "Oh my god, I'm saying it." He let out a cynical, distressed cackle. "Just like I saw. Shit! And I'm going to do it. Oh, Christ. I am falling to pieces." Da Vinci shook his head, his eyes finally starting to cease their watering. "God. I wish I knew more." He paused and looked at her sincerely, hopelessness in his heart. "Do I tell you the truth?"

"You know the Bryson City Hospital isn't too far out from here if you need a lift." Ruby was still firmly holding her can of mace, but his spiral was soliciting a decent amount of sympathy.

He kept rambling about rights and wrongs and fate. It was dragging on and moments stretched into minutes, but eventually, he turned to her and spoke very clearly. "Ruby, if I let you leave here alive, you have to promise never to come back."

"You've got to stop talking like you're gonna kill me. This mace is meant for bears, and I'm afraid if I spray you one more time you're going to go blind for life, but it is not below me if you keep acting like a damn creep!"

"There were two other people with me." Da Vinci felt lucid for the first time since he had wandered upon Ruby. "They are dangerous people, and they will kill you if they see you here again."

"Let me guess. They're hillbillies or commies. No, better yet, communist hillbillies who live in the mountains and eat human flesh, a Serling special." She sucked air in through her teeth and tsk'd. "Man, I knew Marco was with a commune." She rolled her eyes. "Come on. Let's get you to a hospital, so we can bring you back down to earth."

"Okay, okay, Ruby." Da Vinci flinched away from her as she offered her hand to him. "I'm going to show you something and you're going to want to scream. Like you're going to want to scream *bloody fucking murder* like it's the scariest thing you've ever seen, but I am telling you, do not scream or they will find us." Da Vinci didn't wait for her to respond. He instantly went to work untying the bandages around his forehead. "Don't scream."

When the bandages fell away, Ruby didn't scream, but she did panic. Beneath those ratty old bandages was a third eye, smack in the middle of Da Vinci's forehead.

"Ooooh, god," Her mace can dropped to the ground, and she buried her hands in her massive curls. "What did *I* take?" The panic in her eyes was clear as she looked frantically around the forest. "Ooooh, god." Her knees began to buckle.

"This isn't a bad trip, Ruby. I'm real. It's all real. If you can believe in aliens, you can believe in something standing directly in front of you." Da Vinci tenderly took one of her hands and guided it to his forehead. She didn't pull back. Instead, she watched in awe as she felt the wrinkles and crease of his third eye.

"No latex, no spirit gum, no nothing," she mused. "It moves like the other ones, too."

"That's because it's real."

"I believe you."

"What is it? What does it do? Does that mess with your line of sight?" She touched around his forehead delicately.

"It's a third eye." Da Vinci swallowed hard. Here was his big moment. "And with it, I can see the future."

"A triclopes," she whispered. Eventually, she pulled her hand away from him. "I know humans and I know aliens, but you are something in between, my friend." She stared at him with a newfound interest and curiosity. "Why are you here?"

"That's insignificant, Ruby. Insignificance we don't have time for. I need you to listen. We don't have much time." Da Vinci grabbed one of her shoulders as his gaze barreled through hers.

She stood at attention, seemingly ready to absorb every word he said.

"You cannot come back here, Ruby, ever. If you do, you will be found, and it will cause many deaths."

Her eyes grew wide as she looked at Da Vinci in shock, clearly believing every word he said. "What? I would never kill someone." She pulled her arm away from him and backed up.

"You wouldn't," Da Vinci cooed. "But there are many who would. You can never come back to the mountains, and you can never talk about what happened here tonight. Tell no one, no matter how much you trust them." That was all it took. The future's seam was pulled. He told her exactly what he saw, and he let her know exactly how she played into it. Then all she had to do was stay away and the future would be changed.

The gravity of his words came crashing down on Ruby. "I can't. You don't get it. These woods are all I have now. I... This is the only place where I feel right."

Da Vinci considered her thoughtfully. He had his arms out to catch her in case she collapsed. "Ruby," he said coolly, "there are more powers here at play than you can imagine. You can't come back, or they will find you. We all will."

"All the mountains, or just this one?"

"They find you alone on a trail. You're wearing something baggy and puce. The rest is fuzzy." He laughed sadly. "The future has many mysteries, even to me."

"These mountains are a part of who I am." She then shakily added, "I...I feel like meeting you has finally given me answers, like answers I've spent years searching for. I've waited so long for this kind of breakthrough, and I'm just supposed to walk away?"

"People will die if you come back, good people. You can't just think of yourself here."

She parted her lips and shook her head even if she didn't intend to. "When you put it that way, I guess there's nothing else to say but okay."

There was a lightness in Da Vinci, which he hadn't felt since escaping the facility. The future could be changed. He'd just proven it. So, perhaps he could save his friends before it was too late.

He smiled and, without thinking, wrapped the girl in a hug of gratitude. "You have to find your way down one last time. Can you do that?"

She managed a nod. "I'll get there, no trail required." She hesitated before asking, "You can see the future, so I have to ask, are you the last extraordinary thing I'll meet?"

He knew little of this girl's future, only that it had previously intertwined with his own. "Perhaps not." He shrugged. "Goodbye, Ruby."

She let out a loud, cathartic sigh. Her entire body loosened as she pulled away from him. "Goodbye." She began to walk away, only to stop and turn back to him. "Da Vinci, if you're going to be hanging out in the woods, don't eat anything poisonous, okay? A lot of stuff up here looks edible, but it's not."

She was grasping at straws to stay. He'd have none of it. "Thanks, Ruby."

She vanished into the woods, and he should have been relieved. She lived. She wouldn't come back. They would all live. He'd changed his actions and saved his partners in the process, but the idea that perhaps the future was written in stone still plagued him. He could only pray that when he went to sleep that night, he'd find a new vision of what tomorrow would be.

Coup

SEPTEMBER 12, 1963

Deformed and beautiful, Diana sat beside Da Vinci, her cool shell-like skin brushing against his flesh. The air was warm, above them the sun shone, and in front of them, Tim lay asleep in the dirt. For the last hour, Da Vinci and Diana were silent, enjoying one another's company. But eventually, as always, Diana needed to pry.

"Sometimes," she started. "The way you act is reason for concern. You seem afraid and I don't see you afraid often. It's worrying me."

"You're not worried." Da Vinci took his hand in hers. "Curious, but not worried," he said fondly.

"There's something knowing about that smile of yours." She lifted their hands and spread her fingers out, toying with his, a coy smile pulling at her lips. "What aren't you telling us?"

"Hiding something from you? I could never."

"You're worrying me."

"Beautiful, I know you well enough to know there's not an ounce of concern in you right now."

"Oh, what a shame," she replied, trailing her hand up his arm. "Trapped in the woods with no known salvation, and I'm not allowed even an ounce of concern?"

"Not an ounce, at least not yet." He grabbed her hand again, lacing his fingers with hers.

"You're saying there'll come a point...where I will be allotted an ounce of worry?"

"I'm not sure." Da Vinci shrugged nonchalantly. "From this point on, I don't know." He leaned his head back to gaze at the sky and breathed deeply, taking in the sharp smell of pine. "No idea anymore. It's freeing. Before a few nights ago, we were doomed, but I took care of it."

"You took care of it?" She chuckled. "What was our fate before?" She tilted her head, her limp curls falling to the side.

"Death for most of us."

"For Tim and me," Diana corrected him. "That's why you were acting so peculiar, wasn't it? If you were going to die, you'd have told us. You're modest like that." She paused for a moment, but Da Vinci sensed no need to weigh in. He was happy to watch her. "But you took care of it," she repeated. "Well, then, aren't you just my hero?" She craned toward him, and their foreheads briefly touched. "Well, thank you for saving us."

"I do what I can," he teased, then rolled his eyes and offered a crooked smile. "You should sleep. You're only this affectionate when you're drowsy."

"I don't get drowsy. Old women and housewives get drowsy. I get tired." She shook her head gently, sensually. "Wake me up if anything happens while I'm out. And wake Tim up if he sleeps past six hours. He can function just fine off five." Carefully, she pushed herself off the ground, little chips of the skin on her hand sprinkling the ground. She headed toward the bright clearing where Tim lay.

As she walked away, Da Vinci took in the moment the sun hit her golden hair. He protected his partners like a shepherd. For once, his mind was silent. There was no anxiety about the future. There was no anxiety about the past. For a moment, it was serenity, and then it was pain. Every nerve in his body was burning and the neurons in his brain fired with an electric intensity. Tim and Diana slowly vanished from his vision and all the colors around him fogged and blurred together into a fuzz. His entire body shook, and then he was on the ground, face planted into the yellowing grass and dirt. His cheeks scraped against rocks and branches. The only thing he could hear was white-static noise feeding in from the universe. Da Vinci was still struggling to come back to reality when Diana and Tim finally got over to him.

"I'm stabilizing his neck." Diana's thumb was pressed firmly against his jaw, stopping him from biting his own tongue. Her knees were at the base of his scalp to prevent his head from smacking against the ground. Tim nodded and then got to work turning Da Vinci on his side.

Da Vinci's words curdled at the back of his throat, coming out in half-audible groans. At last, there was a screeching sound and an urgency deep in Da Vinci's system that made his heart palpitate. His entire body felt as though it was coming back from numbness with pins and needles buried as deep as the corpus callosum. There was a war in the jungle. There was a plague of blood. And then there was Rigan. The boy was alive.

Da Vinci didn't come out of his fit gracefully, nor gradually. He shot up from his convulsions like a swimmer surfacing for air, with a loud, dramatic inhale and then mania.

"They're back for us. The whole team."

Diana and Tim both jumped the instant the words left Da Vinci's mouth. Their days were about to get a lot harder if they couldn't fight the KGB off.

"Where?" she asked. "Are we safe for now?"

"We're going to find them first, not the other way around." Da Vinci wiped the dirt from his face and cringed as his hand grazed many healing scrapes. "They've got Rigan."

There was an instant standstill. No one needed to speak. It was a fact universally known that they were at a very high risk of fighting one another. There was no way they'd walk to the enemy, but there was also no way Da Vinci was going to carry on with Rigan alive and hostage. Diana kept her gaze steady and on Da Vinci. Tim watched Diana.

"Come on, Diana. That drop from a few days ago should have killed you, and Tim should have hypothermia with how drenched he got out in the storm yesterday, but you're both still alive. You're fucking superhuman. Are you really going to let the KGB scare you?" He egged them on. "You two are practically invincible! And it's just the three of them down there. They sent three field agents to come collect two super-humans and a semi-pro negotiator. And if this adds any merit, I can guarantee that we will be fine afterward if we go down there and fight. I've seen it. Mother-fucking prophesied." Da Vinci was bubbling with excitement, building their showdown. He was unafraid for once. Now, he just needed them to be, too.

Tim and Diana both exchanged a look with each other before Diana spoke, "We'll be fine? You're sure of this?"

"Yes. It'd be embarrassing if we weren't fine after this. We will be fine, and we will get Rigan back," Da Vinci confirmed, already standing and packing up what little they had.

"How do you know they have, Rigan? What did you see?" Tim helped Da Vinci shuffle their few meager supplies away and cover their tracks as they prepared to take off.

"I saw him. He's okay. I saw them, too, just glimpses, but I did see them." Da Vinci was almost giddy. Rigan was never a part of the original massacre he'd seen. Things were changing. He was certain of it. He was saving them.

The three spies wasted no time taking off down the side of the mountain, carelessly stomping through the trail and moving with purpose.

"So, from what I saw, they are at the cavern where we met Rigan the other night. We shouldn't count on him for help. They've got him either knocked out or heavily sedated, but as I said, we are more than capable of handling this. I'm going to lure out their weakling first, you know, old gentlemen's duel. We'll talk around each other so it doesn't look like we're about to kick ass. Then, when the first punch is thrown, you two can jump on out and we'll start this blitz." Da Vinci raced ahead of them.

"The cave?" Diana moped. "That's a good hour away, even at your speed."

Da Vinci hadn't realized it, but he was traveling embarrassingly fast. He'd burn out fast at that rate.

"At least we'll have plenty of time to figure out our line of attack."

"We show up. We kick them into last Tuesday. Our line of attack is perfecto." Da Vinci nearly slid down the side of a bluff in his hurry, but Tim grabbed him before he could lose his footing.

"Slow down." Tim's brows were knit, and he looked at Da Vinci as he'd look at a child.

"Oh, let him be," Diana toyed, the corners of her lips cracking. "How old was Rigan when he was assigned to you? I'm going to guess you two go pretty far back."

Da Vinci had prepared this entire speech about morality in the spy business, but before he could talk, before he could even begin his incredibly well-thought-out monologue, Tim cut him off.

"Rigan was not assigned to him. Da Vinci demanded him. The kid was supposed to be put on a work farm or prison or something dastardly." Tim kept his eyes on Da Vinci, likely to make sure he didn't take a nose-dive off a cliffside.

"Really?" Diana laughed. "You never struck me as the kind of man to demand something, Da Vinci. You're always such a gentleman." She picked up her pace just enough to be beside Da Vinci rather than behind him. "You also don't strike me as the mentor-protégé type."

Tim audibly snorted. "Da Vinci used to demand a lot. He was a primadonna. As for the prodigy—"

"Rigan was just a really nice kid." Da Vinci talked over Tim, hoping to drown out the conversation before it could carry on.

"Rigan was a kid, period. Da Vinci couldn't watch him go to the rack, so he saved him." Tim scoffed.

"The rack?" Diana sounded pleasantly surprised. "What'd he do?"

"You will love this," Tim said.

"You are not telling this story. If anyone is telling it, it's me." Da Vinci spun around to stare Tim down.

Diana let out one soft, melodic laugh. There was a chemistry of happiness in the group that Da Vinci hadn't seen in a long time. He and Tim continued to bicker over where to start the story and how to tell it, but once the two of them got into a rhythm, they started to explain how Rigan came to be known as Marco.

*

"What? What, What, What is so, so, *so* important that I have to miss game five of the series?" Da Vinci plowed through a small side hallway in a downtown DC holding building. He wore an expensive suit jacket and a scowl. His partner, Tim Carroll, followed close behind him, moving quieter than Jupiter missiles. The hallway was poorly lit, metallic in style, and highly secluded from the rest of the city. Despite its soundproofing and depth, there was no doubt that Da Vinci's complaining could be heard throughout the building.

"I ask for one chunk of time off a year and it's the goddamn series. And this time around, my team is in the finals. But am I at the bar with my happy ass watchin' the game? No. I'm here, on some run-of-the-mill negotiation-room bullshit with your mangy ass." Da Vinci chewed the ear off their escort, Adams. "And you know what? I couldn't help! Because he spoke Swahili! I speak eighteen goddamn languages and Swahili ain't any of 'em!" A hint of an Italian accent could be heard on his tongue as he got increasingly frustrated.

Adams was a calm, narrow fellow from the Bronx. He was experienced and always smelled like citrus and pepper. The CIA considered him one of the few people able to handle Da Vinci and his beastly demands.

"Who'd have guessed the vet from the slums would be so high maintenance." He spoke flatly but rolled his eyes. This is how most of Da Vinci's and his exchanges went.

"Ya know what, Adams? If we were not friends, I would have said no, but because we are friends, I hauled ass from Manhattan so I could make it to DC in time to do your stupid interrogation, and it wasn't even that important. So, forgive me if I am upset that I missed what was apparently a perfect game for a case I can't even work." Da Vinci had his hands on his hips and his feet firmly planted like two strong tree.

"Is he always like this?" Adams turned his attention to Tim who only smirked in recognition of being talked to.

Tim rarely sided blindly with Da Vinci, but Da Vinci knew for a fact that he'd also been watching the game. He suspected nothing short of unyielding support.

"He is," Tim replied, "but he does his job well. Is that not what matters, Adams?"

Adams bit his lip for a moment before turning his back and scanning the area. He dropped his voice. "You two are so irritating and ungrateful it pains me. You really think this Swahili guy is why I called you here?"

Da Vinci and Tim both stared at him with deathly glares. "I swear if it was for something lesser I'm going to be *really* angry," Da Vinci muttered under his breath.

"Of course, this Swahili guy isn't the real reason I called you." Adams leaned in and kept his head down. He now had both Tim and Da Vinci's attention. "There's a mob here, and I think you're our best connection in, but it's a high-level case."

"Wait. Is it...?" Da Vinci held his hands out and bit his bottom lip, eagerly waiting for Adams to fill in the blank.

"Yeah, it is, but you've got to give me more time to see if I can get you in on it." Adams's gaze shifted from Tim to Da Vinci. He leaned in closer. "Wait here. I think she just went on break. I'll go talk to her."

"You know her?" Da Vinci gushed. "You know the goddess?"

"Please." Adams tsk'd. "I helped Hera make her name. Of course, I know her. If I can get her approval on this, you'll both be in on one of the biggest organized crime busts to date." At the sound of heels clicking on tile, Adams jetted off, offering Da Vinci and Tim only a wink in assurance that he was setting his plan in motion.

Turning to Tim, Da Vinci was oozing excitement. "Adams knows the goddess and we're going to get to work with her."

"Calm down, you remember what happened with her last partners? And we are only going to get to work with her if he can pull through."

"When has Adams ever not pulled through?" Da Vinci hissed.

"You were about to crucify him just a hot minute ago." Tim probably criticized him further, but the door swinging open down the hall caught Da Vinci's attention. Out of it came Agent Stroud and a tall, dark boy.

"I can't work like this. The kid's impossible. He can barely speak English, let alone Thai!" Stroud strutted down the hall, screaming to no one. His target waited in the doorway of the negotiation chamber, still handcuffed and looking appropriately despondent.

"How old is that kid?" Da Vinci narrowed his eyes with laser precision as he walked toward Stroud. "Stroud, calm down. What's the problem?"

"Thank god they brought in an expert. Niccolò, get this fucker on the rack." Stroud growled. "Kid from Thailand. Broke into a goddamn embassy. Can't seem to understand any language I fuckin' utter. He's got secrets in him, but we're gonna have to beat 'em out."

"How old is he?" Irritated, Da Vinci physically barricaded Stroud from walking past him.

"How the hell should I know? Seriously, this is ridiculous. They're giving old-timers like us cases like *this* in favor of a broad!" Stroud perked up as he saw Tim waiting down the hall. "Hey, Dresden! You seein' this?" Stroud pushed past Da Vinci toward Tim. "Man, you're not gonna believe this!"

For a moment, the boy and Da Vinci made eye contact. He was young. Fourteen, fifteen couldn't be far off. After taking a moment to peek around, Da Vinci approached.

He spoke to the boy in English. "Did Stroud really try and talk to you in Thai? No offense, but it doesn't strike me as your native tongue." Da Vinci leaned up against the doorframe opposite the boy. His tone lazy and his shoulders slumped.

In response, the kid offered out a jumbled combination *eh* and *hms*, his eyes wide and falsely confused.

Da Vinci scoffed. "Cut the bull, kid." Da Vinci switched his language to Portuguese, picking it up from the kid's unintentional dialect.

The boy instantly snapped his head up and looked at Da Vinci suspiciously.

"Don't play stupid with me..." Da Vinci grabbed the kid's wrist. The boy attempted to yank away, but Da Vinci held on with a lion's strength.

He thumbed for the boy's plastic identity band and read it before pronouncing it semi-correctly. "Rigan Hevel. Don't play stupid with me, Rigan Hevel. Stroud may be dense, but I know a faker when I see one and you are fucking faking. Besides, how am I supposed to know what to get you for lunch if you keep faking?" Da Vinci let go of the kid's wrist and continued speaking in Portuguese. "Personally, I was going to grab some burgers from Mel's, but if you're more of a pasta guy, I can swing by Gio's. The restaurant, not the agent." Da Vinci spoke with a campy, cocky rhythm, unintentionally bobbing his head with it.

"Right, because a person of my clearly not-Thai background has had access to burgers and pasta my whole life," Rigan replied in Portuguese, but the eye roll he gave was universal in meaning.

"He speaks," Da Vinci whooped. "So I'll cut to the chase. Why'd you break in?"

"Shun told me to." Shifting to a slightly more comfortable position, Rigan cracked his neck, curls falling every which way as he swayed. His jaw tensed.

"Shun. The Renegade?" Da Vinci's interest was piqued. "You worked for the Renegade? What is he like?"

"You'd be surprised." Rigan spoke offhandedly. "Where are these burgers you mentioned?"

"Hmmmm…" Da Vinci inspected the boy up and down for a moment. "Portuguese, dark as night, let me guess. A Brazilian son of slaves? But the real question is, how did you start out there and end up working for the Renegade?"

"Your friend has a lot of work to do if you're his competition." Rigan dodged Da Vinci's accusation.

"Yeah, Stroud's a crummy negotiator. You never answered me, though. Did he really try to talk to you in Thai?"

Rigan smirked deviously. "I speak fluent Thai." Rigan flipped from Portuguese to Thai, as did Da Vinci. They carried on their conversation.

"Stroud's incompetence has sent more than a few pleasant souls to the rack. You gonna be one of 'em?" Da Vinci crossed his arms and leaned in close, truly propositioning Rigan with a chance to avoid punishment.

"What the hell is the rack? You say that like it means something to me. I don't have a clue what that is."

Da Vinci laughed to himself and then sighed heavily. "Well, you can talk, or I will personally peel all of your fingernails off with rusty pliers and unmatched enthusiasm."

*

"Of course, Rigan decided to talk once he knew what the rack was. They were going to lock him away after that, but you know he'd have been iced by Shun's insiders before he could even leave the States, so I took him under my wing. Ended up helping raise one of the best navigators in the industry." Da Vinci breathed heavily on his fingernails and pretended to wipe them off on his raggedy button-up.

"So you two were the ones I handed the mad bomber off to," Diana mused. "You guys really did an exceptional job on that case."

"Tim did." Da Vinci sighed. "I was off training Rigan at the time."

She looked at Tim with genuine surprise and respect in her expression. Tim did little but grimace in return.

"You were more demanding than I was." She spoke peacefully and walked smoothly. She was thinking of work. Da Vinci could see it in the calmness in her face. She was far from the humid, dense forest that surrounded them. The breeze gently brushed through the trees, the sounds of birds filled in the silence, but eventually it ended—as all things must.

"Quiet..." Tim hushed the group and placed his arm out in front of Da Vinci. Diana had already stopped. "I can hear someone."

Diana and Tim stood still, listening in on the muffled voices coming closer.

Suddenly, they came into view, traversing the rugged terrain of the woods. It was a pair of Soviet agents looking more bored than brute. There was Gulliver, tall and lanky, with a head of light brown hair combed and swept to the side. He was the one who'd shot Da Vinci the night he was kidnapped. And Kal, even taller and significantly bulkier, with black hair that reached his shoulders. He was the one who'd kidnapped Da Vinci. Both wore maroon combat garb.

"About time." Da Vinci began looking for the third member of their team. When he turned around he found himself face to face with an intimidating and familiar woman.

"Retreat is not an option." Nikola broke the silence first.

They were cornered. Da Vinci was ready to run when Diana placed a hand on his shoulder.

"Nikola, sweetheart." Her nails dug into Da Vinci's shoulder, but she stayed in control.

Nikola smirked, her finger pressing against the trigger guard. "Funny that we'd meet again and it'd be like this."

Nikola began to release the safety on her weapon when Da Vinci started screaming.

"Wait! Wait! Wait," he shouted. "Christ! Eaaaasy! Let's see if we can talk this out first. Unbelievable. I'd put money on you not having kill-on-sight orders. They want us alive, don't they?" Da Vinci huffed and pulled his shoulder out from under Diana's hand, then turned a full circle to lock gazes with Gulliver. "We gonna talk?"

Looking between Kal and Nikola, Gulliver stepped between the USA spies and his teammates. "Of course, Niccolò. Do you remember me?"

"Hard to forget the man who shot me," Da Vinci said.

"You're looking a little rough these days. Third eye treating you well?" Gulliver asked.

"Better than you've treated us," Da Vinci snapped back.

Gulliver shifted his weight onto his right hip and buried his glare into Da Vinci. "So, you three will be coming home to us today then?"

"Conditions." Da Vinci had a cold tone.

"Let bygones be bygones, comrades. Come home with us now, or we'll force you." Gulliver extended his arms outward and stepped closer to Da Vinci, as though welcoming him in with a hug. "We are offering you a mulligan. Come willingly and any previous betrayal will go unpunished. As an added incentive, we will also promise the survival of your protégé."

"On what conditions?" Da Vinci repeated flatly. He'd never been the overzealous showboating type.

"Complete surrender." Gulliver rolled his eyes. "You're not really in a negotiating position. Judging by the unruly beard, dirty bandages, and scant frame, I'd say your teammates can't take care of you, and you certainly can't survive on your own." Gulliver was right in that way. "Come home, comrade. We are the backbone of the working class, the proletariat. Save your protégé, save your partner, and save the girl." Gulliver's gaze flicked to Diana before returning to Da Vinci. "Convince them to come back because you three will starve out here before we let you escape."

Gulliver had some of the iciest eyes Da Vinci had ever seen, but he did not waver.

Leaning his face in close, Da Vinci whispered to Gulliver, their partners out of earshot, "Have you considered that I have seen more of your future than you have, Gulliver?" Da Vinci lowered his voice and his devious tone intensified. "I know you and him are shagging, but I'm more interested in how he and Nikola would take it if they knew you were a double agent." Da Vinci took in a sharp inhale. "I know a bad negotiator when I see one, and I know a good negotiator when I see one. You are neither. You're fucking faking." Gulliver's entire body tensed and Da Vinci knew he had him. "If I were to guess, and I need not guess because I know, you're a low-level British Intelligence agent."

"It wasn't supposed to get this far." Gulliver's eyes were wide, and there were clearly restrained words trapped in his throat. "I don't know how to get out."

"Well..." Da Vinci sighed, tired of the exchange. "You've made your bed, now lie in it." Da Vinci swung and swung hard, knocking Gulliver back.

Gulliver's face bled from Da Vinci's sucker punch. "Bloody hell!" Gulliver stumbled, covering his jaw with his hand. "You sleazy git!"

Da Vinci didn't respond, instead he swung for another punch, but he was too slow. Gulliver easily deflected him.

Kal was coming up from behind fast, heading for Da Vinci. Diana wasted no time. She pounced on Kal. They hit the ground and rolled. Kal reached for his gun, but Diana instantly snatched it from him and threw it away from their fight. She was powerful in her human form. Now, she was a monster.

"Are you certain you want this fight?" Diana spoke confidently, then leaned in close and cooed out of habit.

"Your beauty is gone, Goddess." Kal spoke with a thick Russian accent and not a hint of genuine emotion. She threw a blind punch and sent him crashing to the ground.

"Gulliver, go!" In the fray of things, Kal found his partner.

Da Vinci had no intention of letting Gulliver go. His field training was kicking in, and he was ready to tear the Englishman down, but in the background of the madness, Nikola's gun went off and Da Vinci spun around just in time to see Tim get shot. Even though Da Vinci knew it was coming, the shock of watching his partner get shot and then stagger back as though nothing had happened hit hard. He was winded without even being hit.

In that moment of weakness, Gulliver took off.

"Dammit." Da Vinci paused, waiting for Tim to charge at Nikola before chasing after Gulliver.

DIANA'S ENTIRE BODY was on fire with adrenaline, her mind raging. Kal had taken part in tearing her down, and she was hungry for retribution. He fought fruitlessly. He swung, hit, and her skin would crack, but she hardly faltered. Then she struck back with unmatched force. In the background, she barely made out the shapes of Nikola and Tim going toe to toe. She was holding her own, not through punches but avoidance. She'd always been able to keep a fight going.

"You should come back with us." Kal narrowed his gaze, giving Diana a cold glare. "Don't you think letting her kill you is more satisfying than forcing her to work with you again?"

"Go fuck yourself." Diana swung her leg up, and despite Kal initially blocking her, the swing had such strength it still landed against his side and cracked his ribs. He doubled over. She swung up again, and her fist landed in his face, knocking him backward.

Kal smacked the ground. She didn't wait to grab a handful of his hair and yank his face up. "Get up," Diana growled. "Fight me." The past week was boiling in the back of her mind. "You'll be dead by the time I'm through with you."

Diana found immense pleasure in the blood inching down his face. Nevertheless, he stumbled back to his feet and extended his fists. Resilient. She could respect that.

She swung from her right. He dodged down. She threw up her leg, but he quickly grabbed behind her calf and threw her off balance, flipping her backward. Preemptive, she extended her arms and fell into the flip, moving swiftly and landing effortlessly.

As a human, Diana was unreachable, unyielding, adaptable. As a monster, she was undefeatable.

If he was panicking, Diana couldn't tell. He seemed controlled, aloof. Injured as he was, he kept fighting. She charged at him. But, as fate would have it, he was prepared and he got the one clean hit he needed.

As she ran at him, he swung, his fist cutting deep into her stomach. She recoiled backward.

Diana's body twisted from the punch. She hurtled toward the ground, hundreds of pieces of skin and shell flying through the air around her. Her muscles peeked out from behind her chest and arms. That said, it really didn't hurt.

Once on the ground, she reacted fast enough to roll away from Kal's follow-up kick and pull herself back to her feet. Her face was already healing, a new shell growing in over the exposed muscle. She tauntingly shook her head before striking Kal. He was too stunned to dodge.

Within seconds of her hit landing, Diana had him straddled on the ground. Her fists drew back with sharp jerks as she kept throwing punches, not keeping track or caring about what would be left of Kal when she was done.

She would have killed him, too, had Nikola not come up behind her and pulled her off with one clean yank. "Get out of here, Kal." Nikola's face was scratched up, the sleeve of her garb torn clean off, and her arm swollen and bruising. She offered her good arm to him and quickly pulled him up. Kal's face was bloody and swollen. He propped himself under Nikola's arm. Diana was still down after being thrown.

Kal huffed and heaved, only sharp wheezes coming out of him.

"We'll be all right," Nikola assured him. "We need to book it. You'll bleed out otherwise. I've got Dresden off our backs for now, but we've got to be fast." Nikola hesitated for a moment, staring at Diana. She should've been up by then. She should have gotten up and taken them both down, but she stayed still. This was intentional, both she and likely Nikola knew it.

"Let's go." Nikola propped Kal's arm against her good shoulder and guided the two of them out of the woods as quickly as possible.

Dusk was just settling in. Diana turned her gaze to the sky, the sound of Nikola and Kal limping off just a few feet from her. She'd let them escape. Rather than fight, she wanted to lie there and take in the pain of her insides breaking. It was the first pain she'd felt in weeks. The skin on her fists was worn down to nothing but semisolid membrane. She'd done more than bust Kal's face. She destroyed it. If he didn't bleed to death during their escape, she'd be surprised. Tim came into the clearing perhaps ten or fifteen minutes after silence had finally rested in the valley.

"Diana, are you okay?" Tim came over to her with about as much urgency as he could muster on any occasion.

"You got shot and you're still standing. Impressive." She came alive again and cracked her neck as she stood. The majority of her had already healed over. "And good, thank you. Better than in a long time."

"Catharsis does wonders," Tim said. "Where's Da Vinci?"

DESPITE THE SCREAMS of battle, the shattering of bones and noses, cries, shrieks, and blood-gurgling gasps, nothing could penetrate all the static that ran through Da Vinci's mind as he stared down at the face of Rigan Hevel. Things were not as they had seemed.

In the blur of his visions, Rigan looked fine. Rigan looked alive. Rigan looked well, but upon closer inspection, Da Vinci realized he hadn't saved him. He'd damned him. Rigan was grossly beaten, scratches and scabs covered his face and throat, but what was truly unsettling about the boy was the scales forming on Rigan's chest and his face. Three deep slits protruded from his neck, and from them, he breathed. His ears were deformed, fin-like and segmented. His hair was gone and his skin produced a damp, oozy slime. Between his toes and fingers was webbing. Where a smile once resided, now a mouth of crooked shark-like teeth could be found. In a few days, he'd be fully deformed like Tim and Diana. Rigan was too early on in the transformation process for Da Vinci to see it in the blur of his future-seeing visions.

Tim found Da Vinci first. He spoke, but the words were muffled to Da Vinci.

"How is—" Diana's voice dropped off as she came into the clearing. "Da Vinci." She was visibly shaken for a moment but quickly regained composure. "Is he alive?"

He hadn't moved since he'd found the boy. Da Vinci sat, slumped over Rigan's body, still wondering how he could have missed this. Something as big as death and as minor as deformity. Da Vinci had always been blind to what he didn't want to see. "We need to get to shelter." Da Vinci cleared his throat and then said callously, "He's going to need time to heal once this process is done."

Neuroses

SEPTEMBER 19, 1963

"So, scale of one to ten, how accurate is the movie? Honey Ryder, Felix, Dr. No, real or just Hollywood glitz?" Kal and Gulliver sat at the dimly lit corner table in their hotel room. It was covered in playing cards and cigarettes. The radio chimed in the background. The evening telecast was always their white noise of choice. The sky outside had just started to darken.

"Kal, I'm honored you think they based James Bond off me, but that doesn't change the fact that you have the last two, and you need to give it to me." Gulliver looked up at Kal's face, still surprised by its lack of puffiness. Even though Kal suffered serious injury in their scrape with the goddess, he had healed miraculously fast after the introduction of the newly enhanced steroid, all of the invincibility, none of the physical deformities. Once the KGB realized they weren't getting the CIA agents out of the mountains without equal strength, they expedited the improvement process on the steroid. Kal was alive because of it.

"I do not have the last two." Kal kept his gaze on his cards and his face stiff. "It is irrational that you think I do."

Gulliver looked from his own hand to Kal, and then back again, scrunching and unscrunching his face as he reexamined his logic. Finally, he said, "Yes, yes you do."

"I do not," Kal replied.

"Let me see your hand." Gulliver leaned across the table, fighting Kal for his cards. Kal kept jumping his hands around, a suggestion of a smile on his face. Gulliver scrambled out of his seat in an attempt grab the cards.

"I do not know why you are doing this. I do not have the two." Kal quickly stood and raised his hands above his head. Given how incredibly tall Kal was to begin with, Gulliver was struggling.

"You are lying!" Gulliver tiptoed, jumped, and then knocked the cards right out of Kal's hand. Kings, queens, and aces fluttered down to the ground, as did the two of spades. Gulliver spotted it in an instant. "Oh, my god, I knew you were lying!" He wheezed, laughter bubbling in his throat.

"English is not my first language," Kal replied.

"My god, Kal," Gulliver guffawed. Kal was finally losing it. His cool and stoic façade melted away in favor of laughter. "It's numerical," Gulliver finished.

"You are so upset." Kal wrapped an arm around Gulliver's waist, pulling him closer.

"I always get so upset!" Gulliver groaned. "You are bloody ridiculous. The next time you pretend not to speak English, I'll just switch to Russian."

"Numerically, I do not think it would matter." Kal threw his head back, still laughing. He took the moment to pull his hair down from its bun and give Gulliver a quick kiss on the forehead.

Their mirth was just dying down when Gulliver stiffened. The sound of clicking heels struck him to the core. "We're the only ones on this floor. That's got to be her."

"Oh." Kal looked around the trashed room, wine and rum bottles occupying the corners and clothes draped all over the beds. "That is no good. It must have been bad news."

"You don't think the commander—"

Kal cut Gulliver off, "We cannot worry about it now. We need the room to look good before she comes."

Like a switch had been flipped, the two sped off to hide their copious amounts of booze and dirty clothes. Gulliver shoved his stuff into his paisley suitcase. Kal threw most of his in the tub. By the time Nikola's fist rapped on the door, the room looked semi-decent.

"Just a second," Gulliver called out. When Nikola didn't reply with a snide remark or order them to hurry, Gulliver swallowed hard. "This is bad." His heart rate picked up as he worried what could have possibly zapped Nikola's attitude.

"Calm down. We are good," Kal assured him before opening the door on a disenchanted Nikola.

She stood in the hallway for a while before uttering a hello. When she walked in, she patted Kal on the shoulder. "You're going to want to sit, big guy." She grabbed a chair from the end table where a mess of cards and water stains sat. She was going to comment on the mess. Gulliver knew it before she said it.

"If you two are gonna gamble and drink, use a goddamn coaster like the good lord intended." Even though her voice was aggressively neutral, this was a joke. It'd taken Gulliver a while to warm up to her curt witticisms.

She wiped the condensation from the table and then sat, the bottom hem of her pantsuit pulling up just enough to show the tight ankle straps of her pumps.

"Is the commander reassigning us?" Kal asked.

Gulliver was always relieved when Kal asked the questions on his mind for him. They joined her at the table, sitting an "appropriate" space away from each other.

"We're not getting reassigned," she replied.

The anxiety in Kal's eyes left just in time to be replaced.

"We're to return to the Carolina Facility. Expect to be gone for a few weeks."

"Why?" Gulliver had kept his calm for all of a minute. His temper was rarely seen but impossible to ignore when it came.

"Unspecified purposes." Even though Nikola's words had a defeated tone to them, Gulliver could easily see that she was sugarcoating.

There was a long pause while everyone came to the same conclusion.

"Unspecified purposes," Gulliver replied. "We're getting the steroid."

"You two won't get a say in it?" Kal snuck a glance at Gulliver. He'd been getting sloppier over the past few months. If Nikola wasn't on to them already, she would be soon.

"It's been decided for us. We're the best agents they have." Nikola didn't sound convincing in her delivery.

"The best agents?" Gulliver replied sharply, more aggressively than he'd intended, but unapologetic once it was done. "We're not the best agents. We're the agents who know about their fuckup. This is bollocks!"

"We don't have a choice in the matter, Gulliver," she said. "Kal went through it. He recovered faster than the others, and he came out with as ugly a mug as he had before. We're only going to get those three out of the woods if we can match them with equal strength."

Gulliver looked at his hands for a moment before clearing his throat and speaking evenly. "If you believe that, then why do you sound so fucking miserable yourself?"

Nikola tensed. Her tone grew instantly colder with Gulliver. "I'm sorry. Did my kindness make you forget I'm your superior?" she shot back. "I am upset that it was their choice to make and not mine, but that does not mean I'm going to go off and throw a fit because of it." Any form of exhaustion, any form of resignation, she'd had was gone. Gulliver could see it in her eyes.

The only audible sound in the hotel room was the repetitive clanking of a box air conditioner. Gulliver stared down like his eyes could burn holes in the carpet. He buried his hands in his hair. "They can't punish us for their mistakes." He shook his head. "That's simply not fair." His hate was radiating now. His options here were so limited. "They can't do that to me. I don't give them permission to pull my insides apart and make me some kind of half-human hybrid. This is their problem. They can fix it." He had a habit of crying when he got frustrated. He had since he was a boy. Today was no different. His eyes filled fast.

"Comrade," she said soothingly.

"Don't *comrade* me, Nikola! You don't want this, either!" Gulliver's words were bitter. He snapped up from the couch and started for his bag. Soon enough, he was packing everything.

"The situation is less than ideal, but what are your other options?" She stretched back to where she could see him. "Defect? Spend the rest of your life on the run from the KGB?"

"You defected from America. I've defected from the UK. Even Kal has shown more than once that his loyalty to the USSR is abysmal at best. The CIA losing three of their top agents? Not a problem for the KGB. The KGB losing three of their own subpar field agents, two of which are known defectors? Not a problem for the KGB, Nikola! They are experimenting on bodies that don't matter. We are disposable. Once our mission has been fulfilled, I bet they kill us, too."

His words were toxic.

"I feel sick." Kal stood shakily, bracing himself against the hotel's wallpapered interior. If he could have, Gulliver would go to him.

"It's obvious. We're too big of a liability." Gulliver shook his head. "We'll kill the Americans and then the KGB will kill us and pretend like the program never happened."

Kal was paling, his already fair skin growing sallow, sweat drenched his chest and soaked through his button-up in a near instant. "Nikola." His head shook. "I have my sisters." The light in his eyes started to go.

"Don't get worked up over worst-case scenarios. They aren't going to kill us." She stood and approached Gulliver. "And if they try, we'll stop them."

Gulliver snapped the lid of his suitcase shut. He looked back over to Kal, completely ignoring Nikola. "You wanna run? Then get moving, because I'm going."

"Comrades, I'm telling you to rethink this." Nikola stood in front of them. She was shorter than both Kal and Gulliver, but far more foreboding than the two of them combined. "You are making the wrong choice," she said coldly. "You think your family will starve if you stay, Kal? Imagine how dead they'll be if you defect. KIA? At least, your family gets food, clothes, reward for your sacrifice. You defect? The KGB will hunt them down and squash them like bugs." She turned her attention to Gulliver. "Sit your ass down. You're rushing into things."

"You're right. I'm rushing into things! Time is precious and I'm not wasting any. I'm getting the hell out of Dodge!" Gulliver shoved past her.

"Gulliver, stop!" Nikola snatched his arm, her nails digging through the soft material of his sweater. "Stay with us," she hissed.

"Us? Kal is coming with me." It didn't dawn on Gulliver that Kal wouldn't come, until he wasn't. "You're not." His heart was hollowing. The idea of going on without him was wrenching, but one he'd have to get used to.

"I must care for my sisters." His voice was low, sad. "This may be the only way to keep providing for them." Kal bowed his head, his gray eyes vanishing under his hair. "I think you should stay, but I know you must look out for yourself."

"You're right." Gulliver was crying again, despite his stiff upper lip and headstrong choice. "I do have to look out for myself."

"Gulliver." Nikola tightened her grip on him. "Rethink this. Do you really want the entire USSR as your enemy?"

"I've defected before. I'll do it again," Gulliver remained respectful. Two more minutes and he'd likely never see either of them again. He'd never see those agents in the woods again.

Nikola let go, and he pulled his arm away. "Fine," she said, "go out that door, and make yourself an enemy of the state."

"You both owe me at least a ten-minute start after all we've been through." Gulliver walked to the door, and turned the knob with a sweaty palm. Nikola began to shout something behind him, but it was drowned out by the giant group of SWAT agents grabbing for him the moment he stepped outside of the room. There'd been an entire fleet of them beyond their door, waiting for the three of them like vultures.

"Christ!" Gulliver needed to think fast. "I was getting a bloody Coke!" An all right improvisation. He'd have believed it if not for the suitcase in his hand. Luckily, he had back up.

"I changed my mind!" Nikola's voice came from behind the room's closed door. "I want coffee!" Nikola busted out of the hotel room and gave the first SWAT agent she encountered a dirty look. "What are you all gawking at?"

Gulliver, although disheveled, pulled it off. "I swear I am working hard on getting you that coffee, but there is literally a barricade out here." He even mustered a laugh in between balancing the undeniable dread and relief that was washing over him. He'd never get to leave. This was his future now. But, he'd also never have to leave Kal.

The faceless agents eventually loosened their collective grip.

She gave the crowd a once-over, then scowled. "One of you, get me a drink." She then grabbed Gulliver. "*You, get packing.*" She nudged him back toward the motel room.

As the SWAT agents began to disperse, Gulliver and Nikola reentered the motel room, then slammed the door behind them.

"We almost lost you." Kal let out a long, slow exhale. Gulliver could see through his mask of civility and into his heart. This had drained him.

"You two reflect so goddamn poorly on me," Nikola snapped. "I am great at what I do."

It took their new posse of SWAT agents only five minutes to bring her coffee, and then it only took ten minutes for the three of them to pack up their belongings and get out to their chauffeured vehicle. The drive from New York to the Carolinas was long. So, everyone had time to watch as they sped along the highway, the stench of pesticide and cow wafting into the cramped cabin of an Econoline. Gulliver was sandwiched between Nikola and Kal in the back. The two grunts in the front were preoccupied flipping through channels of static looking for a salvageable signal.

"Things will be fine, Gulliver." Kal gently elbowed him, whispering barely above audible threshold.

"Shut up, Kal." He glared out the windshield, trying to stop himself from freaking out. There was no way out. He was trapped. "We're going to fucking die."

"Change is good, comrades." Nikola leaned in, her lips barely moving and her gaze set on the driver.

"Please," Gulliver scoffed. "You've never changed, Nikola. Since the moment we met, you've never stopped playing the part of someone convinced she's better than the rest of us." Gulliver refused to make eye contact with either of them. He'd forgive them in time. He didn't have it in him to stay this mad.

"Mmmmmmm. Wallow in your self-pity then." Nikola's words dripped with sarcasm.

Kal went back to whispering to Gulliver, and Nikola rolled her neck back onto the seat, lifting her face to the night sky. In reality, this was not the first time Nikola had changed because she was told to.

*

There was something spiritual about going to the gym in the mornings. The building had hardly any movement. There was no one there to interrupt, and the floors always smelled faintly of lemon-based cleaner. These were the times Nikola reveled in. This time of year, winter storms kept her confined to the indoors. So, she ran the smoothly finished indoor track. Her tight tennis shoes squeaked, the noise bouncing off the cold, hard walls of the empty building. She threw herself into every step, her heart rate to the heavens and muscles burning to the bone. The way she moved made it look as though her head was ready to bob off her shoulders. She clenched her jaw to help bear the pain. Sweat soaked her shirt and beads of perspiration ran down her face, desperate to fall to the floor. And despite all this pain, she kept pushing, until her ligaments and tendons grew weak and her legs loose and wobbling. As she approached the mile marker, she widened her strides. Her bones feeling like they were about to bow and break in two.

The feeling of crossing the finish line was always the same. Her stomach knotted and her heart beat against her ribs. She huffed, wiping the sweat from her brow. Finishing a run was euphoric, painful but euphoric. She rejoiced in the accomplishment and the burn of lactic acid. She pulled her hair down from its ponytail and started toward the women's locker room. Soon enough, the building would start to fill with agents from all walks of life, and Nikola would be at her desk filing paperwork. It was frustrating, being in administration, but they said it was necessary for her to work her way up the clearance-level ladder.

The silence of the locker room was another calming aspect of the gym. It wasn't silence with machines running in the background, the TV playing on low, or dogs running across linoleum in the kitchen—it was true silence. There was something meditative about it. But, before she could start her day, she had to purge.

She walked into the bathroom stall casually, then checked over her shoulder one last time before sinking to the ground. She sat there for a while like she was waiting for a Pavlovian retch of the stomach. Eventually, as the post-run nausea began to settle in, Nikola stuck two fingers down her throat, against the hardness of the back of her mouth and the wetness of her tongue. She dry heaved once, bile retching its way up the esophagus. She dry heaved again and braced herself on the rim of the toilet with her free hand. This sent her crashing into the bathroom floor as she slipped on the sweat from her palm.

"Christ," she grunted, her hand grazing her now-bleeding nose. Nikola coughed in between deep breaths. She shook, pulled herself back up, and dry heaved until vomit and water filled the bowl as bile mixed with blood mixed with sweat. She kept purging until her throat was raw from the acid and she felt truly empty inside. This was also euphoric.

She flushed away the lost contents of her stomach and walked out of the bathroom stall as though nothing had happened.

At the sink, she let the water run for a moment before pooling it in her hands. It was hot and welcome on her cool skin. The blood and dried spit came off her face and vanished down the drain. The evidence gone. Her shoulders were tense. She kept her hands under the water until blood broke through the dry skin of her knuckles. After rubbing her hands raw, she shut the sink off and went to shower. It was quick and cold.

Once done, she walked into the locker bay, opening her locker and grabbing her work clothes. Her small frame looked skeletal in the tight-fitting dress. When she looked at herself in the mirror, all dressed, she instinctively dug the tips of her weak fingernails into the palm of her hand as the frustration bubbled up. The running, the purge, it made her feel powerful. This made her feel trapped. It always made her feel trapped. She threw her fist out, her bloody knuckles smacking into a wall-bound paper towel dispenser, once, twice, three times. It didn't make sense for her to keep hitting it, but she did.

She bit her upper lip, shaking her head because she knew it was too late. The tears started and she felt even more helpless than before. Gradually, she intertwined her fingers with the damp and matted hair above her temples and gave it a hard tug. Soon enough, she'd be at her desk smiling, grabbing coffee for superiors, her tactical problem-solving still going unnoticed, all in hopes that her hard work would pay off and she'd end up on a real assignment as opposed to administrative duty. She was still fighting for control of herself when her meltdown was interrupted.

"You know there's more paper towels in the hall." A feminine voice floated into the room.

The sound of her voice sent Nikola reeling. She kept telling herself she needed to stop crying before turning around, and because of this, she didn't initially respond.

"Hello?" The woman's voice sounded smooth like a pan of melted chocolate as moved closer to Nikola.

Nikola coughed forcefully before clearing her throat and spinning around. Already muttering a halfhearted explanation. "I've just been under a—" Nikola stopped speaking when she saw the infamous woman in front of her. She was five foot eight and had a license to kill. Today's ensemble was a tight purple piece and hair bigger than her ego. Nikola's face flushed.

Diana inspected Nikola unapologetically. "You're Nikola, right?"

Nikola lifted her brows as she realized that this goddess knew her name. "Yes. You're Hera, right?"

Diana smirked. "Was there any doubt?"

"I'll get out of your way," Nikola muttered, picking up her still damp workout attire and purse. She had planned on doing her hair and makeup there, but from what she had heard, Diana could be difficult to work with. She wanted to get away as fast as possible. Keeping her eyes down, Nikola headed for the door, but Diana stopped her. Blocking her as she'd gone to pass by.

"You should stay." Diana sounded concerned. "You look unwell." She placed a hand on Nikola's shoulder.

Nikola's gaze perked up from the ground and landed on her. She examined Diana momentarily, determining whether to stay or go.

Forcing herself to smile, Nikola bowed her head. "I feel fine. Thanks, though." She shuffled to her locker, her thoughts in a flurry from this chance encounter.

Diana came behind her and sweetly placed her hand on her arm. "Stay, I insist. I have been wanting to talk to you anyway."

Nikola didn't want to be late. She wanted to be at her desk when she was supposed to at 7:00 a.m., but no one said no to the goddess. Not even someone as stubborn as Nikola. "All right." Her mouth went dry. Her head was starting to reel from the earlier purge. She swayed.

"There's no reason to be afraid." She laughed a melodic laugh. "You're shaking. Have a seat." Diana guided her to a bench in the bay and sat, patting beside her so Nikola would join her.

"I, uh…thanks." Nikola sat down, her hand on her head, trying to figure out if this was actually happening. In no world did Nikola see her and the goddess crossing paths, but here it was. "I'm fine, really. I just finished a workout."

"I saw." Diana's smile was gone. "I've been watching you for a few days now."

"Why?"

"I just happened upon you here a few mornings ago when I dropped in early to see the director. You have a decent set of skills, Nikola. You're agile, fast, strong for your size. I was interested after watching you train, so I dug further into your file. You've busted your ass over the last year. You're a great problem-solver, a strong communicator, everyone I spoke to about you spoke highly." Diana shifted in her seat and tilted her face closer to Nikola's, holding her gaze. "And it pains me to say this, but it would be a disservice to you if I didn't say it. You're not cut out to be an agent."

Nikola had been listening with her heart racing, waiting for Diana to say the words "field training," waiting to finally be rescued from her sea of pencil pushing and paperwork, welcomed onto the field as a true equal, but then that last part came and Nikola felt her entire body shaking. Her face grew hotter.

"Excuse me?" she said sharply.

"The purging, the over-exercising. You're not cut out to be an agent. You're too indulgent." Nikola was already ready to argue, but Diana quickly cut her off. "I'm doing you a favor. I'm saving you time. Get out of here and find something else to do with your life, because you will never leave that desk in administration."

"Take your advice and shove it up your ass, Miss Priss. My personal life is none of your business," Nikola spat, already gathering up her bag and workout garb, ready to storm out the door.

"Nikola, don't waste your time. So long as you're going to sabotage yourself, you will never be an agent like me. You'll never be at my clearance. You'll never get the kinds of missions I go on. You will never see that field. Clean up your act or go back to hobunk nowhere. I'm not telling you anything that isn't true." Diana crossed her legs and looked up at Nikola who was already halfway through the door.

Nikola kept telling herself not to go off on Diana. A blow-up like this could get her fired. A blow-up like this would be the end of the career, but the moment Diana said "Hobunk nowhere," a blow-up like this was worth it.

Nikola kept her voice calm and her words calculated in delivering a string of insults. "I know it's hard to imagine a female agent who doesn't want to be *like you,* but they do exist." Nikola turned on her heel and walked closer to the sitting diva. "Some of us don't have the tits, ass, and need to sleep around for secrets. Some of us can do our job without the frills and charlataning." Nikola bent, crouched down to be exactly at Diana's eye level. "So I guess you're right. I'll never be a spy like you. We can't all sleep around like Hera and Adams, some of us are better."

If Diana was shocked, she didn't show it. That doll-like face of hers hardly moved. But, when she spoke, there was a revitalized energy. "You think I seduce so I can do my job?" She laughed. "I can break necks without flinching. I'm the best shot in the CIA. I am why we are beating the reds. I've started wars and ended them. I do what I do to make my job easier. Not because I need to. You want to talk about strength? I am the epitome of it."

"Save it for someone who cares, honey." Nikola slammed a locker and then started toward the door, but she found Diana following close behind her.

"Wait." Diana rushed to Nikola and cornered her in the small doorway to the gym, their faces only inches apart. "I believe I misjudged you. Which was a poor decision on my part, but you gave me plentiful cause." Diana wasn't making the best case. "Perhaps you will be a great agent, but what I am saying is still true. The purging and over-exercising must stop. *Perhaps* I could help you." She sounded diplomatic and well-rounded, but she was still crawling under Nikola's skin.

"In case I wasn't clear enough earlier, I don't want your help." Nikola pushed past her and swung the door open, but Diana pursued her farther. It wasn't until they were out into the main hallway that Diana caught up to her, grabbing at Nikola's arm.

"What if I could get you in on the Jimmy Hoffa arrest?" Diana looked up to Nikola, a serious expression in her eyes but a manipulative knowing in her heart.

Nikola glanced around at the swarms of agents piling in for their morning shifts. In the sea of black, white, and neckties, she felt like the crowd was big enough that she and the goddess could speak as if they were alone.

"Dammit," she whispered, more to herself than anyone else. "Of course, I want in on that." She kept her head down like the conversation they were having was illegal.

Diana's eyes lit with excitement. "Perfect."

*

Four hours into the car ride, Gulliver finally passed out. Exhaustion hit him quickly. Kal had done a bit to cheer him up, stupid impressions, dumb Russian jokes that failed in translation and thus made Gulliver crack up even more, but there was still a sadness to Kal that couldn't be denied. Nikola had been feeling anxiety. They'd be in the hills soon enough. She mustered up what energy she had and spoke.

"Kal, after you got the steroid, did you feel any different? Not physically, but mentally." Nikola rested her arm on the seat behind him.

"A bit," Kal replied. "I'm less worried about destroying my liver now." He laughed.

"Pffft, Yeah, you would." Nikola paused for a moment, watching Kal's attention drift down to Gulliver before looking up to her for help.

"You think he'll be all right?" Kal asked.

Nikola laughed as a knee-jerk reaction. She didn't feel too bad about it, but it was clear that it didn't soothe her partner's anxiety. "You know him better than I do. What do you think?"

"I know what I think. What do you think?" Kal tipped his head forward, a seriousness about him.

"I don't know if he'll be okay or not. But what I can say is, regardless of the outcome, we are going to have to listen to him bitch about this for the next year."

Kal released a low, bellow of a laugh. "We should be fine."

"Fine," Nikola repeated. "That's a way to put it." The car drove deep into the mountains of the Carolinas.

Roswell

SEPTEMBER 26, 1963

When it rains in the mountains, waiting for the storm to pass can take hours. With the altitude of the bluffs, the temperature can drop twenty-some degrees in only an hour. And although Ruby had driven home in worse weather, that night, she felt more on edge than ever before. Since her brush with the three-eyed man of the mountain, she hadn't gone near the park. But a friend needed a ride out to Fontana and she was too indebted to them to say no. It was just to some bonfire in the woods. Normally, Ruby would have attended, but she wouldn't dare risk hiking now. She was ten parts interested in knowing more about the strange man she'd met weeks earlier, but ten thousand parts more terrified of what would happen if their paths crossed again. The pounding rain on her windshield and the clatter of thunder only added to her stress.

She sat in her driver's seat, white-knuckling the steering wheel and singing softly to herself as she sped through the curves of the road. For a minute, she even felt a little safe, the necklaces on her rearview mirror jingling along with the bumps in the road and her heat blasting to keep her warm. But in the midst of this last moment of peace, her tire blew out, and her car skidded on the slick pavement and hydroplaned into a ditch. Her face smashed into the steering wheel and her whole body was suspended as the car's momentum sent her up off her seat. It happened in slow motion yet all at once.

BEFORE SHE WOKE, a monster pulled her from her van.

The vehicle had wedged itself on the border of the woods and the road. Anyone looking in would be concealed and hidden away from the world. So Diana wasn't afraid to approach it. She had half a mind to get Da Vinci and hijack it, but upon seeing who was inside the van, any plans of escape vanished and were replaced by an irrefutable rage.

"We should kill her." Tim examined the girl's bruised body. "We have to kill her." He opened the door of the van and she came slumping out. He caught her before she fell. Steadily, he placed his hands around her neck. He looked to Diana, as though waiting for confirmation, but she'd give him none of it.

"It's got to be Da Vinci." Diana stared at the girl with no empathy in her heart. "We give him an inch and he takes a mile. Now, he's lied to us and put the whole group at risk. We need to know that we can trust him." There was a chill in the air that did not come from the rain but the frigidity in her voice.

"It's Da Vinci, Diana." Tim went to break Ruby's neck anyway, only to be stopped in the split instant before it was too late.

"What the hell are you doing?" Diana had a cruel tone to her voice. She had her hands between Tim's and the girl's neck. "You heard me. Da Vinci is the one to do it."

"He won't." Tim scowled as he resisted Diana's controlling grip.

"Then we abandon him and Rigan to fend for themselves."

Tim let go of Ruby and left Diana to catch the girl before she hit the ground. "You know what I hate most about you?" He paused, but not long enough for her to answer. "You're petty." He turned his back to her and began his ascent into the mountains. "You think now is the time for your game of power and politics, Diana?" Tim kept his back to her, speaking from a distance. "I'll clue you in; no one here has power."

THERE WASN'T SLEEP anymore. Only a dreamlike state existed for Da Vinci. Blurs of men in power, explosions on the water, small-town mothers, and the smell of meat grinding intertwined with the faces of those he knew, wars he'd been in, and other jumbled pieces of subconscious, all trying to make sense of his partial lucidity. Being snapped out of it was sometimes a blessing. So, when Diana woke him, he welcomed it.

"Da Vinci?" Her voice was a lover's coo. She was seated on damp grass, barely visible in the dark. "I need you to wake up for me."

Protected under a makeshift shelter of sticks and tarp, Da Vinci had only a sliver of warmth. He felt for Diana's hand as he came out of his trance. "Hey." He gave her a tired smile, whispering over the muffled sounds of crickets and rain. "What's going on?" He looked at her face, still beautiful and her hair, still a soft yellow. Her presence had a warmth to it, regardless of her cracked skin. For a moment, it was paradise.

"Are you okay?" Da Vinci grabbed for his still-drying shirt. Once he caught sight of the trouble in those big eyes of hers, he hurried to get ready. "What's going on?"

She grabbed his hand and helped him to his feet. "There's something you need to see." She let her hand linger in his for another few moments before turning away. "Come now." She ducked out of the shelter and entered the clearing, Da Vinci not far behind her.

"Diana, wait," he grunted, zipping his damp slacks and shuffling out after her. It was only upon entering the clearing that his stomach turned and the bile in his gut wrenched up and burned his throat. Lying in the clearing was Ruby Starr, badly bruised and unconscious.

He stepped over to the girl, not looking Diana or Tim in the eye. He crouched down to examine her. On her cheek, was an imprint of her steering wheel's logo. "Wait." His gaze turned upward to Diana. "You didn't do this. It was a car wreck?"

"No, but we would have." Diana stepped Ruby and stood beside Tim. Both of them had a cold aloofness in their stance.

"When I saw this the first time... In the first vision I had, it was you two who hurt her." Da Vinci looked at Ruby's forehead, the wounds seemed superficial. "But this time, it wasn't," he said simply. "I would have rather she never come back, but at least this time, we did things differently."

"This time, we'll do things right." Diana kept a hard, flat expression on her face. "She dies. You lied to us. You breached trust. Make it right."

The reality of the situation settled in. Da Vinci's mind began to reel and the weight on his shoulders felt heavy enough to sink him. He turned to Tim who offered him no assistance.

"There is no other way, Da Vinci. She has to die. She knows too much and could lead the KGB right to us." Tim was always honest with him.

"We got lucky the first time," she explained. "We had the upper hand because they underestimated us. If we run into them again, it won't be the same level of child's play. We'll have no element of surprise. Next time we see them, they'll have come up with something to counter us. She's too much of a liability."

Da Vinci brushed off the knees of his pants and threw his shoulders back as he stood. "We're not going to kill her. This conversation will go on and on, but we're not going to kill her." He crossed his arms. "I know this. So, let's just skip to the part where we decide it's in our best interest not to kill the kid." He let out a long deep breath that sounded more like a groan of pain than an exhale of relief. "This argument is going to be a waste of our time, because I know that in a few weeks, she'll still be here."

Diana gave orders, and when they weren't followed, someone always paid. Under her cold surface, a rage was boiling, and Da Vinci knew it. The two men were her audience, hinged on her response.

"You've already proven that the future can be changed. This is no different. We've got to kill her, and if you want us to stick together, it's got to be you who does it." Not a muscle in Diana's face flinched as Da Vinci started his rebuttal.

"She hasn't told anyone, and she won't tell anyone. She didn't even see you two that first night in the woods. If I'm right, this girl will become vital to our survival. We can't kill her now, or we doom ourselves later on." Da Vinci was more irritated at this whole ordeal than anything else. He knew she lived. He'd seen it. This was a waste of time.

"We've spent enough energy on this already," Tim huffed. "This needs to end."

"Tim agrees, Da Vinci. This needs to end." Diana took a few steps back from the girl, giving Da Vinci more space. "Kill her before she wakes up, or you'll have to do it while she's conscious."

Sweat built up on Da Vinci's brow. His heart beat in his ears. How did this play out? How did they get from here to letting her live? He guessed the only way, was if he made it happen. "We don't kill her."

"We don't," Diana confirmed. "You do."

A twinge of resentment hit Da Vinci. He stared at Diana with the same amount of coldness she presented to him. "I don't kill kids."

"But you kill mothers, you kill fathers, soldiers, civilians, collateral damage. You may not kill kids, but you sure commanded the orders that did. The landing at Normandy, the bombings in Dresden, it's no different."

Her words cut him deep enough to harm him, but he kept his head held high and his voice strong. "That was war. It isn't the same." Da Vinci stepped up closer to the two of them, his face now only inches from Diana's. "And you know that."

"It is the same, Da Vinci," she answered. "It's us or them, and you'll choose us like you always do."

"You need to shut the hell up." A hoarse voice came from behind Da Vinci, an indisputable accent strung onto the words. Da Vinci turned just in time for Rigan to grab onto his shoulder. Rigan was weak, but he'd always been resilient.

Diana saved face. "I apologize if my words have offended either of you, but this is no time to show mercy or compassion. This girl puts us all at risk." Diana turned to Tim for support, and although it was rare they agreed on something, he supported her in this endeavor.

"The sooner we kill her, the sooner we can get moving," Tim added.

"Your answer is always homicide. I'm sure she's..." Rigan's voice grew faint as his gaze followed Tim's to the girl on the ground. "Fuck." For a minute, Rigan stood there with his mouth hanging open and his jagged car-wreck teeth exposed. "Fuck!"

This made Da Vinci's heart break. He and Rigan had always shared the same hesitance toward death. The boy was realizing this entire situation was his fault.

"What?!" Tim put his hands out in confusion. "Why are you yelling?"

"She's my local." Rigan's words were labored. His breathing slowing to long, heavy heaves.

"You led her here?" Diana asked.

Rigan bowed his head, and Da Vinci was quick to offer any condolences he could muster up.

"It's okay, Rigan." Da Vinci spoke in Portuguese, excluding Diana and Tim from the conversation.

"Okay?" Rigan turned to Da Vinci, speaking in his native tongue. "It's not okay. They're going to kill her. I did this." Rigan coughed. Just the walk from the shelter had taken the wind out of him, the anxiety induced by seeing Ruby seemed to be overwhelming his still-healing body.

"They're not going to kill her." Da Vinci could feel Tim and Diana glaring, but he continued on in Portuguese, choosing to console Rigan instead.

"Enough, you two." There was an edge of contempt in Tim's voice, coming from years of listening to Rigan and Da Vinci talk *exclusively* to each other. "We need to get this over with."

Ruby woke up to a scene. Tim reaching for her neck and three shrill voices screaming for him to stop.

"Knock it off!"

"What the fuck, Tim?!"

"Stop! Stop! Stop!" Da Vinci pushed on Tim's shoulders but made about as much progress as one might make attempting to move a giant. Diana on the other hand, grabbed him by the collar of his shirt and succeeded in yanking him away from Ruby. Tim looked ready to jump her but stopped on account of Da Vinci throwing himself between the two of them.

"Stop it," Da Vinci growled. "The both of you!" The tension in the air was high, and everyone had a temper that was bubbling over. His inflection teeter-tottered between screaming and sobbing. "We can't kill her."

"Ruby? Are you all right?" Rigan was over her, ready to fight off anyone who sprung at her, but as she came to, she began to scream.

Startled and likely physically strained, Rigan fainted. Da Vinci was quick and lucky enough to catch him. He laid the boy on the ground gently. "Rigan, Rigan, come on…" Da Vinci kneeled down, checking Rigan's now fully scaled neck for a pulse. He was alive but out for now. It seemed each time he came to, he could stay for less and less time. Da Vinci checked Rigan's bandages.

"What is that?" Ruby's voice was high and her breathing was off. She stumbled to her feet and audibly gasped as she found herself face to face with Da Vinci once again. "No." Her voice was low and her tone was riddled with dread. "No," she repeated. "I didn't come back. I didn't break the rules." She nearly collapsed again in agony.

"The rules?" Diana parroted. "What's she talking about, Da Vinci?"

"I told her not to come back on the first night we met her." Da Vinci shook his head and turned his attention to Ruby. "Do you feel all right? You were in a crash."

"You told me things would be fine if I didn't come back," she croaked as her eyes started to well. "You're not going to kill me, are you?"

Diana and Tim both watched Da Vinci carefully now. He couldn't read past their expressions, but he was certain they were rightly pissed.

"You knew this was going to happen?" Diana didn't hold back on the accusing aspect of the situation.

"Not exactly," Da Vinci defended himself.

"But you knew she'd find us again? You knew she'd create complications." Tim crossed his arms over his chest, perhaps showing the most emotion Tim was capable of.

"I thought I had stopped her." Da Vinci could feel himself losing footing in this argument. "I thought things had changed."

Diana looked at him with an icy expression. "This isn't the future you said you changed, is it? The one where Tim and I die?"

"No!" Da Vinci immediately blurted. "I changed that. Rigan is here. That's a change!"

"What a positive change on Rigan's behalf," Tim muttered dryly.

"I am trying, Tim," Da Vinci barked.

Ruby was already gathering the belongings they'd taken from her, including a backpack and blanket. They were quick to notice.

"You're not going anywhere, sweetheart." Diana's words were not a challenge but an order.

Ruby swallowed hard and stepped closer to the group now. She was afraid but brave. "Is it okay?" She pointed down to Rigan.

"It?" Da Vinci replied with an unintentionally sharp tone. "*It* is Marco."

"What?" She joined Da Vinci on the ground. Her eyes widened as she took in all of Rigan's abnormalities. "Maybe what he was telling me was true," she whispered as a note to self, but with trained ears, they all heard.

"Did he tell you about us?" Da Vinci attempted to maintain a bit of tact in his digging, but his attention was divided as he attempted to find the cause of Rigan's distress, re-checking the makeshift bandages for bleeding.

"No." Ruby shook her head and pulled her legs in toward her chest. "Just, just alien stuff—what's really in Area 51 and...and like...I don't know. People tease me about stuff like that a lot, so I thought he was pulling my leg, but I mean, maybe it was true. This is some creature-from-the-black-lagoon-level shit."

"Operation Mogul?" Diana raised an eyebrow and now stepped closer, her body looming over the three of them.

"He's a tale spinner." Da Vinci addressed his partners this time. "It's just something he does." He paused, weighing the anxiety that was tearing him apart with the need to keep going. "Grab the aspirin from your backpack, Ruby."

"How did you..." Ruby grabbed her bag and then dug out a bottle of small white pills. She poured two out for herself and gave the rest to Da Vinci. "Here. You need them more than me." She popped the two into her mouth and swallowed them dry. She meekly looked up at Diana and Tim, clearly trying her best to ignore their physical deformities. "You know, there's some apples and a sandwich in there. If you guys want them." Her voice had the strength of a mouse's squeak by the time she offered the bag to them.

Diana considered it thoughtfully before taking the bag and handing it off to Tim. "Thank you."

Tim went right to work looking through the backpack. There were no secret compartments, no weapons, just a change of clothes, some food, and a copy of Ken Kesey's *One Flew Over the Cuckoo's Nest*.

"I'm keeping this," he said, pulling the book from her bag.

It was clear Ruby had intended to laugh. She had a smile on her face and started to chuckle moments before she burst into tears. "Are you going to let me live?"

"We have to kill you," Tim replied casually, his hand still in her bag. Diana and

Da Vinci snapped their gazes toward him. Both upset, likely for different reasons.

"We are not going to kill you. Don't worry. I know you live. Trust me, I see the future." Da Vinci put his arm out and onto her shoulder, reassuring her that things would be all right. He then turned and smiled at Diana, his demeanor calm. "Might I request a moment alone with you two?"

Diana offered her hand to him and helped him off the ground. "If you must." She gestured for Tim to follow them as they pulled aside, then left Ruby with only an unconscious Rigan as company.

"Can you still see her?" Tim asked Diana as they descended farther into the woods.

"Yes," she replied calmly. "And if she runs, I can catch her, no problem." Tim and Diana then turned to Da Vinci expectantly.

The back of his neck prickled and sweat inched down his back. They were waiting for him to speak prophecy. Her life was in his hands. "I know this looks bad, but you two have to let her live. I can't go on with her blood on my hands. Not when she didn't do anything wrong, and not when killing her could indirectly kill us."

"Then you should have bloodied your hands the first time around," Tim countered.

Diana placed her hand in Da Vinci's. "There's no way around this, Da Vinci. If she's a spy for the KGB, she'll kill us. If she's just a local, she'll still kill us. They'll find her. She'll talk. Especially now that there is more than likely a documented car crash with her name on it."

"She's no KGB agent and you know that." Da Vinci pulled his hand away and began to pace. "I wish you two would stop playing scared, because I know that you're not." He started calculating all the possible ways he could get out of this conversation unscathed.

"We're not playing this game scared, Da Vinci. We're playing it smart," Diana refuted. She and Tim, despite their differences, were both tactile like this. It was clear neither of them planned on backing down.

Da Vinci could feel his face heating up. His stomach churned as the truth came to the surface. "This girl is the only reason Rigan and I live. You two may not feel the cold and need to eat, but we do." He felt the shame flood over him. "She is the only reason we survive as long as we do." This time, he spoke to Diana. "And she is the only way to get ahold of Adams."

That name always grabbed Diana's attention. "She is?"

"How do we know you're not just saying this to save her?" Tim asked.

"You don't." Da Vinci was starting to cry. He didn't want to, but look at the goddamn circumstances. He felt hopeless. "I don't." He broke down, the reality of his visions and the reality of the future setting in. "I don't know what's real and what's not." He folded in on himself. Both Diana and Tim reached out to grab him. He braced himself on the two of them, his sobs heavy. "I'm trying to save us. I'm trying so hard to save us all." His knees gave way, but as he sank, so did his partners. They followed him to the ground, sitting on the soil.

"Is she what you changed? Was she going to be the reason Tim and I died?" Diana held his hand again, her compassion a glimmer of hope in his bleak life.

"I don't know. I don't know," he squawked, his throat hoarse and the tears not stopping. "She isn't KGB. She doesn't lead them to us, but in the future, when you know if you save her, you'll die. You two still always choose to save her over yourselves."

Diana and Tim both exchanged dubious glances. Tim even laughed.

"That's not particularly characteristic of Tim and me, Da Vinci. I fear you may be worrying over nothing." Diana rested her hand on his back, rubbing it gently.

"But you do it," he murmured, pulling away from his partners and sitting up on his own. "You both do it. Even though I tell you not to... But how do I even know that's the future now?" The question was aimed more to the universe than to them. He'd been so frustrated over these last weeks. He didn't understand what anything meant anymore. "Rigan wasn't there in that final fight with them, so that's changed, but neither was Adams. It was just us, and all I have is bits and pieces, and no matter how many times I put it together, it doesn't fit. I keep taking guesses and trying to make logical leaps and bounds, but it never makes sense." He rubbed his forehead, irritating his third eye.

Diana turned to Tim, and an unspoken agreement was made. "She'll stay until we no longer need her." Diana took Da Vinci's hands. "Okay?" Diana met his gaze. Her eyes were a cool, steady gray color, and in them, Da Vinci always felt as though he'd find salvation.

"But that means you could die... But it also means she won't." Da Vinci tipped his head back and looked at the stars.

"What you saw holds no promise, Da Vinci. You have changed the future before, right?" Diana suggested.

"Minimally," he whispered.

"Then she stays for now," Diana said.

Da Vinci could feel his fears crowding around him, but he chose to press on. "Okay." He cleaned away the tears and dirt from his scabbed-up face. Diana and Tim helped him to his feet.

The three entered the clearing, surprised to find Ruby still there, sitting quietly next to Rigan. She turned and saw them, grabbed her bag, clearly intending to make a run for it but stopped short when Diana laughed.

"There's no reason to run. You will not die tonight." She stepped closer to Ruby, eventually taking her soft face in her cool, cracking hands. "I promise you your safety in exchange for goods and services if you will so have it."

"What do you mean?" Ruby asked.

"Food, medicine, and a change of clothes. That's all we want." This move was uncharacteristically soft for Diana, but maybe even she couldn't deny the facts. They were starving, some of them were sick, and they were trapped. They could use her help. So, although Ruby was not set solely free as Da Vinci would have rather seen it, and although she was not dead as Diana would have rather seen it, she was going to live.

Diana went over the logistics of drop-off points and meeting times, and by the time she was done, Ruby only really had one question. "What's stopping me from running away?" Ruby asked innocently. "Not that I would. I'm just curious."

"Nothing," Tim said grimly.

Pulling himself away from Tim, Da Vinci joined Diana. "I'll walk her back to her van. Just to make sure she's safe." He pulled from the pocket of his slacks a long, red scrap of fabric which he'd fashioned into a kind of wrap for his forehead, to cover his third eye. "Let's get going, before they tow your van."

"Oh, my god. My van. Did it survive the crash?" Ruby asked.

Da Vinci laughed, relieved that, given all she had faced that night, the state of her glorified passion wagon was at the top of her concern list.

"The front is a little banged up, but you'll be fine," Diana said.

"Great...Well...thank you," Ruby said before joining Da Vinci on a walk through the great forest. As they followed the trail, Ruby seemed deep in thought, contemplating, curiosity eating her up. Eventually, she asked, "What happened to you four? What made you all...sentient?"

"Sentient...that's a nice way to sell it." Wanting to protect her, Da Vinci lied, "Aliens."

"Wrong. Try again," she sassed. "They'd never."

"Yetis." He thought she bought it for a second, but as they traveled farther, she tried again.

"I just had to plead for my life. I feel honesty is a good thing right about now."

"Communists." There wasn't a hint of play in his voice.

"Like McCarthyist?"

"Like the KGB."

"What are you then?" Her tone softened.

"Intelligence agents." Da Vinci dipped and followed her down the path, her van now in sight from the slightly higher bluff.

"What?" Ruby had to stop for a minute to take it in. "Like spies?"

"That's another word for it." He had little enthusiasm. "We worked for the CIA, and sometimes we were lucky, and sometimes we weren't. This time, we were really unlucky."

"So you are more man than mystic." There was a deep sadness in her tone. She leaned back on a rock formation along the path. "I am so sorry.

I... How did Marco get wrapped up in this? He was fine just a week or two ago."

"He got dragged into this by mistake." Da Vinci's gaze wandered off to the skyline of mountaintops they faced, watching lightning bugs glide through the sky. "His real name is Rigan, by the way."

"Rigan," she repeated. "Is that Brazilian?"

Da Vinci nodded. "That it is."

"He'll be okay," Ruby promised. "I'll bring all the medical supplies I can carry when we meet again."

"About that—" Da Vinci exhaled steadily. "Don't. It may be for the best if you don't come back, Ruby. Do you remember what I told you the first night we met?"

"Yeah," Ruby replied. "I think about it every night when I go to bed, every time I feel there are eyes on me when there aren't, every time I look to the sky, I'm worried I'm going to kill someone."

"I don't think what I said has changed at all. Yeah, they didn't find you on a trail, and yeah, they didn't beat you half to death, but...time corrected itself. You were still found and you were still hurt." He started moving again, leaving the view behind in favor of the trail. They were getting closer. "I can't say for sure, but I fear that if you come back, Diana and Tim will die." He hesitated. "I also fear that if you don't, Rigan will die. I don't know what happens to you." Da Vinci could feel himself getting choked up again, but he swallowed his tears, forcing himself to speak coherently. "It's just something to consider. I don't know what of the future I've changed, but I know that you are entering a dangerous world by taking part in this, and I can't guarantee your safety and I can't guarantee the safety of the others. It may be best if you just go back home and stay there."

Whatever swarm of emotions hit her, rendered her silent. Instead she just stared, expecting answers from him like the rest of them.

Da Vinci could see her struggle. "I offer only my advice and what I've seen. Sadly, what I've seen isn't clear."

Domovoi

OCTOBER 5, 1963

There was something vicious in the way Kal and Nikola circled each other. Nikola looked prepared to pounce at any moment and Kal was already strategizing how to counter her first, second, and third move. Neither one seemed ready to throw the first punch, but as they navigated their makeshift ring, Nikola, of course, could not hold back her excitement. She swung with a swift and sudden jab.

When it hit, he let out an involuntary laugh, not even flinching. It was not that he hadn't expected Nikola to hit him. By all means, he was ready for her to hit him, she was too eager, but he did not expect it to have next to no effect on him.

"Hell, Kal." There was an untamable ecstasy in her voice. She swung and hit him again, yielding the same result. "You're stronger than the both of them." She punched for his ribs this time. Her fist merely bounced back from his flesh, leaving no sign of impact. She laughed loudly. "Does it hurt when I pull your hair?" She threw her arm out and grabbed a few stray pieces of hair, then yanked before Kal could so much as answer.

"Yes." He batted her hand away.

"It wouldn't have been so easy to reach, if you cut it to an approved length." Her words were sharp.

"Don't be a nark," he shot back, leaning into his own fighting stance before throwing a punch with most of his strength behind it. Although Nikola had also been given the steroid, she did not evolve to have unbreakable skin and a healing ability as the others. She came to with a different affinity all together.

She dodged one of his throws and then another. When Kal finally landed a hit, she flew backward, twisted her torso in time to catch her fall, then quickly flipped herself forward and landed on her feet. Kal watched in disgust. Her reflexes were beyond heightened. They were inhuman, swift, agile, and uncatchable.

"That the best you got?" she taunted before charging at him. He'd gone to move, but she was too fast. She hit his chest and flipped herself over his shoulder, then pulled him to the ground and landed on her feet. It happened so quickly, Kal hadn't even had time to react. On the ground, he jabbed his leg out and hooked her ankles, which sent her crashing into the side of their ring, crushing cardboard boxes and rolling onto the hard concrete floor of their training room. Regardless of the hit, she was still on her feet faster than he was.

"Guess not," she huffed. Kal stepped from the blue mat of their arena and joined her on the workroom floor.

He threw another poorly directed hit before finding himself in Nikola's grasp. Her nails dug deep into his skin and drew blood. He yanked his arm away.

"That was unexpected." He looked at the wound, which was already healed over. Nikola punished him for it by swiping at his face.

Kal jerked his hand to his face, surprised her nails had hurt so much. They were unnaturally reinforced. He pulled his hand away to find an abundance of blood. Although his face had already healed, for a brief instant, the injury was awful.

He looked at her with a grimace. "I will crush you."

She laughed, and he swung, caught her off guard, and sent her crashing next to a pair of weight machines. She slid across the floor and grabbed the nearest free weight. When she came to a stop, she sent it ricocheting like a discus right toward Kal. Luckily, he grabbed it before the weight could do any real damage to his face.

"Nikola!" he barked.

"Oh, come on." She rolled her eyes. "It's not like it would have hurt."

"I can still lose my teeth." He sounded dry and uninvolved, but the moment the words left his mouth, he sent the discus spiraling back to her. She laughed in delight before gracefully dodging the weight. She grabbed it straight out of the air, turned the momentum around, and sent it right back to Kal. It was at this moment a blood-curdling scream echoed through the training room.

"What are you two doing?" Gulliver's shrieks reverberated off the walls. He'd been sitting on a weight machine farther out in the room, but couldn't ignore the near-deathmatch going on around him. He looked out of place in the gym with his soft sweater and delicate glasses, better suited for a library than the training center. He was not dressed to fight because unlike his partners, Gulliver's new abilities were found in the mind. He was a human lie detector, able to tell even the tiniest fib from the most convincing half-truth.

Kal set the weight down nonchalantly, like it hadn't been a deadly weapon a few seconds before. Nikola followed him toward Gulliver.

"We're just having fun, Gulliver. No worries." Nikola looked down at him as his spectacles slid from the bridge of his nose.

"You two are supposed to be sparring, not trying to kill each other." He looked around to see weight machines strewn about and tossed out of place and scratch marks along the floor from where Nikola had glided. "Commander is going to have my arse."

"Commander's going to have your ass? Commander is going to have *my* ass," Nikola taunted.

Kal snickered, his gaze running the length of her body. "Where?"

She let out a loud, hearty laugh. "Good point," she replied before walking past Gulliver to clean up the stray weight machines they'd knocked over or broken in their day of training.

"I brought lunch for you two if you're interested." Gulliver dug into his satchel and pulled out a few bagged lunches. Kal's interest was piqued, but Nikola continued to adjust equipment.

"You two can eat. I'm going to clean this place up. It's filthy," she said. Kal's gaze lingered on her. He was contemplating whether or not he should help. Clearly, she knew what he was thinking. "Christ, Kal." Nikola exhaled. "Eat lunch, ya brute."

As Kal sat on the floor in front of the weight bench, he could see Gulliver smirking out of the corner of his eye.

"You weren't really *that* hungry," Gulliver teased. "Glad I swooped in and saved you?"

"Hardly," Kal tsk'd, grabbing his jacket and lunch from the weight bench Gulliver was sitting on. He pulled a sandwich and a few broken chips from the bag. "I have my reasons."

"Couldn't let me get too far into my book, right?" Gulliver poked at Kal with his foot. "I wasn't reading it, anyway. You and Nikola trying to kill each other diverted too much of my attention."

Nikola moved hundred-pound weight machines as though they were nothing, her arms capable enough to carry them without flinching.

"It's crazy she didn't end up unbreakable like you."

Kal drifted his hand up to his shoulder, lying it over where Nikola dug into his flesh. "They are impressive, the abilities."

"There's hardly even a scar." Gulliver ran his hand along the small scratch, sending a ripple of goosebumps across Kal's skin.

"Nikola's practically Boris Shakhlin at this point," Kal grumbled in between bites of sandwich.

"She'll be harder to catch and hold onto. There'll be no more stopping her from rushing in on an objective. It could become problematic." Gulliver had dropped his voice low.

"Could?" Kal raised an eyebrow and let out a deep laugh. "Ah, it already is." He took a bite out of his sandwich and sat, just enjoying Gulliver's company. Things seemed fine until Gulliver tapped his shoulder, in a panic. Kal glanced up from his food to find Nikola strutting their way.

"Kal, I think she heard you."

Like that, Nikola had his attention. She moved forward with an intimidating prowess. "She couldn't have heard me all the way over there." Kal swallowed hard.

"Of course not." Nikola winked.

"Oh, you're in trouble." The words left Gulliver's mouth as a whisper.

"I can hear you, too, Gulliver." Nikola crouched down to eye level as she met with the two of them.

"I think *we're* in trouble," Kal whispered back to his partner as though Nikola was not presently a few inches from his face.

"Who'd have thought you'd also come out with better intuition?" Nikola snorted, snagging her lunch from behind Kal's head. "My rash nature is passion, Kal. You know this. More importantly, you know it's never failed us." She dug her hand into her lunch and pulled a sandwich from the bag. "You two enjoy yourselves. I'm going out." She stood and walked away, then turned back to glare. "And get a haircut, Kal. Any longer and I'm legally obligated to report you blah-blah-blah. You know the spiel. Get a haircut."

Kal continued to devour his sandwich, and Gulliver pawed through his book with his shoulders hunched. They waited until they heard the soft thud of the door.

"As if she didn't hate me enough already." Gulliver buried his head in his hands for a moment before looking to the ceiling.

"She can probably still hear you." Kal chuckled, his mouth full of food.

"By god, you're probably right." Gulliver groaned louder this time, sliding off the bench and joining Kal on the floor. "Now she'll really hate me."

"Nikola does not hate you. Toys with you? Yes. Doesn't respect you? Probably. But she does not hate you. You are good at your job. For her, that is often enough."

"But I want her to like me." Gulliver laughed as soon as the words left his mouth. "Christ, now that's whining." He huffed, grabbing his own lunch. "I'm just saying, I want to be in good standing with my commanding officer, ya know? Especially after what I pulled last week."

"Please, she felt the same way about the steroid. She just didn't dare defy *her* commanding officer," Kal assured him. "But, things turned out good, yeah?"

Gulliver sighed, eating mindlessly. "She's right, though, about your hair. It's way past regulation."

"You don't say?" Kal deadpanned. He picked at the crust on the outer rim of his sandwich.

"Are you going to get it cut or shaved?"

"Why? You got an opinion on the matter?" Kal winked and gave Gulliver a gentle nudge.

"No," Gulliver said defensively. "You've just already gotten a lot of warnings. I don't want them to take disciplinary action against you."

Kal was silent for a minute, the hum of fluorescent lighting filling the room. "How many warnings has it been?"

"I don't know. Five or six?" Gulliver reached for more chips. "I'm sure Nikola didn't run back and file a report, though. I think there are few things that woman hates more than paperwork. There's still plenty of time to cut your hair."

He hadn't meant to, but Kal locked his jaw, his teeth grinding. Had there really been that many warnings? How many until higher-ups started to take notice?

"Kal, it's all right." Gulliver laughed nervously. "Why the sudden change in pace? It's just hair."

"I'm going to go get a shave." Like someone had flipped a switch, Kal packed his lunch. "I cannot be careless."

"Kal, slow down." Gulliver rested his hand on Kal's shoulder. "And also give me your crisps if you're done with them." He reached for Kal's unfinished food.

"I'm going to eat them later." Kal shrugged his shoulders as though he was saying sorry.

But, Gulliver was unmoved. "What a stupid thing to lie about."

"What?" Kal asked, confused.

"Kal, I can see when you're lying. Did you forget? I've been watching you lie *all* week." Gulliver had a playful grin on his face, laughing at the whole situation, but Kal's stomach dropped.

His heart swelled as his chest tightened. "You haven't said anything."

"Because your lies are harmless to me." Gulliver rested his head against the cool metal bench. "I've always had a feeling you weren't here of your own accord. Seeing how much you intentionally sabotage missions just confirmed it." Gulliver traced shapes on the ground. "It's crazy, honestly, that blinding light you give off when you tell the truth. I'm still getting used to it. What is it that they have on you, anyway? You still do a great number of missions so it must be something big enough to keep you from completely ruining our assignments."

"Do you know what a domovoi is?" Kal asked, getting to the subject in his moseying kind of way.

"No," Gulliver answered. "Is it a type of punishment?"

"No." Kal let out a long exhale, a sad laugh at the end of his breath. "Not in the direct sort of way. The domovoi is the spirit of the house, and for a long time, I did not pay tithe to him. I was Sergei then."

*

Work at the mill was slow this time of day. Soon enough, the men would pack up their things and return out to the cold. But even now the embers and irons still glowed bright enough to cast a waterfall of orange around the mill's walls. This was when Sergei typically vanished, going from a giant forge worker to a common criminal in under twelve meters. He'd bow his head to his line partners and disappear for a moment to the secluded rows of lockers lining the walls, hints of orange decorating his hands as he reached into the bags and wallets of men he knew and men he didn't know, never taking more than a ruble. Coins here, coins there, it was always enough to add up to something. An amount miniscule enough that those who realized something was missing would account it to an error of the mind, not a thief. He'd come back with food from his own locker, assuring the men he was merely peckish, and then finish out the day in the mill, leaving four or five rubles richer. Stealing was that easy and that hard.

"You need a lift home, Durova?" a dwarf of a man with snarled teeth and a dirty hat asked.

"I'm fine," Sergei assured him, knowing very well that he'd stolen from this same man only twenty minutes ago. When the day was over, he hurried out of the factory, getting away from the crowd of coworkers and friends. He headed for a bus station on the opposite side of town. On his way, he would take four more rubles. One from a stout woman in a large coat, two from a sleek-looking fellow headed to the upper east end of town, and one from a beautiful woman by the name of Catharine. The town was large with sweeping Victorian-style buildings and a rich culture. Even though Sergei was significantly taller and broader than the average man, he was able to hunch himself over and play the part of an anonymous, generic commoner as he walked through the town. He only pickpocketed a few coins here or there, never anything extravagant. When he arrived at the bus depot, he was able to relax on the cool metal benches, watching his breath dance against the backdrop of sweeping metal beams and snow. There was a decent lot of people gathered around. The bus was always so crowded. He waited until he was on the safety of Bus 20 before taking a few measly kopeks to finish his day out, now ten rubles and eighteen kopeks richer than he was before.

For most of the bus ride home, he stared out the window, disregarding the abundance of conversation going on around him. The great skyline of the city gave way to large snow drifts, which eventually gave way to endless mountains. There was nothing but the bus, the road, and the few people left in it. Eventually, mountains gave way to farmland. Neither flora nor fauna interrupted this vast land of delicate snow. After two hours on the bus, they finally lurched to the route's final stop. Sergei and a few stragglers hurried away. From there, it was a mile walk to his meager beginnings and current home.

There wasn't much outside of the house. It was an old, wooden barn, and in the warmer seasons, potato sprouts could be seen for yards and yards away, but for now, as the winter settled in, there was nothing.

Sergei waited outside for a minute before opening the door. He checked his pocket, ensuring his money was tucked inside his jacket. His boots were well cleaned from the snow, and the scent of the factory had mostly drifted away with the wind. With that, he entered. Inside, two girls were curled before an open fireplace as a draft cut through the house. Sergei was quick to close the door and step gently through the house. He hung his jacket and removed his shoes before settling into the kitchen. At the sink, there was an unattended plate with two biscuits and a glass of juice beside it. His youngest sisters would believe this was their offering to the domovoi: a mythical house troll that controlled fate. His eldest sister, Alexandra, would leave the plate of biscuits out so that once Sergei returned home from his day at the mill, he'd have food waiting for him. He ate in silence over the sink, occasionally turning to watch his two younger sisters toss and turn at the fireplace. This was the best part of his day.

Once the food was gone, Sergei returned the empty plate to the counter, snuck back over to his jacket, removed the currency and coin from his front pocket, and then slid it into the breadbox—Alexandra and Sergei's personal hiding place for what little savings the family had. If Alexandra asked him about where the money had come from, he would play pretend and say that the savings had always had that much money in it. It'd worked before, and he believed it would work again. Once it was hidden, he made his way to the fireplace and collapsed into a recliner. He drifted further off to sleep as the warmth of the kindling wrapped around him. Right as it seemed he was about to escape into dreams long since forgotten, two hands slammed down onto the arms of the recliner.

Sergei jumped awake, gasping as he came to. He was surprised to find his oldest sister before him. "Alexandra," he heaved, his heart still pounding from the surprise.

"Come. Away from Lada and Elena," she said in their native tongue as she began down a short, narrow hall toward the back of their home.

Sergei's mind was still fuzzy with the soft tinge of slumber. He stumbled up and followed his sister. It was not often she woke him. It was not often anyone woke him until the sun began to rise and Lada and Elena needed to get ready for primary school. He moved his jaw mechanically, reawakening all the sore joints of his body.

"What is it?" He followed her right into the room of their parents. Since their death a year ago, the room remained untouched, a temple to a time that was.

She sat at the foot of their parents' bed, waiting for him. "Something is wrong."

As though he had just been drenched in water, Sergei came alive, his mind racing with what could have possibly happened during his shift at the mill. His thoughts first, as always, jumped to his youngest sister, Lada.

"What is wrong?"

"Someone said they saw you at a tavern the other night..." She patted the bed next to her, asking her younger brother to sit by her side. "As head of this household, I am implored to ask why."

Alexandra had two icy gray eyes and fair-as-fair hair, as completely opposite to Sergei as one could be. She always wore black. The family always wore black. But, despite all her prominence and all her power, Sergei had no trouble lying.

"I was never at any tavern." He spoke with a false shock in his voice.

"Have you been courting someone?" She gave way to lightness now, laughter disrupting the emptiness of their home.

"Have you?" Sergei teased.

"This isn't about me," she replied cockily. "This is about you." She pulled herself back together and reverted to her previously more formal self. Sergei enjoyed spending time with his sister. Before their parents passed, Alexandra and Sergei were inseparable, causing trouble in the market, disrupting their neighbors' barn life, running petty cons. Things were fun. Life was enjoyable. But that was years ago. This was now.

Sergei still had just a faint smile when Alexandra spoke again, her voice raining down tension. "Catharine wouldn't lie to me, Sergei." Alexandra paused, a frown on her face. Although Sergei's age and hers were only four years different, it sometimes felt impossible for them to reach one another. "Sergei," she repeated again, focusing in on him. "What were you doing there?"

"I go to work and come home, Alexandra, that's it. Catharine was mistaken." Sergei could feel the sleep starting to take him again. In only five or so hours, he would be back on his way to the mill. It was exhausting. He hurried the conversation along. "You have nothing to worry about, sister. Things are fine. I am fine."

"I would understand if not, though," she said wispily, her gaze scanning to the walls of their parents' room. "Sometimes, I just come in here and sit at night. I miss them so much. There are vices worse than drink. We could figure something out."

"Everything is fine, Alexandra. Drinking isn't my vice," he answered. "I am going to go back to sleep."

"There's one more thing." Alexandra still sounded worried. "I think one of the girls has been stealing from their school...maybe even classmates. Our savings has been going up by about twenty rubles a week. I've been counting. And you know I'm not very good at disciplining the girls, and they like you so much," Alexandra pleaded, but Sergei knew better. She was more than capable of disciplining the girls. She was looking for a confession rather than assistance.

"That's from me." Sergei shuffled his feet against the cool wooden boards of the floor. "I added the money. It's just from odd jobs is all. I've been helping a few of the men after work. Alexandra, you are good at this. Do not worry."

"When?" She didn't miss a beat, as though she'd played this conversation in her head before. "You leave home at the same time you always have, and you arrive back the same, too. Your pay is the same, so certainly you're not doing it on the mill's time, so when?" Alexandra held his gaze with a serious expression. "If you have ever had any respect for me, Sergei, you'd tell me the truth."

Sergei paused. He could feel his mouth going dry. "I have my ways of finding time, Alexandra."

She watched him closely. "You've been stealing it. From the men at the tavern, from factory funds, from women on the streets. I'm not sure which, but it's one of the lot, isn't it?"

Sergei looked at her for a minute, his mouth slack-jawed. "I could be pawning our parents' belongings." He offered her the halfhearted alternative, still trying to catch up with the conversation. How had she found out?

"This temple is untouched." She held her hands out and gestured to the walls of the room. "So how have you been doing it, Sergei?"

Struggling to find his words, Sergei began to piece together how his sister had figured him out so quickly. He'd always had a habit of underestimating her.

He returned to her side and sat on the end of the bed. "Is it obvious, or are you clever?"

She sighed, but smiled. "You're obvious to me, but I'd bet you've nothing to worry about at the factory."

"Mmmmm," he huffed, tired and growing more tired. She was right. No one could read him better than Alexandra. Before their parents died, they had practically functioned on the same brainwave. "So..." He waited for her to speak, respectfully holding back his own opinion on it.

"So what?" She shrugged.

"So it's good then?"

"What do you want me to say, brother? That I want you to steal? Because I won't."

"But I can still stay here?"

"Of course, Sergei. We are family. I would have you nowhere else. Besides, with the money, we can buy Lada and Elena beds of their own. You could even move out of the chair." She slapped his knee, and for Sergei, things felt right again.

"How does the saying go?" she asked. "Small thieves hang, great thieves escape? So, don't hang, Sergei."

*

"Funny thing is, they don't hang thieves anymore." Sergei looked right through Gulliver. "In special cases, they don't even put them in the gulag. Sometimes, they end up right here. Sometimes, they're KGB agents." There was no show, no confidence in his tone. Sergei was reliving every misstep that got him to this training facility, with these partners, in this place, and this time. He was exhausted again.

Gulliver looked more emotionally traumatized than Sergei did. His eyes welled, but no tears would escape him. "So," he croaked, "you're telling me I can't have your barbecue potato crisps, because a house troll who lives in our hotel room needs them more?"

Sergei chuckled. Softly at first and then loudly, bursts of laughter rumbling from his gut to the barren walls of the room. "Yes. Yes, you cannot have my chips because the house troll may need them more."

"You're just being a kiss-ass." Gulliver busted out laughing with him, sadness still deep within him. "You want him to give you like a cooler car or-or-or at least better hair regulations!"

"You've figured me out." Sergei pretended as though his plot had been foiled and kept smiling until their laughter had died down. He found Gulliver's hand with his own and held it.

"Speaking of which." Gulliver panted, catching his breath, and still just a bit giggly. "I have decided you're getting it cut. A shave is way too manly. You think people cross the street to avoid you now? That'd be even worse."

"Oh." Sergei chuckled, rested his head against Gulliver's, and found himself happy again. "All right. Whatever you say."

Bottom of the Sea

OCTOBER 17, 1963

Although there were many waterfalls throughout the mountains, few were as great as the hidden gem of the backcountry. Roaring in with a twenty-foot drop and white water for miles, the waterfall had claimed many lives over hundreds of years. But despite their notoriety, there was Ruby, treating this dangerous river like a wading pool. She was lying flat against a boulder, her legs dangling off the edge and her toes barely skimming the top of the water. There was a pure look to her: soft, at peace, seemingly careless. Had Rigan looked normal and not like a creature of the night, he'd have taken the opportunity to spook her from behind. However, he didn't need her screaming and macing him, so he called her name.

"Ruby Starr, to what do I owe the pleasure?"

"Rigan!" She hopped off the boulder faster than she likely should have and started shuffling over to him. Water splashed everywhere. "Give me a second!" She moved effortlessly but with purpose. The moment she hit dry land, she pulled Rigan into a hug, but seemed to instantly regret her choice. "You're damp." She pulled away with a slight cringe. With teeth as well-shaped and sharp as glass shards, Rigan imagined he frightened Ruby, but he hoped that she saw past all of it in remembrance of the boy on the motorcycle.

"That's normal," he said.

"No wonder you don't wear a shirt." She brushed at her floral top as though that would somehow dry it. "I'm so glad to see you up. I'm glad to see you alive. Tim didn't mention you were going to be the one meeting me this time." Their drop-off arrangement led Ruby not to their camp but to an agreed meeting point halfway down the mountain. Not only because Ruby did not have the time to make the full hike, but also because Diana was uncertain she wanted Ruby knowing where the camp was.

"They weren't sure I was going to be able to walk." Rigan shrugged. "But thanks to the likely illegal amount of painkillers you brought us, I'm up and talking again."

"Is it bad that I brought more?" She handed off her backpack to Rigan.

Rigan glanced into the open sack, then did a double take and gawked at not only the sheer amount of things Ruby had managed to stuff into her one small bag, but at the alarming amount of men's clothes and hardcover books.

"How can you afford this?" he muttered under his breath.

Sadly, no matter how low Rigan tried to keep his voice, it still was obviously not quite enough for Ruby to miss it.

"Um, Earth to Rigan. First time we met, you gave me two hundred dollars?" Ruby looked at him as though he was speaking another language. "Did you forget?"

"You didn't spend any of it before finding us?" Rigan's words came accusingly. He immediately regretted speaking. There was an obvious expression of hurt on Ruby's face.

"What's that got to do with anything?" She had her hands on her hips and she was drilling into Rigan with her glare. "You're not going to do this, too, are you? Tim and Diana both cross-examined me the first time I brought supplies. I thought we were good. Haven't I answered enough of questions?"

Rigan's stomach dropped as he realized that was why he was asking so many questions. Of course, they'd already investigated. They hadn't told him they had, but they had. They were two agents better than Rigan. There was no reason for him to ask her all his normal questions, learn her history, demand names and childhood homes.

"Did you get mad when they accused you of being from Florida, too?" He snickered and she rolled her eyes.

"I am so over you four saying I'm from Florida. I'm not. I'm Ruby Starr and I'm from Maine. I'm a nameless waitress."

"Sure," Rigan teased. "What kind of hippie-commune parents name their kid Ruby Starr?"

"Okay, first off, mean, and second off, uncalled for." Ruby laughed as she turned away from him. "I am going back to my river rock, because at least at my river rock, no one is sassy and rude." She stepped into the stream and started toward the same large boulder she'd been on before.

"Oh, no, water, a fish's sole weakness." Rigan followed her and even caught up, making it to the boulder while she was still hobbling across.

"I am going to fight you off there in five seconds if you do not move. Hiking three hours while carrying twenty pounds worth of fresh fruit and other foods with the necessary vitamins and minerals does wonders for a lady's leg strength."

Rigan waited for her to clamber onto the rock before admiring her nonsense. "I'm just saying, what kind of parent names their kid Ruby Starr? Sounds like something a flower child would pick out for themselves." Ruby narrowed her eyes as she tried to push Rigan from the rock, but using his sharp claw-like nails, he dug into the boulder and held his ground. "What's so bad about Florida? Don't bother lying. I know I'm right."

"Besides the people?" Ruby snorted. "A lot. A whole lot."

Rigan looked at her curiously, examining the worth of prodding. She had his attention. He wanted to know. "Like what?"

"Please." Ruby tsk'd. "Like the world traveler hasn't been to Florida."

Rigan huffed, leaning back and lying against the rock. His abdomen was killing him, he hadn't healed completely, but he pushed through it. He was tired of seeing only three people for days at a time. Ruby was a beacon of light in the shadows of the woods.

"I love Florida. It reminds me of home. What's your deal?"

"Hmmm...too awful to tell." She shrugged. "Some things are never meant to see the light of day. My story is one of 'em."

"Too awful to tell?" Rigan leaned in. Now, she had his full attention. There was something in the way she moved and the tone of her voice that clued him in that he was electrically close to getting to hear this story. "Is the story sad or just awful?"

Ruby sighed and pressed her fingers to the bridge of her nose. "I did something awful." She seemed to shut down suddenly. "But that was the past and this is the now. And now I am a good, positive person who does things like help spies trapped in my mountains." She sounded as though just one quirky statement could change the entire path of the conversation, but Rigan was still mulling over her previous words.

"You did something awful." He kept his voice low. "Ruby. Me? The people upstairs? We do awful things. You're what? Middle-class, black, female, young. You're a hippie at best. We're monsters."

"What?" Ruby snorted. "Come on. Tim's greatest pleasure is when I bring him paperback romance over new cutting-edge fiction. Diana just seems desperate for an eyelash curler, and Da Vinci let me go that first night I met him. And you." She eyed him smartly. "Don't even get me started."

Rigan hummed, lowly, subtly, more to himself than anyone else. "Tim got into the spy business so he could stalk women without legal repercussion. Diana has killed more people in one day than most agents do in their entire career. And she did it on a whim. Da Vinci has put more people on the rack than any other negotiator I know. And his signature move is pulling molars out with pliers. And don't even look at me. The people I've waterboarded for intel. I can't even begin to count. Whatever you did can't be as bad as what we've done."

"I don't believe that for a second." Ruby put her hands behind her head and lay back on the rock, the two of them now watching the clouds together.

"You don't believe Diana and Tim wouldn't have killed you if Da Vinci and I weren't there? You didn't feel any fear the first day just Diana or just Tim showed up for the supply drop?" Rigan asked, not to be assertive but to make her think. He assumed he succeeded when there was a lull of silence between them.

"I just didn't know them yet," she finally said.

"So, assuming everything said was true, still think your actions are too awful to be said?"

"Why's it so important to you, anyway?" She nudged his side with her elbow and propped herself up.

"Because you ape out whenever it's brought up. Besides, I'm sick. Humor me." Rigan smirked and made Ruby roll her eyes.

"Yeah, sick in the head," she shot back. Eventually the sound of her words faded into the hills and there was nothing left to hear but the roar of the falls and the rubble of water for a moment. "You're not going to hear this and then hate me, right? Even if I did something really awful. Now that I'm spending half my days climbing up a mountain, it's best that the people on top actually like me."

"No judgment," Rigan assured her. "Unless what you did is really, *really* awful."

"Oh, my god. Stop." Ruby shook her head as she switched to a seated position. "See this is why I'm not telling you."

Rigan was laughing as he pulled himself up and sat next to her. "Ruby, I'm fucking with you. Just tell me."

"I know you're just fucking with me, but if you ever 'just fuck with me' about what I'm about to tell you, I will hate you, and when the rest of the gang gets cool things like books and magazines, you will get nothing but fish products. And then you'll have to be a cannibal and you get to enjoy that entire moral dilemma."

Rigan, being someone who loved anchovies, took a moment to consider her deal. However, his curiosity got the best of him. "Tell me."

"So, one night, I almost killed my ma."

"Oh, my god, what? In no scenario was that what I imagined you saying."

Ruby wailed, ignoring Rigan's interruption and carried on, "So for like...almost a year? Maybe two?" She paused and seemed stuck in her own head, as though working through a difficult math problem. "So like up until ten months ago, I did a lot of LSD. Like, a lot." Her face relaxed after a moment and she carried on. "Almost every night, I was sneaking in through our bathroom window, stumbling around, making a mess, and my parents would pretend like they didn't hear it, and I'd sneak back in bed, wake up, and do it all again the next day, and..." She took an indulgent few seconds to remember. "It's scary how much I remember. I can still taste the peppermint coming off the lips of the boy I'd kissed goodbye and the olive curtains on the slightly too-small window I squeezed through, the sound of boots on linoleum, harsh fluorescent lighting." She sighed. "There's no dignified way to tell this story.

"Then the next day, they would sit me down and have a long talk about my future and my choices, college, stuff like that. It was always the next day because there was no point trying to talk to me when I first came home." She grew rigid. "I can see it so clearly now. Every day that goes by, I understand it a bit better." She took a long breath. "That night, I just went too far. It messed me up bad. When I got into the bathroom, I hit the floor just like that." She smacked her hands together for added effect. "My bracelets made so much noise against the tile, it was echoing in my skull. I didn't stay on the ground for long, though. I picked myself up pretty quick. And then I saw my reflection. I don't know if it spooked me or if I thought it was something else, but I just knee-jerk reacted and bashed the damn mirror in with the palm of my hand. After the initial shock, I picked up all the pieces and carried them around. Blood was getting everywhere at this point."

She ran her hands over each other, her thumb caressing the palm of her other hand. "So like any rational druggie, I got into the tub. I didn't run myself a bath. I just wanted to bleed all over my nice clothes in the tub rather than on the floor. I even kept the pieces of mirror nestled in my blouse." She sighed, laying herself back on the rock, staring into the sky as though it would take the weight off her shoulders. "I thought I was going to die. It seemed like I sat there for hours, decades even. I was scared. So, I started screaming. Rational thought? Not my strongest suit when I'm that messed up. Next thing you know, Ma and Pa are busting open the door. Ma has got a pan and Pa has a bat. I jump out of the tub faster than any high person should. Then I charged at my ma, glass in hand." Ruby's eyes began to well with tears. She was working hard to fight off any kind of emotion.

"There were no words and no connection between me and my actions. I looked at my family like they weren't mine. I thought they were...you know...imposters. I thought they were imposters of my family, pretending to be my family. I ended up slicing Ma's arm open. They nursed me back to health that night and then told me the next day I could quit and stay, or keep using and leave."

"You chose to leave?"

"Wouldn't you?"

"No," Rigan scoffed. "Food, house, a loose tolerance for drug usage. You had it made."

"Man, forget you." Ruby rolled her eyes. "My parents gave up on me way too quickly. Look at me now. Healthy, got a steady job, got four illegal felons chilling out in the woods that I bring food to. I have it made now. Got to ride a motorcycle not too long ago." She winked. "They were stupid and old-fashioned. I still survived."

"Ahhhhh," Rigan cooed. "My bike was pretty sweet. There's something I miss."

She paused for a minute before speaking. "You don't think I'm awful now, do you?"

"I think you're petty." He snorted but then gave way to a more serious persona. "Ruby, when I was eleven, I took what little savings my family had, joined an organized crime ring, and left them for dead." Rigan shrugged. "If they were able to survive the week with little to no food, they may have lived, but if they starved, then that's on me, for the rest of my life. So, no, I don't think you're awful."

"Rigan." Ruby frowned, flopping around on the rock, looking for a comfortable position. "How do you live with that? Does it ever haunt you? Do you feel bad?"

Rigan looked at her, surprised any of those questions had left her mouth. For a second, he just stared, and then he shrugged. He almost spoke, but she cut him off.

"How'd you get your tattoo?" Breathlessly, she pointed to the octopus tattoo on the left side of Rigan's chest. "Less heavy stuff, yeah?"

"Do you really believe in aliens?"

Ruby and Rigan had a stare-down for a moment as both of them clearly wanted to divert the subject from themselves. It was tension, but it dispersed into bubbly laughter, like a soda-fizz that had calmed down.

"You next," she said. "You're better at this."

"Well, it begins in the Caribbean."

*

When he first laid eyes on her, he knew he'd follow her to the ends of the world. Isabelle was five-foot-nine and had legs that went on for days. In the crowds of the Caymans, she stood out like a blinding ray of light. Rigan was drawn to her immediately. Although he and Da Vinci were there for work purposes, there was downtime in between stakeouts and torture mills. Isabelle was how he chose to spend his.

"You eat like the wolf hunts." Isabelle was just barely peeking out over her sunglasses. "You eat as though you'll never see food again."

Rigan was presently scarfing down a plate of rice and fish as though he was competitively eating against his dainty partner. "Oh," he said, attempting to appear distraught. "I'll just stop eating at this point." He gently placed his fork and knife down and glanced at Isabelle like a wounded animal.

"Could you imagine if I ate like that? We'd be stared at no matter where in the market we went." She teased him, picking a piece of shrimp off his plate and popping it in her mouth. "Have you seen the turtles that come up to shore in the nighttime?" She picked at his plate of food, taking only small ladylike bites.

Rigan wiped his face off with a handkerchief before nodding. "A few times. Why?"

"I haven't," she said. "I'm going to go see them tonight and wanted to invite you along if you're interested."

"Finally, something I can show you," he teased. "About time."

"So, is that a yes?" She laughed behind closed lips and dragged her fork along his plate before picking up another piece of shrimp.

Rigan hesitated. "Do you hear someone?" Rigan turned around, and as expected, Da Vinci walked toward the two of them with a warm, charming expression on his face.

"Excuse me, Miss. It seems I need to take my partner for the time-being. I'll be sure to return him once we're done." He bowed his head, his attention never leaving the woman.

"Oh." She sounded sad. "Where are you going?" she asked Rigan.

"Just work stuff," He sighed, staring Da Vinci down for a moment, displeased by this interruption. "Right?"

"Of course. Environment can't save itself," Da Vinci mused. "Come on, Marco. We'll be back."

She turned to Rigan with kind, understanding eyes. "I will hold my breath until you return."

"You would suffocate," Da Vinci grumbled.

"Forgive me." Rigan took her hand and gently kissed it. There was something so Victorian in their relationship. Their romance seemed rooted in longing stares and sweet nothings. But Rigan had to turn his attention back to Da Vinci. They left Isabelle for the time-being.

Things were fine and cordial and warm right up until they got back to their hotel room.

"Kid, I get that the new-and-exciting appeal is there, but you have an unhealthy attraction for that woman." Da Vinci groaned, yanking their suitcase of weaponry out from their hotel safe. "Like grossly so. You know we're leaving in a few days, right?"

"Like you haven't gone through a parade of women over the past week." Rigan pulled a few spare maps from under his mattress.

"Exactly, a parade. I don't have an unhealthy fixation on any one." Da Vinci rolled his eyes.

"The only one with an unhealthy fixation is Dresden."

"Now, listen here..."

Da Vinci went on to explain some type of break-in. A few big names, a few minor grunts, a general mission objective, but Rigan's thoughts were already back at the market, wondering what Isabelle was doing. Sometimes, she rested on the beach, her feet in the sand. Other times, she snacked in the market, a pastry in one hand, coffee in the other. And on rare occasions, she sang. Her voice was that of a siren. He'd never met a woman quite like her before. Da Vinci and Rigan completed their mission. It was fine. It was routine. Everything was as expected. That was two of three assignments taken care of. One more needed to be done before they left the islands. Luckily for Rigan, that was still a few days away. When they returned to the hotel and cleaned up, he was quick to bolt out the door and head to the open-air market, not even giving Da Vinci a chance to voice his concerns.

He found her dancing to the beat of a steel-drum band set up on the outskirts of the market.

"Isabelle!"

"Marco!" She wrapped him in a hug and pulled him out of the shade and into the sun. "Dance with me." Her wild hair blew in the light sea breeze. It was at that moment Rigan knew he was in trouble. She had him—hook, line, and sinker. He joined her, gently taking her hand and spinning her under his arm.

"Check this out!" Isabelle pointed to right above her elbow. Newly tattooed there was an outline of a large sea turtle. "I got it down at this cool little dive by the beach! You should get one, too," she gushed. "It'll be golden."

Rigan took her arm and examined the ink for a moment. He had never seen a tattoo on anyone who wasn't either A. a mission objective or B. trying to kill him. But that was just Isabelle. She was a whole new kind of person to Rigan. Even more endearing, she was a woman, out on her own, getting a tattoo in 1958. It just wasn't something you saw back in the States.

"O-okay," he replied. "What should I get?"

"You should get another sea creature." She started leading them away from the street band and closer to the shops at the end of the market. "You could get a turtle like me."

Rigan mulled it over for a second, and although he loved telling Isabelle yes on all accounts, he decided against her recommendations. "How about a giant octopus?"

"A giant octopus? That sounds perfect." She giggled before ducking under a low-hanging tapestry and pulling Rigan into a deep kiss. For a moment, they lingered there.

As she pulled away, she said, "If you're going giant, it should be fighting a pirate ship."

"A pirate ship?" He raised a single eyebrow. "I could tell you stories about pirates you wouldn't believe."

"It's settled then." She took him by the hand and guided him a few stands farther down the line. "There's this shaman-type guy who does them. It's really something."

They stopped in front of a rather small, open tent with a chair and a few ink blots around. As they stood there waiting, an older-looking man with a deep tan and calming eyes came up from behind.

"Back again so soon, chérie?" he said.

"Yes." Isabelle smiled gracefully, hints of excitement in her eyes. "He's going to get a matching one," she cooed. "A big octopus and a pirate ship."

"Quite an order to fill." The old man patted a seat farther in the tent. "Sit."

Rigan reclined in the seat, unbuttoning his shirt. "How much do you think this'll run me?"

"Oh, don't worry about that," Isabelle cooed. "I'll cover you." She took his hand and tilted her head. "You can squeeze away. The tattoo *will* hurt no matter how tough you may seem." She gave his arm a light punch. "My hand can take it."

The entire process of getting the ink done was surprisingly fast, and although it did indeed hurt, Rigan was more than happy with the end product.

"Now you'll always have something to remember me by." Isabelle ran her thumb over his hand, her eyes sad and her face long, but a smile still pushed its way through the pain.

"What?" Rigan frowned. They held hands as they walked through the market, Rigan's shirt unbuttoned just enough to show the corner of a thick black bandage pad.

"Oh, you don't have to play so coy." She ducked in between two stands and guided them onto the white sandy beaches of the shore. "You're here for work. If I were to guess, I'd say you'd be gone in what, two? Three days?"

Rigan's face flushed as he kept his attention on the ground. "I'd been meaning to tell you." He took both of her hands and stared into her eyes, a sadness overtaking him.

"I am smarter than I appear."

"I-it's not like that. I didn't think you weren't smart. I just didn't know how to tell you."

"It is all right, Marco." She dropped one of her hands away and began leading him farther down the beach and away from the market. "Come with me." She smiled. "The sun will be setting soon. I wouldn't be surprised if the green sea turtles have already come to shore." There was something so heavenly in her smile. When she looked at him, he felt as though she could see him for who he truly was. He didn't know how he'd live without her. Her hand fit so perfectly in his. In a place like this, with the skyline of mountains and waterfalls, with the music-filled markets and ever-turning tide, Rigan wondered why he'd chose to leave. He briefly considered it. What if he ran away with her? But as the cold reality of the situation settled in, he knew he couldn't. Working with Da Vinci was the only thing keeping him from deportation, prison, and a potential hit from his former boss. Some things couldn't be, but for the time-being, he and Isabelle weren't one of them. With the waves lapping over their feet and the sun setting in the distance, he drew her in and kissed her.

And after a moment, she threw her arm up, knocking Rigan in the face. After that, she wrestled him to the ground, her manicured nails digging into his skin.

"Isabelle!" Rigan choked, flailing his arms as he attempted to fight her off. "Isabelle!" He swung for a hit but missed. He attempted to throw her off of him, but as her limbs spread over him, he found himself pinned. It was then that she grabbed his head and pulled him under the water, holding him by his hair and ignoring his many half-landed hits.

He was choking, trying to cough up the salty sea water flooding his throat. "Is-Isa—" Only syllables were getting out in between the moments he was able to thrash just enough to breach the water's surface. He fought her until he felt his limbs going numb. His mind was emptying. He was dying. He tried to call out for help, but was met only with a rush of water in his lungs. Everything was going black until Da Vinci yanked him out of the ocean.

Isabelle was lying on the shore, bleeding profusely from the back of her head, a bloody rock not too far from her body.

"Y-Y—" Rigan wheezed, his neck already bruising. "Y-ou, knew?"

"I suspected."

*

"After that, we didn't talk for days. We did our mission and got out of there." Rigan paused. "We're fine now. Clearly." Ruby and Rigan were both lying on their backs, pressed flat against the boulder, their elbows barely grazing.

"My real name's Robin Harrison," she admitted abruptly. "You're right. I picked the name Ruby Starr for myself. My family is from Florida, and they've been trying to contact me for months. They've sent countless PIs, called the cops. That's why I freaked out when you said I was from Florida."

Rigan placed his hand over hers. "Thank you."

They watched as clouds passed overhead. In time, she turned over onto her stomach and looked him in the face. "Do you think about her more now?"

"What?"

"Now that you are the way you are. Do you find yourself thinking about her more?"

Rigan contemplated the question, eventually he shrugged. "No. That was a long time ago, and she tried to drown me so that helped me get over her." He exhaled deeply and turned his head toward Ruby, propping himself up on his elbows. "I think about our first trip to the mountains. Play it over and over in my head."

"Was that the last time you were normal?"

"Yeah."

"Do you ever think it could have gone any different?"

Rigan laughed, his gaze lingering on her heavenly face. "All the time."

Right Behind You

NOVEMBER 6, 1963

Darkness lingered in the morning and rain clouds festered in the sky of the Smokies. Ruby Starr had an abundance of water bottles stuffed into the pockets of her diner uniform and her parka, but Tim was more interested in the contents of her backpack.

"A plethora of supplies this week," Tim said. "Diana finally talked you into bringing her curlers?"

Since the agents had taken her under their wing, Ruby had picked up more than a few shifts to cover their luxury expenses. Now, she was bringing them produce, clothes, sanitary products, and books on a weekly basis. This week, she had even splurged and brought them a collection of "manager's special" canned mystery meat. It wasn't that great. In fact, it wasn't even a fraction of what they were likely used to, but it was something.

"I was hoping it was enough food. I know last time you mentioned Rigan's ample appetite." She poked through her bag.

"Boy always eats more than he should." Tim sighed. "More aspirin?"

"Yeah, Diana mentioned that Da Vinci is coming down with a cold and she's just being cautious in case it turns into something big."

"That's news." Tim narrowed his eyes as he focused on the bottle for a moment. "I guess it makes sense. It seems as though he's the only one of us who is warm-blooded."

Tim dug his hand into the bag and pulled out a newer but severely well-loved book. "What is this?" He flipped it over to read the back, noticing a torn, bent backside. "Do you bend your page corners?"

"Only when I don't have a bookmark. But man! You haven't read this? It's great. It's by this lady named Victoria, and it's seriously all about how hard it is to be a young woman in the here and now. I brought it for Diana, but only because I assumed you had already read it. You've got to give it a read." She dived into the backpack on her own and pulled out a collection of poetry.

"Victoria Lucas..." Tim held the book in his hands, staring at it for a moment before skimming through the pages. "I think I'll keep this one for myself," he mused. "That said, I have something for you." Tim pulled from his back pocket a thin envelope addressed to Fairbanks, Alaska. "We need you to get this in the mail, but we need you to travel at least a hundred miles north of Bryson to send it out."

"A hundred miles?" Ruby let the words come out a bit more distraught than she intended. "Tim, that's a long way to go. Especially with the passion wagon still all beat up."

"Anything in that range and we risk it being found by the KGB. Diana's written it in a cipher. If you can get it through, there is a chance we'll be escaping very soon."

"Who's it for?" she asked, taking the envelope from his blue, veiny hands.

"Adams. He's a friend of ours. If anyone can get us out of here alive, it is him."

Ruby bit her lip, staring for a moment at the letter and calculating gas and time frames before decided it was a task she could handle. "All right. Does it need...postage?"

"Mhm." Tim nodded, digging into his back pocket and pulling out stamps. "You brought us these a few weeks ago for a reason."

Ruby's face reddened. "Oh, I forgot about these. I wanted to get you guys these cool ones with cowboys on them, but they were all out." She looked at the waving American flag as though she could just barely see a horse and lasso underneath. "Next time."

"Assuming Adams writes back," Tim scoffed. "Diana and Da Vinci have high hopes, but Adams is notorious for his committal problems."

"Man, is that *another* book?" Rigan's carried over as he entered from the opposite side of the stream, walking across as though it was nothing and then breaking on shore with the gentle waves. "Ruby, you have got to stop bringing him romance novels. It's time he branches out and finds other hobbies."

Tim looked at Rigan with a serious expression on his face. "Don't just pop out like that. You could end up hurt."

"What? You going to shoot me?" Rigan laughed hard while his friends remained silent. "What'd you bring him?"

"It's this artsy little book." Ruby beamed. "It's so good you should read it once Diana and Tim are done with it."

"That reminds me." Tim pulled a book from the inside of a ratty suit coat Ruby had brought them. "This is yours then." He handed a slightly water-logged copy of *One Flew Over the Cuckoo's Nest* to Rigan.

Rigan looked at it skeptically and then turned his full attention to Ruby. "What's it about?"

Ruby looked at him, surprised that he didn't address Tim, but at this point, she started to accept that the group just had a universal issue with Tim. Diana never spoke highly of him. Rigan always harassed him. The only one kind to him was Da Vinci.

"Asylums and just institutionalization and Native Americans. It's just... It's hard to explain, but you have to read it no matter how poorly I sell it."

Rigan wore a rascally grin. "I've been to asylums like you wouldn't believe." Rigan sounded ready to say more, but Tim cut him off.

"Remember, Ruby has to go home alone tonight," he said coolly. "No reason to scare her."

"Oh, no worries. I sleep with a bat by my bedside, anyway," Ruby assured them. "Ever since I met you guys, I feel as though danger is always looming."

Rigan and Tim went for an obvious jab about how she would one day attack the very aliens that came to collect her, but as they both spoke over each other, the joke was lost in translation, leaving both acutely irritated.

Rigan flipped the book over in his hands, leaving a sticky residue on the cover as the natural moisture of his hands rubbed off. "Honestly, Tim, I'm surprised you had this at all. It's not your usual grab. Maidens, knights, Anna Karenina."

"Anna Karenina is not my cup of tea. Just because it is old and has a woman's name in the title does not mean it is in my required reading collection."

"Coulda fooled me." Rigan was already skimming his new book.

"What is your required reading list?" Ruby mused, leaning over Tim's shoulder and peeking into *The Bell Jar*.

"Oh, a wide va—"

"Romance." Rigan didn't look up from his own book as he weighed in on the conversation. "Tim is always falling in love with someone, fictional or not." He rolled his eyes. "He wouldn't be Tim if he wasn't."

Tim shrugged. "Rigan's right." He laughed dryly. "A lot of the Bronte sisters' work. A bit of Dickens, Austen, of course." He stopped just as a sprinkle of rain began to fall.

"So did he ever?" Ruby turned her attention to Rigan now, her curiosity running wild.

"Ever what?" Rigan closed his book. They paid the rain no mind.

"Really fall in love." Ruby smiled shyly for a moment but unable to hide her hunger any longer. She was excited to hear this story as she was certain Tim had to have fallen in love at least once.

"Oh, plenty of times like—" Rigan was cut off by Tim.

"I think it is only fair I tell this one." He laughed very quietly. "I think Ruby would agree."

Ruby's gaze lingered on Rigan for a moment as though still considering hearing his version of the story—as it was often more exciting and heavily embellished—but she then relinquished, turning the spotlight to Tim.

"So, tell me about the women you've loved."

This time, when Tim spoke, he sounded vacant, as though off somewhere else for the time-being. "It was really only one...one woman."

*

Holly controlled the dance floor, bobbing her head and swinging her hips in a slow, cool way. She had sweeping platinum-blonde hair hanging down to her shoulders, straight and glossy. It swayed with her every move. Tim watched quietly from the bar, suppressing a smile. He often tried not to give himself away so fast, though he rarely was able to. Her presence did not demand the attention of every man in the room, but that of Tim, nonetheless.

"You're hopeless," the bartender said while pouring a glass of scotch. "Think you'll talk to this one?"

"She's not my type," Tim assured.

"I don't believe that a second." The bartender slapped the glass down in front of Tim, a cheesy smile on his face. "A man like yourself must know all sorts of things about romance."

"A man like me?"

"You come in here on the weeknights and read the classics, your textbooks, old fiction, all the sorts. A scholar is never one without romance."

"You work weeknights?" Tim answered, faking a surprised expression. He knew Irv, the bartender, worked weeknights. He chose not to talk to him because he didn't want to look like one of those sob stories who view their life from the bottom of a bottle.

"Mhmmm," Irv replied. "I see the way women look at you. You're a very interesting man, Mr. Carroll. You pique interest, but you never follow through."

"Women don't look at me." He sighed, pulling out a notepad to aimlessly scribble on. Despite his large stature, Tim always had a way of making himself appear small.

"Now, that's nonsense. The one out there. What's her name? Harriet?"

"Holly Scott. She's new in town and happily taken. She's rather keen on the guy to her left, Keith Richardson. They're going steady." Tim gestured back to a tall, young jock dancing to her right.

"You go to college with these two? Or have you just done an awful lot of research, Mr. Carroll?"

"For the love of Christ, Irv, call me Tim. We've gone through this. But to answer your question, I don't go to school with them. Information just travels down the grapevine to me. I've changed my mind on the scotch. Can I get a rum and Coke?" Tim slid the glass back to Irv and found himself staring at the slow moving, sensual young lady on the dance floor. She had the kind of darling eyes that won hearts over in mere moments. Each step she took had a youthful bounce to it.

Frank Sinatra's familiar tune spilled from the speakers and flooded the whole bar. People rushed to the dance floor. However, Holly and Keith rushed off.

"One beer and a cider for the lady." Keith pulled open his wallet and gave Irv a ratty ten-dollar bill.

"See, MSU," Irv said to Tim but gestured to Keith's varsity sport's jacket. "Told you I wasn't losin' my mind. This cat—" Irv pointed to Tim. "—tried telling me your jacket wasn't a local college, but I knew."

Suddenly, all attention was on Tim. His face started to drain of heat. Tim couldn't tell if he was feeling more nervous or embarrassed. He took his hat off to busy his hands. "I should have recognized you. I always see you at UM's football games." He spoke coolly, despite his nerves.

"You go to Michigan Tech?" Holly raised a single brow in interest; she disregarded Keith's half-mumbled "Let's get out of here" and sat down next to Tim, "What's it like there? My brother's going there and won't tell me a thing. I'm Holly, by the way. Holly Scott, I just moved here from south of Chicago." She shook his hand.

Tim then pretended to know nothing about her. "Nice to meet you, Holly. I'm Tim Carroll, and the campus is just beautiful. It's a si—" He was cut off by Keith.

"Holly, we need to go." Keith looked visibly irritated that their time was being wasted.

"Just a second," she huffed and spun around in her seat toward Keith, placing her hand on his knee. "I just want to ask this kid some questions about UM. You know I'm going to work at a college some day and I want to make sure I pick the right one. Besides, after we finish these drinks, we can head on outta here." Tim picked up an underlying tone of suggestion in her voice. His stomach churned at the thought of that ape pawing at the poor girl.

"You want to work at a university?" Tim answered, impressed. "What for? Teaching?"

"Yes." She batted her eyelashes at Tim. "I love astrology, the stars, the science. It's all fascinating, and don't get me started on the zodiacs. You look like...a Cancer, am I right?" She smiled big again, and Tim laughed.

"You're right! July twelfth!" Tim answered like he was impressed. In reality, he was a Virgo, but he wanted her to think she was correct, just so he could see her eyes sparkle again.

"You know the zodiac signs, too?" Holly asked.

"By heart. I find the idea of fate and destiny to be an extremely fascinating and comforting topic." And thus sparked a beautiful friendship. Holly and Tim nearly talked each other's ears off about the idea of a divine god, a fate worse than death, predetermined soul mates, and Jung personality types.

Even the stoic-looking Keith chipped in a comment occasionally. He amused Tim. Keith had quite a zany personality for a meathead. At one point, Keith balanced a glass on his forehead so intently that he almost fell out of his chair keeping it steady.

Their little section of the bar constantly erupted into laughter. Keith had comedy, Holly had charm, and Tim had intelligence. Irv almost never moved, keeping a watchful eye on the conversation and the top of their drinks always overflowing. He even let them stay an hour after closing time and called a cab when their night finally ended.

They piled into their yellow chariot and the fun didn't stop.

"I've just had a ball with you tonight." Keith chuckled. "We've got to do this again sometime."

"Ooh let's! Let's! That'd be a gas," Holly cooed with excitement. "Why not after class this Thursday? Same time, same place?" She smiled expectantly at Tim.

"That sounds like a good idea," Tim replied.

When they finally reached MSU's campus, Tim waved, sad that they had to go. Once they piled out, the taxi driver sped toward Tim's dormitory at UM.

Tim had a rare lightness to him. His typical friends were hermits, rarely leaving their dorms or their weeknight seats at the bar. Keith and Holly were a different kind of people, the kind of people who went out and did things! He left the cab with a hop in his step. He was excited about the colorful friendship that had just started blooming. He even tried to stamp out the glaring envy he felt for Keith and the way he got to dance with that sweet, smart doll.

Thursday rolled around and Tim sat on the same barstool, waiting and waiting and waiting, worried that Keith and Holly had been pulling his leg. He started to think that they might not show and it'd all been an elaborate ruse.

"I haven't seen you here all week." Irv came out from the back of the bar, cleaning a shot glass. "You seemed to have a real blast with..." He waved his hand as he searched for the word. "Oh, what was her name?"

"Holly and Keith," Tim replied. "They're supposed to meet me here tonight." He tried to sound calm, not allowing himself to get nervous.

"I don't think you care much about Keith showing up." Irv laughed.

Tim kept his expression serious. "Keith is a really funny, great guy."

"But come on. Holly? You two had sparks the other night, talking about, oh, what's that astrology nonsense?"

"The zodiac signs," Tim replied. "I'm not that kind of guy, Irv. Keith seems pretty great, anyways." He fell silent, content with his thoughts. Irv stepped off to do his work. The night seemed to be a bust until there was a sudden series of fast taps on Tim's shoulder; he spun around to see Holly with big eyes and a sweet smile.

"Tim!" She excitedly hugged him. Keith smiled like a schmuck, picking Tim's jacket off the barstool he'd been sitting at.

"Put your jacket on," Keith boomed. "We're heading to a barn shindig, right on the outside of town."

"It'll be a spin," Holly sang, already starting out the door.

Tim pulled his jacket on, followed behind the two, and piled into a cab they'd called.

"So tell me, how is UM treatin' ya?" Holly crossed her legs and snuggled under Keith's arm.

"Everything's aces. I'm looking forward to graduating."

"What are you studying, again, Tim?"

"Mathematics," he replied, a little embarrassed. He felt like a nerd around them. Keith was a communications major. Holly was still trying to find herself a college to attend. The three started talking about school and the future lives they imagined for themselves. They could have stayed in that cab all night, but alas, they didn't. The three of them arrived at the party, fashionably late.

Keith exited the car, his arm nestled around Holly. "Let's dance, doll." He took her hand and gently spun her. Tim realized that he might have made a terrible mistake in coming. The two began dancing. Luckily, they took extra precaution to ensure that Tim wasn't left out. Holly led him out, and he seemed to mesh in well with the other groups of students dancing around, weaving and bobbing their heads to Ritchie Valens's wail.

Tim felt no pressure that night, the weight of school rolling off his back. It was odd how long he'd stayed cooped up in his dorm, studying in the daytime and then drinking at night. The barn filled with more and more people as the night went on. Tim met a couple dudes whose attitudes and egos seemed bigger than their oversized jawlines. He also met a couple of janes, all with voices higher than the heavens and a fondness for Tim's knowledge of early 18th-century literature.

Toward the end of the night, Holly found him. "Tim, it's been a blast! But I've gotta shimmy on out of here," she shouted over the crowds of partiers.

Still grooving along to the beat, Tim replied, "I concur! This is the most fun I've had in months!" Tim chuckled at himself. He sounded like a homebody. Granted, he *was* a homebody.

"Well, I'm glad! We want to see you again! Meet at Fallon's next Saturday?"

"I will see you then!" Tim called over the crowds of dancing fools, not aware that this would become his weekly routine.

Every Saturday, they'd meet up. Keith would constantly quip and make an ass of himself for a good laugh, and Holly would parade around in the latest fashions from hoop skirts to starched white button-ups. Her intelligence always kept her one step ahead of them, and her charm kept her miles above the rest of America's supposed sweethearts. Tim was playing a dangerous game. He was not just in love with her; he was mystified by her.

*

"Did you tell her you loved her?" Ruby interrupted Tim's eloquent flow.

"If you would let me finish, you would find out." Tim kept his voice calm and ignored Ruby's constant barrage of questions after that.

*

Keith lost his charm shortly after the third or fourth month of friendship. His jokes were now stale, and his formulaic way of telling stories was so predictable that Tim could spoil the punch line before Keith had a chance to utter it. Holly thought it was hilarious. Oddly enough, so did Keith. The only one who could feel the tension was Tim.

They were sitting at the Fallon Inn. Tim and Keith downed Coke and rum like it was the last night on Earth. Holly sat politely sipping on cider and spinning the ice cubes in Keith's glass. The vocal level of the bar was through the roof, and Tim could barely make out what anyone was saying over the music. But, the boisterous environment did not stop Keith from demanding all of the attention.

"Keith," Holly started. "Keith." She paused, waiting for a response. But, Keith was too enthralled in telling Irv the story of the previous night's football game to pay her any mind.

"I'll listen." Tim put on a smile and clinked glasses with Holly. He wanted to take Keith by his stupid letter jacket and slug him. "What's going on? You look particularly glum tonight."

"Oh, it's nothing." Her voice had a rich, smooth tone. "Just irritated." She rolled her eyes back to Keith but followed her annoyance up with a laugh. "What's on your mind, though? You're awfully quiet lately. You haven't gone to a bash with us in a couple weeks. Is something going on? Is there a girl?" Her voice filled with excitement.

"No." Tim laughed it off. "There's no girl."

"Then what's troubling you?" Holly looked at him with her brows furrowed and her dainty lips in a pout. They were beautiful, red lips that matched so perfectly with her soft white sweater.

"If anything is giving me trouble, it's you." Tim's voice was muffled, nearly inaudible with the sound of all the college kids rushing to the center of the dance floor.

"What?" Holly replied unable to hear. She leaned in closer, resting a hand on Tim's knee, "What did you say?"

"I said I loved you." Tim's voice shook, sounding broken. It was a shame that Holly didn't hear him again.

*

"What?" Ruby replied, disgusted. "You didn't repeat yourself after that?"

"I had done what I could." Tim shrugged nonchalantly. "I told her I loved her, but she could not hear me over the loud music at the bar and her boyfriend's god-awful laughter."

"What happened after that?" Ruby egged him on.

"She asked what again, and I told her it was nothing and laughed. She seemed to think everything in the world was all right the second someone laughed," Tim answered.

"And after that?" Ruby sounded distressed.

"She did dump him." Tim nodded. "Only so much shit a girl that smart can put up with."

"Did you make a move?" Ruby asked.

"Are you joking? You bet he did," Rigan groaned.

*

She thought the world of him, but surprising as it sounded, there was only so much love and affection Tim could take. They lay in bed one night, Holly cuddled up in a nightie and Tim in boxers, gazing into each other's eyes, smiling every couple seconds like two love-struck fools. She'd say something along the lines of "I'm so glad you're not like him." He'd say he loved her. At first, Tim didn't mind.

Tim was just thankful to have her. He didn't mind the occasional mention of Keith. He'd wrap her up in hugs when she had her back turned. She'd call him "such a gentleman." He even surprised her with a carriage ride through Detroit one snowy winter night, but then they fought. What it was about didn't matter. Whether Tim was in the right or not didn't matter. As soon as the argument was over, Tim left without explanation.

They spoke a couple times after that, but Tim never provided Holly with closure. The love in his heart was snuffed out by the unattractiveness of confrontation. He'd gone from loving her to hating her in one brief flash.

*

"What?" Ruby groaned.

"Oh, my god, that's such a Tim thing to do." Rigan rolled his eyes and shifted his weight from one hip to the other. "I really should have seen that coming."

"What a crappy love story!" Ruby scolded.

"Believe me, Rigan's is worse." Tim snorted.

"Stop." Rigan got visibly tense at anyone's mention of Isabelle.

"But, Tim, why?" Ruby was in ruins. "I just don't understand."

"Love should be effortless," Tim answered. "I am not a man who fights like that. I am not a man who bends. I need a woman who can complement that."

"You need a waif," Rigan scoffed. "Nothing too complicated for Tim. He can't handle it."

"All love is complicated, Rigan." Tim looked from Rigan to Ruby. "All love is complicated regardless of whether or not there is conflict."

"So that's it? You two never reconciled?" Ruby had her head rolled back and seemed ready to pull her hair in frustration.

"No." He shrugged. "I am who I am. You think that story is bad, you should hear what happened when I went home one night this last September."

"Oh, shut up," Rigan snapped. "Boo-hoo. I'm all blue and gross. You love being trapped here. You can read day in and day out."

"I'm sorry. Do you not think I miss electricity? Heated blankets? French fries?" Tim taunted. "Because believe me, I miss the whole lot of it."

"Bet you miss women, too," Rigan shot back, visibly proud of himself.

"I'm going to bring you the worst love story ever next week. I swear to it," Ruby hissed.

"Until then." Tim pointed down at his copy of *The Bell Jar*. He began to walk away but then called back to Ruby, "Don't forget about the letter—a hundred miles, Ruby."

"God, this is just like in the Philippines," Rigan huffed, crossing his arms over his chest. "You're not going to believe the shit Tim pulled in the Philippines."

Tim walked toward camp, his thoughts already wandering. He began guessing why certain choices were made for the cover of the book, the binding. It was a world he felt comfortable in, but his meditative walk was interrupted by two familiar faces.

"Is that Tim?" Da Vinci's voice raised an octave as he hurried down the steep side of the bluff to catch up with his partner. "Tim! We didn't miss her, did we?"

Diana was coming down from behind Da Vinci, moving to his side once she caught up.

"No, she and Rigan are down there. Rigan's about to tell her about the Philippines." Tim gave his halfhearted equivalent of an eye roll.

"Oh, maybe we should leave." Da Vinci stood on his tiptoes to peek down the bluff. "Better to leave them alone."

Diana laughed, deep in her throat. "I'm sure Rigan wouldn't mind." She ran her hand along Da Vinci's shoulder. "I came in at the tail end of the Philippines story last time. I wouldn't mind hearing how it begins."

Da Vinci's face lit up. He had on a pleasant smile. "Well, if that's the case." He started maneuvering down the bluff. Diana followed him, her hand in his.

Decay

NOVEMBER 21 THROUGH 29, 1963

Da Vinci asked Diana to pull the Corvair over in front of a small and shady pub on the west side of DC. Tim had just recently blown up and stormed out of the car, allowing Diana and Da Vinci some much-needed time alone.

"So, tonight's mission was a big success." Da Vinci had a boyish way about him when he was with her. "I'd say that's reason enough to celebrate. Why not come get drinks with me? The pub here plays music till three. We could dance to some Jerry Lee Lewis. I know you think he's just the berries."

"Just the berries? I'm old, but not that old," she teased.

"Are you saying I am?" Da Vinci acted dramatic, playfully offended. "I rescind my invite if you're just going to sit there and insult me to my face."

"Would you rather I do it behind your back like Dresden?"

"Oh, too close to home, Hera. I like to pretend Dresden and I are actually really good friends."

"Yeah, me, too." Diana raised a thin eyebrow and parted her full lips into an earnest smile.

"I can't believe he's still on you about the security breach." Da Vinci exhaled.

"He has a right to." She shrugged. "You two really saved me. Lord knows where I'd be if the CIA canned me."

Da Vinci rolled his head to his left, staring Diana down. "You'd be working for the KGB in under twenty-four hours of termination, and I refuse to accept anything less."

"Hmmmm…" Diana hummed lowly and then let out a rich, decadent laugh. "You're probably right."

"But in all seriousness." Da Vinci's smile had a coy nature to it. "Do you want to come and dance for a while? I'll pay for your meter."

Diana's gaze drifted to the far right. Her expression showed that the gears were spinning and grinding in her mind. Da Vinci was captivated. Her bright golden pin curls lit up when other cars passed by, their headlights hitting her hair just right.

She gently traced the curve of the steering wheel, until she found and turned the key in the ignition, killing the engine. "I have enough time tonight. We've fallen behind on our paperwork."

"But you turned the car off," he teased, a big schmucky smile taking over his face. "Which means you want to."

"Alas, needing and wanting are two different things all together," she replied aloofly. She drummed her manicured nails along the dashboard. "You should get going before it gets too dark out."

"God forbid I get jumped. A geezer like me? All the CIA training in the world couldn't help me take down a common criminal."

Da Vinci was stalling for time and Diana was catching on. Every time she dropped him off, he invited her to go dancing or join him for drinks. Some nights, he'd be a lot more forward and ask if she'd stay the night. She only accepted sometimes, but he knew that she would always consider.

"You crack me up," she cooed, sliding along the bench seat closer to Da Vinci.

"I can tell by how much you laugh at my jokes," he jabbed.

Diana smirked.

"What do you want?" Da Vinci teased. "I can tell you're about to ask for something."

"So quick to assume," she replied.

"But I'm right." Da Vinci looked out of the front window, pretending Diana wasn't practically on his lap.

"You are." She leaned her head back against the cool driver's side window, face to face with Da Vinci. "I want the file on Marina and Brahe's recent missile obtainment."

"Oh, my god, why *that* one?" Da Vinci groaned. "I miss when you asked for the stuff that was easy to get."

Diana and Da Vinci both laughed, and Diana intertwined her hand with his, while playing with his soft, dark hair with her other.

"I promise this is the last time I'll ask for a couple months. I just have a hunch about something, and I think this can help me confirm some suspicious activity on Brahe's part."

"You think he's defecting?" Da Vinci asked with an edge of excitement in his voice.

"I may have a hunch." She rolled her eyes and laughed again. "We'll just have to wait and find out."

"Now, I have to get the files. I've been dying for some in-house drama. Adams has been holding out on me." He mimicked her body language, tilting his head off to the right. "But I'd be lying if I said you didn't scare me sometimes, collecting all these files and secrets."

"Niccolò, you can't be serious." Her eyes grew wide and her face twisted, displeased. "You think I'm going to try to defect?"

"Not defect, but maybe start freelancing. You've certainly got the skill for it. Not like you've got an ace of a team that you'd regret leaving," he replied.

"Niccolò." She had a sultry way of saying his name. She traced from the back of his head to the jaw of his stubbly narrow face with her hand. "You're right. I do have the skills for freelancing, but no cause." She shrugged. "We've got things easy here. I'm just antsy to get back out into the real world. Things are nice now, but it's too many missions, not enough coups, invasions, large-scale rescues. It's fine, but it's nothing compared to what we're built for."

Da Vinci kept his mouth shut, knowing there was more on her mind.

"If I can reveal Brahe, I'm hoping we'll end up back on those kinds of missions faster."

"Do you really miss those missions, though, or are you just trying to get back at Dresden?" Da Vinci's voice didn't falter.

"Oh, please." She giggled. "Dresden isn't worth my time or yours, for that matter."

"So that's it, just trying to get back into good graces? A narrative I can support." Da Vinci rested his head against the passenger-side window, his gaze falling into hers. "Won't you come dance?"

"Not tonight, but tomorrow? You know I'm good for my word." Her smile revealed two rows of perfect teeth. "We can grab dinner down at the Hometown."

"Promise me a burger from there and I'd say yes to just about anything." He grabbed her hand and kissed the top of it. "Until then?"

She threw her arms around him and pressed her lips to his, smiling when they eventually pulled apart. "Until then." She slid back to her side of the seat and waited until Da Vinci had vanished into the bar before pulling back out into the nighttime traffic.

*

"What if I stayed?"

"Stayed?"

"The night we went missing. You asked me to come into that pub on the west side of town. What if I stayed? Do you think we could've taken them?" Diana rested her head on Da Vinci's chest, the two of them lying out beneath the stars.

"We would have been drunk off our asses. If anything, we would have been easier targets." He shrugged. "There are some things that can't be changed."

"Who took you? The night they came for you, was it Nikola?" Diana drew circles on his hand with her finger.

"No, no." He shook his head. "It was the big brute and his negotiator. They were set on convincing me without physical force, but I was noncompliant. So, they shot me."

"I took them both down," she said. "Kal and Gulliver. I beat them no problem, but Nikola got me on my way out to the car. I'm guessing they had her positioned behind another vehicle. I didn't realize it was her until we saw them out here with Rigan."

"There's no use dwelling on what we cannot change." Da Vinci dropped his voice and shifted himself uncomfortably. He cleared his throat. "It's something that can't be and will never be undone. It's our job to just keep pressing on."

Diana was silent. Her eyes glassed over. "I haven't felt real pain in so long." She pulled her hand from his and held it out in front of their faces. "These were down to nothing on the day we fought them. I pounded Kal's face into nothing and all that was left was soft membrane, but it never *really* hurt that much, and after a bit, it healed right up." Diana looked to him but saw that he had no intention of responding. He seemed to still be listening. "If they capture me, or Tim, for that matter, they'll be able to torture us indefinitely. We could be alive for decades just locked away."

"You talking like that terrifies me." Da Vinci focused on the stars. "You will feel pain again, Diana. You can die." He paused for a moment, biting his lip before speaking. "You've always been able to, and nothing about the steroid changed that."

"It's just such a high pain threshold, Da Vinci."

"Sure, you're stronger, but you're not invincible. They'll come up with something to kill us. I'm certain of it, and when they come, we have to pray we'll be stronger than they are." He propped himself up on his elbows, using slow and careful movements. "There, you have your answer. Now, don't do anything reckless."

"What?" She pulled away from him. "What's that mean?" She leaned closer in. "What do you know?"

"I'm not giving you any ideas." Da Vinci shook his head. "I told Rigan what to look out for when we sent him to ring Adams, and he ended up worse off than before. I can't risk that with you, too, Diana. Just trust me and let it be." He took her chin in his hand and kissed her forehead.

"So no chance of me finding out what's going on in that big brain of yours?" The slight smirk on Diana's face and her increased leaning in was enough to make Da Vinci swoon. She knew it. The other day, he'd told her that she was beautiful before the steroid, but now she was "ethereal," something that never was and never will be again. She might have been taking advantage of that fact. There was a sudden genialness to the two of them that hadn't been there for a long time, but this moment of timeless bliss was cut short by the sound of rustling rhododendron.

Diana turned to the brush around them, pink flowers bobbed before them. She put her finger to her lips and stood, signaling for Da Vinci do the same. From then on, it was just waiting. They listened as the footsteps got closer. There was something urgent to them. Whoever was coming was plowing through the woods. Diana and Da Vinci were in position to strike when Ruby burst through the bushes and into their clearing.

"Surprise! Look who brought good news," she sang, an envelope in hand.

Diana relaxed, still frustrated that earlier that week Rigan and Tim just decided it was time for her to know and brought her to camp without clearing it with the rest of them. Luckily, she'd grown very fond of Ruby and allowed it.

"Is that from Adams?" Diana swung from lethal to friendly in under a second. She stepped close to Ruby and picked the envelope from her hand. It was. "Good," she said as though the wind had been taken right out of her. "Thank god." She felt cautiously optimistic.

"Let's go get the others. We'll open it together." He pressed past Ruby and Diana.

"Get the others?" Ruby scoffed, turning to Diana. "You're going to open it now, right?"

Diana smirked. "You and I think alike, sweetheart." She slipped her thumb under the envelope's flap and opened the letter. She only peeked, but the look of delight on her face must've given her away.

"Good news." Ruby let out a long breath. "That's a relief. I would've peeked myself, but I couldn't even understand the first one."

Diana tucked the letter away and chuckled. "It's a cipher. I'll teach you how to break it later tonight."

Ruby squealed and followed behind. The next twenty-four hours were the happiest Ruby and they had. Adams was coming.

When Ruby showed up the next day crying, everyone assumed it was because whatever special connection she'd had with them was coming to an end. They'd return to the CIA, undergo treatment, the world's finest scientists would work on them, and then they'd be real again, but no. Not even Da Vinci seemed ready for what she told them.

"Ruby, what's wrong?" Rigan took her in his arms, and although the top of her shirt was already getting damp from his skin, she stayed there, heaving.

"K-Kennedy," Ruby struggled to be heard in between the long, heavy sobs.

"What's going on?" Da Vinci rushed over to Rigan and Ruby. Diana followed close behind him, more curious than concerned.

"Kennedy's been shot! Killed!" Ruby gasped for air. "He's gone." Her words teeter-tottered between sobbing and screaming. Ruby was still weeping, hugging Rigan as though her life depended on it. "There—there weren't even commercials on TV. It's just been nonstop. I-I ca-a-a-ame here to-to get away from it. I'm so-o-orry." She pushed her face into Rigan's shoulder.

Diana felt void of anything but dread. She turned away from the group and walked toward the woods. "Kennedy's dead?"

"Diana." Da Vinci followed her but knew better than to touch her. She was moving farther away from the group. "Diana, wait."

She stopped on the brink of the woods. She was drifting, spinning worst-case scenarios until she was partially paralyzed. She wiped away what little tears she had left.

"I know how important he was to you and the others," Da Vinci seemed to be pulling whatever trite cliché came to him. "But you have to think of i—"

"That's not what this is about." She shook her head, a cry condemned to her throat. Her words came out calm and articulate. "We're never getting out of here. Go tell Tim. He'll say the same thing."

"We don't know that."

"Adams won't come. He'll be tied up with the investigation. Brahe, Reginald, Minerva, Nike, none of them, Da Vinci." She was shaking. "None of them will come."

"This is just a setback. This investigation may not take as long as you think it will."

"Do you know that?" She spun around, holding back tears. "Do you know that, Da Vinci? Did you know about this? Because if you did, then *fucking tell me!*"

"You think if I knew this was going to happen, I'd have been celebrating yesterday?" he growled back, his face instantly reddening with embarrassment.

"Da Vinci Moretti, the man who sees all and says *nothing*." She paused before her stare flicked over to Tim. He was already walking toward them.

"Seems like we've got some planning to do," Tim said evenly.

"You're right. Come on." Diana turned to address Da Vinci. "Take care of them. We'll be back."

OUT IN THE woods, Diana and Tim pressed on, waiting until they were completely out of earshot before beginning.

"So we are screwed." Tim still looked behind them, as though worried they'd been followed. "Like this is Bay of Pigs levels of fucked, Diana."

"Believe me, I know." She sighed, sitting on a fallen tree trunk. "What the hell are we going to do?"

"Start planning our plea bargain with the KGB." Tim shrugged and sat next to her. "Do not even bother trying to tell me you are not thinking the same thing."

Diana took a long, sharp inhale and then let out an equally tense exhale. "There won't be a plea bargain, Tim."

"Please, you are the Goddess. Not *a* goddess, *the* goddess. The KGB wants you. And that's all I'm giving you, because complimenting you feels like drinking gasoline."

"Not after what we did to their agents." Diana ran her hands through her matted hair.

"So we are as good as dead?" Tim then added, "Or as close to dead as we can get?"

"We're as good as relentlessly tortured for decades on end."

"You don't think we age, either?" Tim asked, curious. "I was just thinking we were unbreakable, not immortal." Tim seemed to be waiting for a response, but she didn't even acknowledge that he'd spoken.

He twisted his mouth into just a shadow of a crooked smile. "Perhaps you're right." He shook his head. "There is no death in our futures."

"Just this—waiting."

"If we keep ourselves moving, we might be able to buy enough time for the CIA to get back in order."

"Da Vinci'll freeze to death by the time the CIA gets itself back in order," she scoffed. "Besides, with Kennedy dead, there'll be some kinda coup."

"There had better not be," Tim grumbled. "The last one was a mess."

"Won't be ours to clean up." Diana laughed at her own joke, ignoring Tim's molten anger.

"We can't live like this."

"We're not living." Diana laughed again, this time just a bit more off-kilter. "Not dyin', either."

Tim grimaced. "You are beside yourself. Come get me when you are actually willing to talk about a plan."

Tim stormed off, but she stopped him right as he seemed to be leaving earshot. "Tim? Not a word to Da Vinci."

"Wouldn't want him to know you are coming undone at the seams." Tim's words were jarring. "I doubt you truly care."

She waited until Tim was gone to pull out a small, red pocket knife she'd taken from Ruby a few days earlier. One of the fortunate parts of having a non-agent pack mule was that getting close to her, getting what she needed from her, was easy.

There was safety in death. Diana had known this since she was a child. Carefully, she took the blade to her arm and began to carve away, little pieces at first, and then large chunks as her flesh grew back. The littleness of what she knew, compared with the unreliability what she guessed, ate her alive. Diana depended on logic and certainty. Without these two things, she was at the mercy of imagination. There in the woods, she crafted a tempting solution. This was nothing shocking. It was something premeditated. Something she'd been thinking about for weeks now. How far could she push herself? How far could the KGB push her if they ever got the opportunity? More importantly, how far could Nikola?

It was a sermon of slicing and not feeling for a few minutes. She was dissatisfied with her lack of response. She raised her arm mechanically and drove the blade deep into her skin. Now that she felt, small tinges of pain hit as muscles snapped apart like broken rubber bands. It was barely anything, but it was a beginning. She quickly yanked the blade out and healed from the inside out. The act mesmerized Diana. She did it again and again. Stabbing the knife into her legs, arms, and stomach. Her stab wounds healed again and again. What started as a hypnotizing fascination quickly became a harsh reality.

"Shit," she whispered, taking the blade, driving it in, and slicing upward. The wound healing as the blade moved along.

"No. No. No." Her muted desperation led to her frantically flailing away at her arm. She cut and cut, chunks of shell and membrane falling to the forest floor. She waited for the arm to finally fall off, but the blue membrane remained and her arm grew back over.

There was a hushed terror overcoming her as her arm failed to fall. She could feel the pain now. The KGB could inflict pain if they wanted, but they couldn't kill her. These were her worst fears confirmed. She kept her breathing steady, but inside, her heart trembled. In no world did she ever imagine death as a luxury, but here it was. Without a second thought, she raised the blade and drove it into her chest. A sharp gasp escaped her lips, but the situation lacked gratification. For a few seconds, there was pain, but then her heart healed and pushed the knife out of her chest and onto the ground without assistance.

She could feel another cry welling up in her throat, but she resisted. Instead, she took the blade and drove it into her chest a second time, a weak whimper escaping her lips as it penetrated her skin.

"Fuck." She sat there for a moment, pulling on her hair. She felt as though sitting there and rotting away to nothingness might be the only solution, but instead, she picked herself up, scooted the fallen pieces of shell and membrane away, and started back toward camp. Da Vinci was quick to meet her when she returned.

"Hey, is everything all right? Tim said you had a crack-up."

Diana raised her eyebrows in surprise. "Tim would say any woman was in hysterics if it'd benefit him," she scoffed. Light, believable laughter left her lips. "I'm fine. I'm just trying to figure out what to do." She shrugged. "We've got to escape one way or another."

THE NEXT DAY, Diana asked Ruby for a lighter. After that, the days blended together. Diana ran on autopilot. A few harsh remarks here, a laugh or two there, harmless flirting with Da Vinci, a conversation about supplies with Ruby. It'd been at least a week since the blade episode. Despite going into the woods with the intention to test the flame against her flesh, she had not yet done it. As much as she hated to admit it, she was nervous. What next if the flames didn't touch her? The longer she waited, the more nervous she got.

The group functioned fine without her being there in full mental capacity. Tim, Ruby, and Rigan were convinced they were going to navigate their way around the KGB to escape. Diana had more than a few reasons the plan wouldn't work, but she kept her mouth shut, because she knew that, in his now-exterior heart, Tim also understood the plan wouldn't work, but the illusion of hope stayed.

Eventually, Diana made a move. That night, she took a large step in ensuring her own mortality. She waited for Da Vinci, Rigan, and Tim to fall asleep. It was her turn to stand guard, but she left them. It was the perfect opportunity to slip away unnoticed. Since her lash out on the 23rd, Da Vinci had been keeping a close eye on her, closer than usual. She vanished into shrouded, green woodlands, surrounded by unglamorous vines and dying trees. Soon enough, there'd be snow. Some days, Diana could feel herself going away with the trees and woodland life. It was all getting cold. She chose the bank of a mostly stagnant pond, not too far from their current site for her experiment, convinced that when she started to blister—and she was certain she would—she'd be able to dip her hand into the water, preventing the flames from engulfing her whole self and the dainty floral dress Ruby had given her.

She pulled out the small, silver lighter, handling it like a relic of the old world. She flipped it open with one of her nails and immediately protected the flame, careful not to let the wind get to it. Not powered by the want-to, but the need-to, Diana dipped her fingers into the flame.

And she felt nothing. Nothing but the residual panic when her heart drove the dagger out of her chest. Thinking on her feet, she switched the flame from her fingers to a location where her skin was softer, along her previously carved-up arm, but no blistering came. She did not feel the warmth from the fire. The flames treated her skin like Teflon. For a long while, she just stared in shock, but after a moment, an uncontrollable sense of anger overtook her. She balled the lighter up in her fist and threw it yards away. Then, she ran her hands through her matted hair and pulled at it, desperate to feel something. Her scalp began to flake and pieces of shell with hair fell at her feet. She made the choice not to cry. She kept herself under control. The next thing to happen wasn't planned. It wasn't thought through, but she felt as though it had to happen.

Carefully, she made her way over to the decaying side of the stagnant pond. At first, she just dipped her toes in, and then she took a deep breath and dove. The temperature of the water was unreadable due to her thick shell-like skin, so there was no immediate shock when she submerged herself in the pond. It was another world down there, filled with algae, mud, grime. Where there was no control in the woods, there was some down there. The world was so peaceful at the bottom of that pond. Everything just gently swayed. There was no chaos. Diana let go of her breath and allowed the water fill her lungs. She'd been waterboarded before. The nearness to death was overly familiar, but when the sensation of drowning took over, Diana didn't thrash or fight to reach the surface. She kept floating down.

She woke up to the water parting and Rigan diving down to get her. He moved like an animal under the water, his webbed limbs helping him reach the bottom of the deep, dark pond. When his arms looped around her, she didn't fight. Once they were back on land, Rigan only needed to compress her sternum once. She vomited up enough water to kill and then some.

"How long was I und—"

"One night. I stop watching after you for one night and *that's* when you chose to try to kill yourself," Rigan scolded. "All I wanted was one night of rest and you decide to try to kill yourself."

"What?" Diana's eyes were still adjusting. Light breaking across the horizon in the east. She'd gone under shortly after dusk. She hadn't drowned at all. She'd fallen asleep. She wasn't any closer to dying than she had been before.

"Da Vinci was afraid of this. He asked me to watch you, and the one night I take a break, you go and do exactly what he was afraid of," Rigan huffed, then took her hand and pulled her up from the ground. She was groggy, but more than capable of walking. "Come on."

They walked in quiet. The songs of the early-morning birds filled the void. Diana watched as hints of the sun took over the night sky and rolled in through the mountains.

Eventually, as they found themselves almost to camp, she said, "You won't tell him, right?"

"Huh?" Rigan seemed to be coming out a trance.

"You can't tell Da Vinci." She sounded distant, but she meant what she said. "It will break him."

Rigan looked her up and down for a moment as though inspecting her and her motives. "You really care if he knows?"

"Yes."

"Why?"

"I care about him." She crossed her arms and stared at Rigan, more desperately than intimidatingly. "He is troubled enough. He doesn't need my trouble, as well. What I did was my own doing, and if I choose to continue, it's still my own doing."

"You really want to die?" Rigan asked.

"No." She shook her head. "I just want to know that I can." She cleared her throat, residual water still lurking in her lungs. "If the KGB gets me. There'll be no cure, no opportunities, it'll just be torture. It'll be torture and endless pain. I need my own cyanide pill. I need to know that's not my future."

"Yeah. I get that. I wish I didn't, but I do." He turned his back to her and started walking again. There was silence for only a second before he spoke again. "Diana, can you be honest with me?"

Her interest was piqued. "Depends. What do you want to know?"

"Do you think we're going to get out of here?"

"The CIA won't be coming. With the Kennedy assassination, they'll be tied up for weeks, even months. An escape is unlikely."

Rigan shuddered. Her words must've confirmed his fears. Tim had been leading him and Ruby on, but Rigan was trained to be skeptical. "Thanks for being honest with me."

Da Vinci and Tim were already awake and in the clearing when Diana and Rigan reached camp. They'd been waiting for her. She had a speech planned out in her head, but upon seeing the fire embers, the fort, the backpacks of food, the people, she was overcome with tears. This was it. This was their future.

"Diana." Rigan offered out his arm for her. "It's okay."

She shook her head and turned away, heading back into the woods, trying to get her thoughts back to the peacefulness she'd found at the bottom of the pond.

RIGAN CAME TO Da Vinci and Tim, seemingly confused. "What do we do?"

"I'll go after her." Da Vinci bowed his head. "I'm the one with the answers." He sighed.

"Don't bother, Da Vinci," Tim said. "You know nothing is wrong."

"Nothing is wrong?" Rigan's eyes narrowed. He glared Tim down. "She tried to kill herself. She is overflowing with tears."

"Diana is not depressed, Rigan," Tim responded. "She is pissed. If you believe anything else, you are only fooling yourself."

For a moment, Rigan was silent. Tim might have been right, but that didn't stop Da Vinci.

Da Vinci plowed into the woods, knowing exactly where to find Diana. She was curled under a bare oak tree. There was just a bit of frost on the ground where she sat.

"Don't expect an apology, Da Vinci. This was something I needed."

"You're wrong," he replied, his voice shaking with the cold. "All you need to do is stop."

"You are so naïve, Da Vinci." Diana brought her legs in to her chest. "You don't get it. I'm not sorry, because we are never getting out of this hellhole. Look at me, Da Vinci. I'm a freak." The words lingered. In her life, she'd been called many things. Some derogatory, some not, but freak was never a word used to describe this goddess. "You turned out fine, Da Vinci. If the KGB weren't waiting outside these mountains, you could walk on out of here. Go back to society. I can't." She paused, but then added, "I need to know that there's still something human left inside of me."

Da Vinci rummaged his hands through his hair, eventually covering his ears. "Don't say that." He frowned. "There is so much human left in you. More—" He stuttered for a moment. "More than there was just a few months ago."

She laughed, clearly surprised by his honesty. But, before she could speak to him again, he began to cry.

"I'm sorry, I'm sorry, I'm sorry." Da Vinci was sobbing. Seeing her exactly as he'd seen her weeks before in one of his visions broke his heart. He'd even warned her. Don't do it. I know you will. And yet she still did. "I'm so sorry, Diana. I shouldn't have said anything. I'm so sorry."

"Da Vinci," she said softly. "What's wrong?" She took his hand and guided him down to the ground beside her.

"You know that future? The one I said I fixed."

"Yes."

"I don't think I changed it." He swallowed hard, feeling the weight of his words. "I think I caused it. I tried to stop you from this, this mad race to kill yourself, but no matter what I said, no matter who I sent, we still ended up here. Nothing I do, nothing I don't do, changes what I see. It always comes to term one way or another." He could feel the dirt and grime of days past sliding off his face with the tears. "I've seen you die hundreds of times, Diana. You've got nothing to worry about." He tried to detach himself from the conversation, but the more he spoke, the more he broke. "Our future is imminent and unchangeable." He felt the most agonizing pain, like a dagger being driven into his heart and twisted until his former self ceased to exist.

"I'm so sorry, Da Vinci." This was the first time Da Vinci had seen Diana act timid. She reached out and caressed his face, wiping away a tear.

"Are you going to keep trying to kill yourself?" His voice was weak.

"No." She shook her head, watching him closely.

They sat in the silence of the early morning for a while, but then she spoke again.

"How do I go?"

"I'll tell you only what you already know. You die trying to save Ruby."

"But how?"

His head shook. "I'm not going to risk causing that. I would never be able to live with myself."

"So you outlive me," she said flatly.

"Yeah." The inside of Da Vinci's mouth was dry. "I wish I didn't."

She scooted closer to him and curled into his side. He lifted his arm and wrapped it around her shoulders, then squeezed her tightly, and they stayed like that as the sun rose.

Ghosts

DECEMBER 2, 1963

"How bad is he?" Ruby handed her backpack off to Rigan and hurried up the mountainside. The drive had been long and she was eager to get moving.

"What are you doing here so early? Don't you have work?" Rigan slung her backpack over his shoulders and joined her in the race to the camp.

"There are more pressing matters at hand! I just made a three-hour drive in under two and you're being sassy with me." Ruby's words had a bite to them. "Now, tell me how he is. Did the aspirin help at all?"

"He's deteriorating," Rigan mumbled. He picked up his pace and got a few steps ahead of her. "The aspirin did the best it could. It's one of those things we're going to have to wait out and hope passes."

"Is there any chance I could sneak him out of the park? I could get him to a hospital." Ruby's boots held strong against the slick surface of icy bluffs.

"You'd both get shot." Rigan shook his head and offered his hand out to help her over a steep slope.

She took it and hoisted herself up. "The KGB has that much spare time on their hands? They're just camping out around the park?" Ruby sounded dubious.

"They don't have that much spare time. We're just that important." He sighed. "We'll have to be extra careful from here on out. We're stationary for the time-being."

"Isn't that like the worst thing for you guys, though? Diana and Tim are always going on about it."

"Exactly." His claws dug into a thick tree as he pulled himself over a small drop. "But he's too sick to move."

"Dammit," she spat.

Ruby and Rigan moved like a machine from then on, Rigan turning back to help her over the steep bluffs, watching to ensure that she didn't slip, and then Ruby always knowing when to pull herself and when to comply. The higher they got, the heavier the snow became. Down at road level, there was nothing but a few patches of ice and some frost, but as they approached camp, they found themselves trekking through blankets of snow inches thick. As they approached camp, they found Tim out in the woods. He was startling in the world of white.

"You're here. Good." Tim approached them without hesitation. "I need Ruby."

"What's going on?" Rigan looked toward the camp. "Is he still okay?" There was something grave in Rigan's voice.

"Calm down. He's stable," Tim answered. "Diana and I have a list of herbs we need. I'm thinking we can get most of them farther down in the mountains."

Ruby's face was flushed from the sprint up the mountain, and the cold was starting to get to her, but she did get a smile out. "Of course, what are they?"

Tim pulled from his pocket a slightly damp list and handed it off to Ruby. She tried to silence her chattering teeth.

"Okay." Rigan exhaled slowly. "I can get you down there and get us to most of the herbs. Once Ruby warms up at camp, she can come down and fill in any gaps in the list."

"O-oh, no, I'm fine," she assured, wrapping her arms around herself. "I'm just a bit chilled."

Tim snorted. "Funny." He nudged his head to the north. "Head to camp and meet us down there in ten."

Ruby looked to Rigan for a minute before turning her attention to the clearing beyond Tim. "Don't-don't kill each other," she chattered. Tim and Rigan began their descent of the mountain at full speed.

INSIDE THE FORT, Diana watched over Da Vinci, brushing her fingers through his damp hair. He was laid out on her lap, nestled under a few quilts Ruby had dumpster-dived and a pile of too-big shirts. When he spoke, Da Vinci didn't seem too worried about his health, but his partners had begun to suspect that he did not fully understand what was going on. He was feverish and constantly talking like the kidnappings hadn't happened, asking when their next departure was and if *Dresden* had talked to the commander the night before.

At his worst, Da Vinci would wake up screaming, his third eye open and moving frantically. The thought of a mercy killing made Diana's stomach churn, but if he didn't get better, she worried that it could easily come to that. He felt clammy and skeletal in her arms. He was as limp as a corpse when hugged or held. He twitched in what she could only assume was a fit of nightmares when suddenly, Ruby popped her head into the fort.

"Wow, it's like crazy warm in here." Ruby sounded as though she'd discovered a pleasant surprise.

"Well, when you spend months at a time in the jungles of Vietnam and the tundra of the Arctic you learn to build a damn good fort." Diana did not look up at Ruby.

"Months in the jungle, is that a true story or a Rigan story?"

Diana let out a thick, warm laugh. "A Rigan story," she tsk'd. "I hated missions that had me sleeping anywhere but the Ritz."

Ruby joined Diana on the damp, dead-grass floor of the fort. "How is he?"

"He is not well." Diana got hung up on her words. Although they were always physically protecting him from gunfire and other agents, this kind of care for Da Vinci was different. This was intimate. There was a new level of fondness between the team that Diana didn't often see on or off the field. It scared her. "But we're hoping the heat will break his fever."

"Yeah, It's like a sauna in here."

"That's good to hear. None of us could really tell. We had to just eyeball it."

"I-uh-I brought some aspirin, but Rigan took it back down the hill with him. I'll make sure someone goes and brings it up."

"Hm, that should help the fever." She paused for a moment, her gaze still resting on Da Vinci. "Is that all you were here for?" Although most days Diana would opt for a long conversation with Ruby about the news and the nightly shows, today was different. Diana wanted to be left alone. Having her attention divided even one other way from Da Vinci was too much. She wanted all eyes on him.

"Yeah." Ruby shifted uncomfortably before reaching for her jacket. "I-I'll be on my way then." She put her jacket back on but was quickly stopped.

"Sweetheart." Diana mulled her options over for a moment. It didn't feel right to just send the girl out into the cold. "I was talking about supplies. Please stay and warm up. You look just about tortured over there."

"Ohthankheavens." Ruby huddled back to the fire.

Diana pressed her plump and cracked lips closed. She had on a knowing smile. "Why suddenly so afraid of me, Ruby? Rigan hasn't been telling you any stories, has he?"

"No more fear than usual," Ruby joked. "I'm just stiff from the cold. Believe me. If my teeth weren't so chattery, I'd be talkin' your ear off."

It was then that Da Vinci stirred, mumbling quickly. He thrashed around. Diana tsk'd. "It may actually be better if you head down the hill soon, though." Diana shifted her legs, attempting to move Da Vinci's head off her lap. "He's getting restless."

Ruby watched him. "Is he going to be okay, Diana?" She bit her lip and looked to Diana for help. "Be honest with me. I can take it. Based on what you've seen before. Will he be okay?" Ruby had misty eyes. Her hand mindlessly smoothed the blankets surrounding him.

"It's too early to tell. He needs to be allowed some rest," Diana cooed, attempting to cue Ruby that it was time for her to leave.

"I wish you could reach me if he gets worse." Ruby brushed herself as she stood up from the damp ground, grass stains on her skirt's hem. "I'll come back tomorrow."

"That's a good idea, sweetheart." Diana bowed her head as Ruby left. Da Vinci grew more restless. He thrashed back and forth, his body drenched in sweat. He let out a strong cough, one that seemed to rattle his insides. He curled closer to Diana.

"Are we going to leave soon? Where's Dresden?" he asked her, his dry lips moving under his mass of beard.

"Not yet, Da Vinci." She brushed his hair, careful not to graze his forehead. "Do you know what is going to happen?" She leaned in closer to him. "Do you know how you get better?" She had her hand pressed to his face. She couldn't feel whether he was hot or cold, but she assumed his fever hadn't broken. "Do you know how we get out?"

In response, he muttered something about the Germans. He wasn't with her anymore. Using her free hand, she grabbed a bottle of aspirin and pulled the cap off with her teeth. She gave him two and forced him to drink them down.

He swallowed and made a face as though she'd just given him cyanide. "Where's Giovanni?" Da Vinci raised his hand to her face but held it with no tenderness. He groped around like he didn't recognize her or where he was. "Where's Giovanni?" This time, he sounded distraught.

Diana didn't speak. Instead, she just continued to brush his hair until the aspirin kicked in. Although he was not healed and his health did not improve, he did calm down and slip back into his restless slumber. For a while, she stayed like that, propped against the back of their fort while snowflakes fell through the entrance, on the very edge between awake and asleep.

She didn't leave this state until Tim and Rigan came rushing into the fort.

"What's the hurry? Are you worried about getting wet?" Diana let her mouth pull into a lazy smile. "Aren't you always wet?"

Rigan gave a salty laugh. He kneeled down in front of the fire. "No luck with the herbs, but we wanted to bring this up." He slid off Ruby's backpack and set it beside Diana. "We won't have any protein tonight. There's no time to hunt."

"We'll be fine." She directed her words more toward Tim as an order rather than to Rigan as a comfort. Then asked tentatively, "Who is Giovanni? He keeps calling for him."

Tim answered while stripping out of his wet shirt and jacket, revealing a chest covered in external veins and a bulbous, beating heart. "The agent?"

Rigan looked at Tim then Diana for a moment. There seemed to be a hesitant air about him. Eventually, he responded. "Giovanni was his major in the war." Rigan cleared his throat. "He named his son after him."

"Da Vinci has a son?" Diana couldn't hide her shock. She'd spent months at a time with him, but this she hadn't known. "Is he alive?"

"Which one?" Tim asked for clarification, even though it was an answer he couldn't provide.

"His major died on the western front, but his son is alive. He'll be turning eighteen soon." Rigan watched Da Vinci with a sympathetic and pained look. "They haven't spoken in a long time. But Da Vinci still sends him a check every month."

Tim bent down and placed his hand on Da Vinci's chest, maneuvering through the layers of blankets. He felt for a heartbeat. "Did Ruby bring anything for him?"

"Fever reducers, but that's about it." Diana stirred through the backpack and pulled the tiny bottle of aspirin from it.

"That isn't going to do much." Tim joined Rigan on the ground. "What a shit way to go."

"This doesn't have to be the way he goes," Rigan snapped. "It won't be. It can't be. He would have told us if it was." He seemed revitalized. "Let's get back to searching."

"I'd like to rest," Tim replied. "Why don't you go, Diana?"

Diana didn't plan on moving, but she nodded in agreement, anyway. She began to shift Da Vinci off her lap, when Rigan stopped her.

"Tim." Rigan's face hardened, his jaw clearly clenched. "It's you and me. If he wakes up, he'll want her."

"It has been an exhausting day, Rigan. Let me rest." Tim locked gazes with Rigan and kept the mood between them cold.

"Tim." Rigan stood, towering over him. "Come on."

They reached a standstill, but between the two of them, Rigan was the one who would not bend. "I want to rest," Tim answered steadily. "Go ahead without me and I'll be there in a minute."

Diana gave Rigan a weak smile. "I'll be sure he keeps his word," she promised. "I wouldn't have felt safe leaving Da Vinci, anyhow."

Rigan rushed out of the fort and into the woods, leaving Tim and Diana alone.

For a moment, they stared each other down. Diana's gun-smoke-gray eyes were calm, unmoving, curious. The normally deadpanned Tim had a scowl on. "You may have Rigan fooled, but you do not have me. I know what kind of monster you are. The moment Da Vinci comes to, you will be right back at our throats, barking orders, pushing him to his limits, manipulating him." Tim paused, shifting his head from one side to the other. "Or the moment he dies, you will blame us or, worse yet, Ruby."

"Are you truly trying to judge me for having self-concern? I'm surprised you'd dare to be so hypocritical." Diana held intense control over her every syllable. "My interest in Da Vinci's well-being is personal."

"You are correct. I am self-concerned, too, but I don't conceal that fact behind false compassion. I don't leave people as husks of what they were when I'm done with them."

She remained silent, still tasting his words. He spoke again before she was prepared to answer him.

"Save whatever it is you have to say." He picked up a dry button-up from Da Vinci's pile and began to put it on. "Don't bother telling me you've changed, because we both know you haven't." He chose to salt the wound. "I'm sure we are only days away from you suggesting a mercy killing."

Diana's calm vanished. She sneered at Tim. "Leave."

Tim let out a smug laugh before pausing at the entrance of the fort. He wasn't moving fast enough for her.

"Get out!" she screamed, shaking the structure of their shelter.

Tim shook his head. "Don't be upset because I told you what you already know." He exited before she could say anything else.

She sat shaking, a cold rage storming within her heart. This would have never happened in the field. She had lost all footing in these mountains. A few minutes passed before she realized Da Vinci was mumbling at her.

"He's wrong, you know." Da Vinci was lucid for this fleeting moment. He grabbed one of her hands and gave it a gentle squeeze, careful not to cause any cracks. "You're so good to me, Diana." He smiled. "So good to me."

She brushed her hands through his hair once again, tucking the stray strands behind his ear. She gave him a kind smile. "I'm trying."

"That's all I ask," he replied. "I hate when you and Tim fight. You two fight so much." He let out a loud wheeze of a laugh that eventually gave way to coughing.

"Are you feeling all right?"

"You're so good," he repeated, his grip on her hand weakening. "You're both so good. You just can't see it." He started to shake. And like that he was gone again. At first, there was silence, and then there were tears.

He was sobbing. Softly, quietly, but he was sobbing. "Where's Giovanni?" He looked through her rather than at her. "Is something wrong?"

Diana did the only thing she could. She lied. "Everything is all right, Da Vinci. Everything is fine."

"You're lying." He paused, taking a large, deep breath before screaming. "You're lying!" Da Vinci pulled away from her hand. "What's wrong? Where am I?"

"Da Vinci," she hushed, her voice breaking. He kept crying out, his body now thrashing. "Da Vinci." She came undone as he pulled away from her. He moved out from the blankets and squirmed when she slammed her hands down on his shoulders and shook him. "Da Vinci, stop! Stop! Stop, goddammit!"

It snapped him out of it. He gasped, his eyes wild as he looked at Diana as she leaned over him. "Diana. It's okay." His voice was already falling off as pain slashed across his face. His eyes rolled back and he went limp. Not dead, but unconscious for the time-being. She sighed and hoisted him back up from the grass and readjusted the blankets around him.

She took a moment and breathed. "But Da Vinci..." Her voice was faint. "It's not."

*

The sound of feet stomping against hardwood reverberated against the walls of the small Southside dive. The smell of alcohol, cigarettes, and sweat all tinged the air, and in the middle of this madness was an expertly constructed ring. And at the center of that were two broads ready to tear each other apart.

Nikola moved with prowess. Her kicks swift, her punches thrown with grace, and her body contorted in a sort of melodic fluidity. But, no matter how talented the opponent, Diana always knew she'd win, and there was no better place to do it than Olympus, surrounded by their peers—the highest-ranked agents—and the political elite.

Most nights, the two trained in a small gym downtown. They'd spend the first half of the night lifting weights, and the second half doing cardio. Now they were finishing the night off like they always did, by beating each other's face in. Most nights—in fact, all nights, Diana managed to pin Nikola, but tonight seemed to be tipping in the opposite direction. Nikola dodged every blow Diana dealt. There was a lethal amount of untapped determination in Nikola, Diana had always seen it, but now everyone else was gaining access to this well of rage.

Bracing her feet against the cold mat, Diana swung hard. Nikola deflected her fists and jabbed at Diana's ribs. The crowd hollered. Their screams shook the walls.

"Get at 'er!" All their voices blended together.

"Come on!" A kind of a blur.

"Go! Go! Go!" Based solely in the existence of drunken delusion and a need for violence.

Diana backed up in time to avoid Nikola's blow to the ribs. She took that split second to grab Nikola's wrist and twist her arm behind her. Nikola contorted her body, relying on a double-jointed shoulder to squirm out of Diana's grasp. They continued to exchange throws. Nikola dodging and Diana deflecting. It was then in that familiar routine that Diana made a mistake. She swung at Nikola from behind, but Nikola did not spin around as she suspected. Instead, Nikola ducked and leapt into Diana, bringing them both to the mat. From there, they struggled. Diana swung with her tightly clenched fists. Nikola had barely escaped a near-critical blow to the face by rolling under the ring's ropes. She wasted no time jumping back into the fight. Diana sat up in time to throw a hit; Nikola grabbed Diana's wrist and shoved her down, it looked as though she had her pinned. Nikola started to count. The crowd was losing it. Most bets were on the goddess. She couldn't let them down.

Diana had a hint of a smile on her face. "Hmph." She smiled and then thrashed, wiggling one hand free and throwing it against Nikola's face. Easy as that, they were back to sparring on the floor, an old-fashioned wrestle to end the night's title fight.

"Tell me," Diana whispered into her partner's ear. "Have you ever kissed a woman?" She flipped Nikola and pinned her for a moment.

"Is that..." Nikola paused, then shoved up. She managed to push Diana back a few feet. "Rhetorical?"

"Entertain the thought," Diana wrestled for dominance.

"You can't—" Nikola huffed and shoved Diana off her. She pinned her on her own. "—seduce your way out of this one." She laughed and counted away. "Three...two..."

"I don't need a way out," Diana grunted. "I need time." Before Nikola could get to one, Diana had flipped her on her back and let out a deep gasp for air as she pinned her down. Three...Two...One...and the crowd goes wild.

"Dammit." Nikola relaxed, resting her head on the mat. "Couldn't let me beat you this one time?"

"And risk my reputation?" Diana tsk'd and then gave way to a giggle. "You'll beat me when you earn it, sweetheart." She stood and helped Nikola up to her feet. They soaked in the glory, the screams surrounding them, the chants of victory, the disappointed sighs of money earned, now lost. Diana smiled and turned her attention to Nikola. "I'm grabbing a drink before we go. You want anything?"

"Nah, I've gotta go talk to Artemis, anyway. I'll catch up." Nikola stepped out of the ring, a cocky smile still on her face.

Diana exited with a smooth swoop, not giving anyone the time of day as she stepped through the club. She carried herself with an intense elegance and aloofness. She had to if she didn't want to be talked up or talked to.

When she arrived at the bar, she bared all her weight on the counter's lip. "A dry martini, please." As the bartender made her drink, she could feel the man on her left staring. She could see the struggle to contain the words trapped in his throat trying to escape. She turned to him, prompting him to talk.

"Let me get that for you." He was a shorter man, more than a few years older than her. His hair was messy and his shirt partially untucked, but he seemed harmless.

"You think I pay for my drinks?" Diana had a playful look in her eyes.

"Oh, my god, Niccolò." Adams spun around. His fiery hair untamed and a knowing look in his eyes. "Amateur mistake."

"Niccolò?" Diana repeated, her interest piqued. "I've heard nothing but good things about you. You really speak ten languages?"

Da Vinci smiled. "Twelve, actually. Working on Thai right now."

Diana hm'd in acknowledgement, then switched her attention to Adams. "You come all the way out here just to see me?"

"Pffft," Adams scoffed. "Please. In your dreams, Hera."

"Hmmmm." She winked. "A shame." The bartender returned with her drink, and she swallowed it down. "I'll see you two around. I'm sure of it." And like that, she left.

Finding Nikola was no issue. It was always hard to miss the amazon of a woman. "Let's get going." Diana pulled Nikola away from a breezy blonde.

"What's the hurry?" Nikola asked, sounding irritated.

"Adams is here." Diana scanned the room. He was already gone. "Besides, what's there here for us?" She gave Nikola a devious smirk.

The two of them quickly headed out into the cold DC night.

The walk from Southside to Uptown where Diana lived was long, which tonight was a plus. It gave them time to talk.

"You should cut your hair." They were the first words from Diana's mouth once they'd left the bar and the last words Nikola probably wanted to hear.

"We are not talking about this," Nikola grumbled, pulling the hood of her jacket up. She always did that when she didn't want her ponytail played with.

Diana spoke again, and this time, her playful nature was practically siphoned from her. "I'm serious."

"So am I," Nikola joked with her suddenly stiff partner. "I'll chop my hair when you chop off yours."

"I can't cut my hair. It's important to the part I play." Diana's thoughts drifted to the shower, the ritual of haircare products she went through to keep it a desirable texture, a desirable volume, a desirable color. "And yours could be important to the part you play if you'd just cut it." She came up closer to Nikola, linking arms with her.

Nikola shifted away from Diana, their arms now barely connected. "I like my hair the way it is. End of this conversation."

Diana regained her likeable composure. "Just hear me out."

"I'm not going to cut it," Nikola snapped, defensively reaching up with her free arm to touch the top of her hood.

"Listen." Diana giggled, trying to lighten the mood. She nudged Nikola. "You're not like me. You don't need long locks. You don't need lots of makeup. You don't need the sex appeal. Because that's not your game. Believe me, as someone who tried to train you in charm and charisma, I know this. And I say this not in the negative way but a factual one. You can't tell me you haven't sensed that perhaps you're not a bombshell kind of agent." She spoke as politically neutral as was possible.

Nikola sneered. It was often suspected that no one was more aware of Nikola's weaknesses than Nikola. "Well, screw you, too, Hera. Not everyone was blessed with a body like yours. Not everyone wants to be that kind of agent."

"Body has nothing to do with it," Diana countered. "It's just not your strongest suit. You're too honest, too raw to procure secrets the way I do. You can't put the mask I wear on without looking like a fraud. You've got other strengths, though." Diana came to a full stop at a small stoop in front of a closed-down office and sat. "Come and sit with me."

Nikola appeared hesitant to join Diana, but eventually, she did. "You're not talking me into this."

Diana rolled her eyes. "Just listen." She rested her hand on Nikola's knee. "You have a very different kind of strength, Nikola. And it's not better than mine and it's not worse than mine. It's just different. So, cut your hair. Chop it off. Keep it short like a man's. Invest in a few well-tailored suits. Lose the earrings, the bracelets, the eyeliner. You've got a jaw sharp enough to kill. When you enter a negotiation chamber, you strike fear. You're six feet two for Christ's sake. Stop trying to soften yourself. Stop worrying about being likeable. Stop wondering what they think, and know that you are stoppable only if you allow yourself to be." Diana's grip on her knee tightened, their faces inches apart. "You have the potential to hold a lot of power, Nikola." Diana then pulled away and waited for an apology.

"I'm not cutting my hair." Nikola's face remained stoic. She kept her hands balled into fists. "This is over."

Diana kept her expression calm, but she was becoming irate. "Why not?" Somedays, it felt as though nothing between Diana and Nikola happened without a fight.

Nikola didn't say anything. Diana recognized Nikola was ignoring her.

"It's vital to your advancement as an agent." Diana was right about earlier; Nikola was too raw. This rawness made her easy to read. It was clear something about this idea was making her uncomfortable and dragging her further and further away from the conversation at hand. "Where are you running off to, Nikola?"

"Somewhere where I'm not expected to talk about my hair," she said calmly, seemingly pleased with herself.

"Oh, goddammit, Nikola, out with it, now." Diana gave Nikola's shoulder a light smack.

"I don't like getting my haircut. So, it's a no." Nikola ran her hands through her hair, pulled down her hood and let her champagne-colored ponytail fall to her midback. "A strong no."

"I can't train you if you aren't willing to even cut your goddamn hair," Diana scoffed.

"I'm a great agent." Nikola shrugged. "I'll manage."

"Nikola. What's wrong?"

Nikola gave a loud huff. Diana had pulled the strings that got her out onto the field. She'd gotten her onto the best missions, stood up for her when she made mistakes, and trained her in combat. Nikola owed her this.

"It's my mother," Nikola started. "When I was younger, it was just her and I. We lived in a small doublewide, somewhere in a shithole trailer park." She let out a weak exhale and then inhaled sharply through her teeth. "I was a kid so, of course, I threw hissy fits as bad as yours. Most days, if I acted out at home, it was the belt, but if it was out in public, she'd drag me to a bathroom stall and beat the shit out of me with the back of a wooden hairbrush, everywhere but the face." Nikola spoke with an enviable stillness. She was clearly distanced far from whatever feelings she'd had at the time. "It was like that for seventeen years. When I finally got a chance to leave, I did. Within a few months, I was with the CIA." She let out a dark laugh. "Anyway, can't get near hairbrushes now. They make me anxious."

"All the more reason to cut your hair." Diana scrunched her face and even smiled a little.

"Go into one of those ritzy beauty parlors you go to? Pay sixty bucks to sit around hair brushes for half an hour?" Nikola jeered.

"God, is that why you have a rat's nest of a ponytail?" Diana winked and took Nikola's hand. She kissed the top of it, listening to Nikola's rhythmic breathing. She admired how brave Nikola was to tell her this. That was a weakness, a big one, and she trusted her enough to tell her. It moved her. She decided to share her own story. "I had my first abortion when I was seventeen." She sighed, resting her head on Nikola's shoulder. "Hollywood, California. The dad was out of the picture and I'd already moved away from my parents' place. At first, I tried to just miscarry, throwing myself down stairs, lifting the heaviest things I could find, but no luck."

Both Nikola and Diana were holding their breath until the story to continued.

"I used a crochet hook, but coat hangers, knitting needles, they're all the same. I could have ripped my uterus open, or I could have hemorrhaged and died on the floor of my apartment with a towel between my legs. But I didn't." Diana let out a long, soulful hum. "I didn't feel guilty. I still don't. I did what I had to, but I did feel numb. Once it was over, I tried to kill myself, better to feel pain than nothing, right? I drove out to the hills and went right over the median and off a slope." She twirled her hair around her fingers. "The next thing I knew, Adams was pulling me from my broken windshield. He took me under his wing, promised me freedom of choice, a career, fame. I took it." She shrugged. "That's how I ended up with the CIA. And after years of training, after years of *sacrifice,* I'm here. No one can control me now. I'm untouchable." Diana licked her lips. "Sacrifices have to be made if you want to be indestructible, Nikola." They were quiet again, looking up into the sky of DC. Many minutes passed between them before Diana spoke again.

"I bet that's why you purge."

"What?" Nikola replied. "I haven't purged since..." Nikola's voice sounded suddenly delicate.

"Did you purge then? When you lived with your mother?"

"Yeah." Nikola kept her eyes down and out of Diana's line of sight.

"It's all about control, Nikola." Diana lifted her hand from Nikola's and instead grazed her partner's chin. "Look at how far you've come. No more purging and no more fear." She spoke knowingly. "Because soon enough, you'll have more control than you know what to do with."

"All I have to do is cut my hair," Nikola replied sharply, sarcastically.

Immediately upon Nikola's remark, Diana's lips met with hers. Their mouths melted together for only one, sensual moment before Nikola's face hardened.

"Don't."

"What?" Diana softened her expression as she looked at Nikola in confusion.

"I've seen what you do to the people you kiss." Nikola shook her head, her face now burning with a blush.

"You're worried I'll hurt you?"

Nikola's expression changed to an emotion Diana had never seen her genuinely portray until that day. Nikola was scared.

Diana frowned. "I'd never." She shook her head, her curls cascading over her shoulders. "Not with you." She touched Nikola's face tenderly. "Never with you."

They both sat, staring at each other for a few seconds. But to Diana, it felt like an eternity had passed by the time Nikola finally leaned in to press her lips to Diana's again.

*

Diana scooted herself and Da Vinci closer to the fire. He was sweating heavily, and it finally seemed like he was coming to.

"I destroyed her," she whispered to herself, grabbing the bottle of aspirin. She fed Da Vinci two pills and then swallowed six of her own. "And if you give me the chance—" She hushed him. "—I'll destroy you, too." From there, they sat together as the snow collected outside the walls of their shelter.

Avarice

DECEMBER 10, 1963

Gulliver pinched the tiny red straw in his scotch glass. He spun his drink mindlessly. "And so I told them I won't be returning for at least a few more months." Gulliver said *and* like he was adding on to a previous statement, but the words came from nowhere.

Sergei looked around the dive bar they were sitting in, seeming to search for the party Gulliver was talking to. He smiled when he returned his gaze to Gulliver.

"Who? Your family?" he asked.

"Afraid so."

"How'd that go?" Sergei asked, pressing his fingertips lightly against his glass.

"They're getting tired. The work is slow in Nottingham. They say they miss me a lot." Gulliver took another sip of his scotch, hoping to drink himself blind enough not to see the truth when others lie. As the days passed, Gulliver was growing more and more discouraged by people and their inability to be honest. Sergei was a beacon of truth amongst the thieves and the liars.

"Did you tell them why?" he asked.

"Dear Mum, dear Father, I, your only son, Roderick, have been granted sentient abilities, which enable me to see your every lie and half-truth. Therefore, I will not be returning home in fear that it will entirely tarnish the sacred image I have of you two. As it has tarnished the image of literally everyone I have talked to in the last month. Except Sergei. P.S. I'm a queer double agent. Toodles, cheerio, miss you dearly, RW," Roderick knew Sergei would likely worry at the usage of their real names, but they were out. It was the middle of the night. So what if they got to be Roderick and Sergei for the evening?

The bartender shot the two of them a funny look. Sergei then gestured back to the tender, signaling that perhaps his friend had had a bit too much to drink and was now acting *ridiculous*. Sergei took Roderick's glass and the bartender went back to the jane he was serving.

"Goddammit, I wanted another scotch," Roderick hissed. "I've had all of half a glass."

"We'll get out of here soon," Sergei assured him.

"Inviting me back to your place? That's so rash. We hardly know each other." Roderick winked.

"That did not stop you from writing to your pretend parents about me."

"Believe me, I'd sing your name from the heavens if I could." Roderick lightly punched Sergei's arm before slamming back the rest of his drink. "I'm satisfied. Let's go."

"I am still finishing my drink." Sergei rolled his eyes and shotgunned the half-full White Russian on the bar lip, threw a few bills down, and then headed out into the cool Virginia night. They hurried into the Karmann Ghia parked in the far back of the lot. Its plates were intentionally not lit. Sergei climbed in the driver's side and Roderick in the passenger's side.

"Could you grab a pass?" Sergei gestured to the glove compartment.

"Of course, this hotel seems especially excited to tow u—" Roderick's voice was cut off by a loud snap.

Sergei had one hand pressed to the steering wheel, ready to drive off. In the other hand, he gripped the top half of the newly snapped-in-two stick shift.

"Ooooooooh, god. Nikola will have your head."

Sergei widened his eyes. Seemingly frozen until he decided to rip the topper off the broken portion of the stick shift and shove it onto the still-attached portion of the stick shift, his strength making the task easy.

"I love you, but I think she'll be able to deduce what happened, even with your clever cover."

"Never. My execution? Flawless." Sergei snorted, then revved the engine and peeled out of the bar's parking lot.

They were right about the hotel's parking policy. Upon arriving, there was a compact sedan being towed away.

"So you're going to let me have whatever I want from the minibar, right? Since you denied me that last scotch?"

"Sure." Sergei shrugged and stepped out of the car.

Roderick hurried about behind him. "That was a joke. Do you know how expensive hotel-room booze is?"

"Imagine if we skipped out on the bill." Sergei paused for a moment and leaned in closer to Roderick. "Imagine if we"—he lowered his voice to a near whisper—"broke the law."

"Oh, my god, Sergei!" Roderick snorted and slapped Sergei's arm.

"Please, yell my blatantly Russian name louder. I don't think we're suspicious enough yet." Sergei snickered. "Should I yell that we're about to go back to our hotel room and undress? Queer and communist, the kind bumpkins of the Carolina backcountry will be grateful for our contributions to society."

"Oh, my god." Roderick felt his face heating up. His eyes were starting to well from holding back a laugh. "Stop." He tried to control his face and act serious, but it was not happening. "Come on." He pushed in on the hotel's doors and entered the lobby. The front desk was empty, and the only noise was an ice machine running on loop.

"I bet there's booze behind the desk." Sergei didn't wait for Roderick to even reply to his musing. He just slid over to the top of the counter and landed on the other side. He crouched down and brought up with him two half-full bottles of bourbon. "I was right."

Roderick cackled again, his laugh as bubbly as his stomach. "Oh, my god, you don't even like that stuff. Put it back. We'll drink from the tiny bottles in the minibar."

Sergei put the bottles back and slid over the counter again. They walked through the dimly lit halls like fiends, often laughing too loud and certain they were up to no good.

"This is us." Roderick stopped at room 23 and slid the key into the lock with no problem, but upon turning it, there was no satisfying click. The key wouldn't move. He turned and looked at Sergei. "Bloody thing won't budge."

Sergei scooted closer to Roderick, took hold of the key himself, and turned it. The key bent and snapped in two as opposed to turning.

"You are on fire tonight." Roderick elbowed Sergei's stomach before trying to turn the knob again. It didn't move.

"Here." Sergei shooed Roderick away from the door. Once he had a grip on the door handle, he tried turning it with no success. "We're going to have to break in, but do not worry, we can fix the door once inside."

Sergei shoved toward the door at the same time Nikola opened it. They collided and went tumbling to the ground.

"What the hell, guys!" Nikola hissed, his body crushing her.

Roderick looked as though he'd just witnessed sacrilege. His entire face lit with red. "Oh, my god, Nikola. We're so sorry."

"Don't just lay on me." She tried pushing Sergei off her to no success. He lay there limp. "Kal!"

He laughed as he pressed off the ground and stood, then offered his hand to Nikola.

"I don't need your charity." She batted his hand away. It became clear that she was in no joking mood.

"What-what were you doing in our—Gulliver's room?" Being partially buzzed kept Sergei pleasantly light.

Nikola's gaze shifted from Sergei to Roderick and then back to Sergei. "Gulliver is room 24. You are room 22. I am in room 23." She was showing him the door when she spotted the broken key sticking out of the lock. "And you have graciously broken my doorknob."

"Oh no, your doorknob. God forbid someone try to break in. You're defenseless with your superhuman agility and unlawful firearms." Sergei shot back. "Do you have any booze?"

"None for you." She ushered him out of her room. "Get out. I've got better things to do than babysit your drunk ass."

Her door closed with a sharp click and Roderick and Sergei were once again out in the hall.

"Seeing as how I no longer have a key to my room...it looks like I'll have to stay in yours." Roderick leaned carefully against one of the hall's beige walls.

Sergei's room was a mess, unlike Roderick's which was always kept in the cleanest of order. Sergei had clothes scattered all over the floor and half-full cups of coffee on every end table. It drove Roderick eight different kinds of crazy, but he loved Sergei enough for it not to matter.

Sergei headed straight for the minibar under the giant dresser covered in newspapers and mission notes. "Here, let's see if there's scotch." He rummaged around. "Ah, no luck. Looks like you're just going to have to drink tea like the limey crumpetfucker that you are." When Sergei spoke, he was doing his best, poorly executed English accent on top of his already thick Russian accent. So, more than anything, he just sounded like he was having a stroke. Roderick was quick to approach the fridge and snag a mini-bottle of scotch.

"Look there's vodka for your Lenin-loving arse." From the time Roderick popped open the bottle's cap to the moment Sergei kissed him, only fifty seconds had passed. Their bodies intertwined, and Roderick found himself desperate to set the alcohol down on any available table space and quick to kick his shoes off. Sergei slid his hands from around Roderick's neck down to his hips. They stumbled their way over to the unmade bed in the corner of the room. Sergei pulled Roderick's sweater over his head and then peeled his own shirt off. Even though Sergei was cold, Roderick could still hear his heart beating in his chest. They kissed hungrily, Roderick enveloping Sergei in his arms. They had just hit the bed when the phone rang. Roderick let out a long, loud sigh.

"Ignore it," Sergei urged.

"We can't. What if it's the commander?" Roderick groaned, flopping his head back onto a pillow as though nothing worse could have possibly happened.

FOR A COUPLE rings, they waited to see if the phone would stop on its own, but the rings kept on. Sergei picked up.

"Hello?" he said.

"No." It was the cold and curt voice of Nikola. "No. You two do not get to wake my ass up in the middle of the night and then go next door and have loud sex. That is *not* how this works."

A laugh started in Sergei's stomach and came out as a deep, cool chuckle. Even though Nikola would pretend not to know about the two of them for Roderick's sake, she had no issue bringing things up with Sergei.

"No, don't laugh at it. Shut the hell up and screw quieter," she huffed. "Besides, you two shouldn't be fooling around right now, anyway. We need to be ready for tomorrow."

"What's tomorrow?" Sergei turned to look at Roderick for answers, but he shrugged just as unknowing as Sergei.

"Pffft, shit." Nikola laughed loud enough that they could hear her through their own wall. "Well, I'm glad you guys picked up the phone for at least someone. No wonder the chick was freaking out when she finally got ahold of me."

"What chick?" Sergei started piecing information together in his head, but he stayed calm for Roderick's sake.

"Caulfield, the new navigator. She found them. We go in on the twelfth." Nikola spoke as though she was only dedicating half of her attention to the conversation. Sergei guessed she was likely reading—in fact more than likely, *rereading* mission plans. They were finally going in on the agents they'd turned in just months ago.

"Oh, okay." Sergei nodded even though Nikola could not see him. "Well, thank you for telling us." He hung up, carefully planning how he would break the news to Roderick, but Roderick was already growing paler.

"It's them, isn't it?" Roderick timidly pulled his sweater back on. "They've found them."

Sergei nodded and joined his partner on the bed, offering out the previously uncapped mini-bottle. "Here, drink this."

Roderick drank it all in one quick gulp much to Sergei's surprise.

"All right," Sergei let out a wheeze. He took Roderick's empty bottle and got back up, but this time, instead of heading to the mini-fridge, he went to the sink and filled a cup with water. "Now, drink this."

Roderick sighed and took a sip. "Water already. You must think I'm about to cry."

"I know this situation hasn't been easy on you." Sergei talked with a low voice, careful not to speak loud enough for Nikola to hear the two of them. "But if you truly want out, there is still time, but not much. All you have to do is put a call out to your commander back home. Nikola and I can escape before they get here. You can go back to Nottingham. It is not too late."

Roderick sighed and flopped back on the bed, not bothering to finish his water. "I'm not going anywhere, Sergei. You've got nothing to worry about."

"I am more worried that you're staying." Sergei took Roderick's hand as he sat beside him on the hotel bed. They held each other's gaze steadily. "Something is wrong."

"Everything is wrong."

Sergei grimaced. "Now is no time for melodrama. Everything is wrong all the time. You get up and go on."

Roderick lay there, focusing in on the hazy lighting. "You're damn right." A hint of a smile crossed Roderick's face for a moment only to quickly vanish. "We're in trouble."

"You don't have to be." Sergei shook his head. "You should have never stayed this long in the first place. If I hadn't been here, you would have been gone a long time ago."

"Quiet down, or she'll hear you," Roderick huffed. "She hears everything now." He began scratching at the collar of his sweater. "The fibers on this thing are like steel wool."

Sergei was having none of his diversion. "Why aren't you going?"

"This isn't just about us, Sergei. I stayed for other reasons."

"Like what?" Sergei lay back next to Roderick. "The glamorous living arrangements? The constant state of fear of being outed? The stern yet benevolent team captain?"

"It's more than that." Roderick shook his head, turning so he was face to face with Sergei.

"Roderick, there's no need to lie. I will not be hurt if you go. I will hurt, but I will not be hurt. I'd rather die knowing you're safe than have you follow us out onto that field this time around. These other agents aren't going to be merciful."

"Of course not. They want us dead, and they just might get it."

"Then go, Roderick." Sergei ran his thumb over the top of Roderick's hand. "I love you, but I know that it's your time."

"I'm not going anywhere." Roderick smiled and any warmth left in him was gone. There was something hollow about that grin, something secretly eating him away, and even though he could try and fool Sergei into not seeing that, it was clear; Sergei always knew.

"What is this?" Sergei asked. "You need to go."

Roderick shook his head. His stomach turned. "I love you. Isn't that enough?" Roderick stood, the bed creaking as he got up. "I'm not going anywhere because I love you." He switched subjects. "Is there more scotch in the minibar?" Rather than wait for an answer. He bent down and pulled out another full bottle.

Sergei sat up and any playfulness, any curiosity, was gone. There was nothing but concern plaguing him. "You should be running. Why aren't you running?"

Roderick considered the bottle in his hand. After a minute or two of silent staring, he unscrewed the top and sucked down three big gulps before Sergei cut him off, gently placing a hand on the bottle and pulling it away from Roderick's lips.

"You are going to be a riot when that hits your gut." Sergei was deadpan, but there was still an intense sense of concern in the way he grabbed Roderick's hand and sat him back down on the bed. "Why aren't you running, Roderick?"

The truth came like a bad aftertaste, all at once and not the least bit welcomed. "Because I defected from the UK four months ago."

They sat there and let the minutes stretch on forever. The words were still sinking in, finally, and Sergei let out a long breath.

"Why would you do that?" There was a distress to him he didn't often like to show. "Why?"

"Do you remember what they said to us when we first started this mission?" Roderick pulled his knees in on himself, curling tightly on the edge of the bed. "They said fame. They said fortune. They said super squad, the greatest spy team the world has ever seen. The goddess and the protégé working together again. It was going to be great, and we were going to be a part of it. Why would I miss out?"

It didn't hit Sergei so much as wash over him. "So I had nothing to do with it?"

"Ha." Roderick let out a long, exasperated breath. "I wish I could say I did it for love, but no, it had nothing to do with you. I did it all for me."

Sergei let out a long breath, releasing an anxiety he'd been holding onto since the moment he and Roderick first kissed. "So, I'm not to blame?"

"No." Roderick lay back on the bed and cuddled in next to Sergei, a frown on his face. "You were never going to be to blame for whatever ends up happening to me, for better or worse."

"So...let's say, at the end of this mission, you happen upon world domination. Do I still get mentioned in your address?"

"Sergei." Roderick sat up, his body now guarded from Sergei's arms. "This isn't a joke. We're going to die tomorrow."

"Thursday. We don't die till Thursday."

"Stop," Roderick croaked.

"Roderick." Sergei sat up. "We're going to be fine. Look at me." Sergei took his partner's hands and held them. "We are going to be fine. I will not let you die." He paused. "Now, was that a lie?"

Roderick smiled weakly, but he did smile. "No."

"It's not a lie because it is true. I will not let you die, and neither will Nikola. You are there to make sure we are not bested on a mental field, and we are there to make sure we're not bested on a physical field. We will all take care of each other. No one is dying."

Roderick's tears were already drying. "This unyielding optimism is unlike you, but comforting."

Sergei smiled. "Only for you, Roderick. No one else can know."

"Oh, of course." He giggled and leaned forward for a kiss.

Belly Up

DECEMBER 12, 1963

"You'll be getting out of here soon enough." Ruby lay on the grass across from Rigan, a fire roaring between them in the camp's small shelter. For the moment, it was just the two of them. Da Vinci had started to see minor improvements in his health and had been venturing back out into the woods with Tim and Diana's assistance. "What do you think you'll do first?"

She's beautiful, even buried under a silly winter hat and layers of scarves, Rigan thought, not yet ready to talk and ruin the moment.

"Post-cure and everything. Should have been more specific." Ruby tilted her head as she looked at her scaly friend on the other side of the flames.

"Shower." Rigan didn't even hesitate.

Ruby rolled her eyes to the back of her head. "Ugh, Rigan, post boring stuff like shower, check my bank account, hunt down the agents who did this to me."

"Hunt the agents down who did this to me?" Rigan snorted. "I take it you asked Tim what his post-cure plans were."

"He's very determined. He does not like the blonde one at all. He's determined to kill her. It's scary, but makes for an interesting conversation. I'm just glad I'm not on his bad side, ya know?"

Rigan redirected his attention to the question at hand. "Post-cure." He sighed. "I try not to think about it. What if it doesn't happen?"

"That's no attitude to have." Ruby flattened her arms and pretended to smack the ground with her face. "You've killed me with your lack of imagination. See what you've done?" Her voice was muffled, but her words were audible enough for a good laugh.

"How about get out of the spy business?" Rigan asked.

"That's still boring. Here, listen to what I have planned for you after your grand escape and then answer." She cleared her throat. "One, get pancakes from the small place off 12th. Two, catch up on *The Twilight Zone*, because Talky Tina was amazing. Three, listen to the whole Ruby and the Romantics vinyl, not just "Our Day Will Come." Four—"

"Take you dancing." Rigan shrugged at the thought. "If we ever get out of this place and I'm acceptable to go out in public. I'll take you dancing—" He paused. "—in Morocco."

"Morocco?" The grin on Ruby's face went from ear to ear. "That's like halfway around the world."

Rigan already regretted the words. "This is a dangerous game." It felt as though his world stopped spinning. "I can't go getting invested in this possibility of escape. We don't even know if Adams will come."

Ruby groaned. "One step forward, two steps back. You guys all need to have some optimism. Positive thinking will lead us into a new era, ya dig?" Ruby pushed off the ground and sat straight up, now clearly able to see Rigan's face over the top of the flames. "No one wants to even entertain the idea that you guys might get out of here. You have to understand. Kennedy's assassination investigation is all wrapped up. Your guy could come any day now." She grumbled a little bit more but then let out a sudden laugh that surprised Rigan. "Assassination investigation. What a tongue twister."

"Or he could never come," Rigan countered. "We would have heard something from him if he was on his way. There's just a way the CIA does things. We plan everything."

"So four, take Ruby dancing."

Rigan smirked, the tips of his jagged teeth peeking out despite his insecurity about them. "All right, if there's an escape and a cure, I will take you dancing."

"In Morocco," Ruby added. "I'm holding you to it."

"Don't get your hopes up. Things don't always work out like in the pictures, Ruby." Rigan leaned his head against the damp wood holding the fort up. Tim and Diana were excellent builders. They were designed for this kind of survival.

"I bet you've been in situations worse than this and you've made a great escape. You were an international spy, for goodness sake. You're lying if you tell me you haven't pulled off a few great escapes."

He was miles away now, a smile on his face. For a moment, he forgot, and he was happy. "I do have a story for you. If you care to listen."

Ruby lazily smiled. "Tell me."

*

Getting on the boat was the hard part. That's what Da Vinci told him. *The Albatross* was a mammoth of a ship, populated with true world leaders, from the cleanest of the clean, to black-market organizers, high crime bosses, and defected spies of unmatched notoriety. It was a once-in-a-lifetime chance to get intel, and the CIA had trusted none other than the nation's best agents—Adams and Diana. But, because they were both mysteriously unavailable, Da Vinci and his protégé would have to do. Far from the best but impressive up-and-coming rookies. It was their audition to truly enter the world's stage for intelligence work.

"You're sure we're going to get in?" Rigan whispered to Da Vinci as the two approached the cruise liner on the shore of Paris.

"We're 'the help,' Rigan. Yes, we're going to get in." Da Vinci adjusted the ruffles on the front of his shirt. His normally subdued Italian accent was now over the top and being played up with purpose. The two were dressed in server attire.

Rigan rolled his eyes and did as he was told. They approached the two beefy, sharp-dressed men watching the boat's ramp. After a few intentionally strained exchanges, they were let on. Rigan was disgusted by how they got there but thankful to be on the boat. Now, they could get to work. Rigan was meant to look in the rooms for intel. Da Vinci was supposed to scan the boat for Demeter, a recent CIA defect. It was his job to make sure she didn't divulge any information to the other members of the cruise. Once he had her in his sights, he needed to take her down. A task he felt grossly unready for.

The two walked back toward the liner's staff kitchen, the blueprints practically branded into their brains from months of prep. They snuck in without trouble and switched out of their stiff suits to more comfortable cook's clothes. Once finished, it was time to split up. Rigan went to the rooms, and Da Vinci headed for the banquet hall.

The dock was plastered in a slew of suits and gowns, tall men, short women, hoity-toity conversations about corporate finance and supermodels. They were all so wrapped up in themselves, it was easy for Rigan to slip by them and walk into his assigned rooms. And by god, the CIA was right. Rigan found himself with illegal weaponry trade documents, proof of companies' toxic dumping, and most importantly, after hours of searching rooms, he'd found the files Demeter stole when she defected from the CIA. Everything was going as planned until Da Vinci went flying by the door. He screamed something completely unintelligible as he ran by, and for a moment, Rigan just sat there dumbfounded. But as Demeter sprinted past the door at full speed, dress now torn up the side and brown hair flying wild, Rigan knew what had happened. Chaos was about to erupt.

Rigan shoved the files he'd found into his bag and stormed out of the room. He headed the opposite direction of the wild chase happening between two seasoned agents, slipping in between passageways and ballrooms until he got to his target point. Da Vinci needed Rigan. There was no exception. Rigan knew the layout of this boat better than anyone else. It was up to him to get the two of them out of there safely.

"Come on, old man," Rigan shouted, grabbing his partner's arm and pulling him into a small, concealed passageway. It was used for staff to get from one place to another. It'd take Demeter all of five seconds to figure out where it was, so this gave them just that to get ahead. "What happened?" Rigan swung doors open and dragged Da Vinci through the kitchen and back through the banquet hall. They snaked through giant groups of people, trying to blend in and get lost in the crowd.

Da Vinci huffed, trying to keep up with Rigan's impressive pace. "So, I thought Demeter didn't know who I was. For a hot second, it even seemed that way. Things were going smooth right up until she recognized me. Apparently, I was wrong about having not met before. We have met, numerous times, I was probably drunk. So we're now officially found out."

Rigan opened his mouth to speak but instead gasped and lost his balance and stumbled as the boat lurched from port. "Why are we leaving? They're not scheduled to depart for another two hours."

"Dammit, she must be doing t—" Da Vinci was cut off by the sound of Demeter plowing through the crowd of banqueters and shouting orders. "Run," Da Vinci squawked.

Da Vinci and Rigan turned to leave, but a barrage of Russian diplomats blocked the door. They were tall, brooding, everything Rigan and Da Vinci were not equipped to handle.

"Comrades." Da Vinci spoke in quick Russian. "Please, if we may."

"Don't bother." Demeter's voice was that of a queen, well-spoken and authoritative. She'd always been an intimidating negotiator. "Take care of them." She crossed her arms and watched from a distance as the diplomats began circling in on them.

"What's our plan?" Rigan asked through gritted teeth. One, two, three, four, five. Five to two. They were in deep.

Da Vinci cracked his neck and then his knuckles. "We're just gonna have to fight our way out of it." Da Vinci pulled from the back of his jeans a small handgun. Rigan did the same. They were both quickly reamed from behind. Not from the Russian's but a staggeringly tall beast of a Thai man.

"Shit." Rigan grabbed Da Vinci and forced him down. The two ducked just in time to dodge one long, hard swing from the man.

"Who is that?" Da Vinci hissed.

"My old boss." Rigan's heart started thudding louder than the ship's engine. "What do we do?"

"Your old boss. Holy shit, kid. No wonder you didn't want to talk. I'd be scared of him, too." Da Vinci wheezed. "So we got no guns. We're gonna have to—" Da Vinci and Rigan were yanked up by the scruffs of their necks and then dropped. They landed on their feet, slightly disoriented.

"There!" Rigan stared at a large glass case filled with old pirate-like swords and a giant harpoon. The only issue was the diplomats and mob goons and goddess between them and the weaponry.

"Smart thinking. Go for it and don't worry about me," Da Vinci ordered. "I can get a few of 'em down, no problem." Da Vinci and Rigan moved like clockwork, dodging whatever was thrown at them. "You get outta here the second they're down, all right?"

Rigan grunted in acknowledgement and Da Vinci was off. The first brute got a hit to the stomach, the second bashed in the face with a ricocheting elbow. They both swung in retaliation but Da Vinci was quick to dodge. They sparred for only a moment longer, because as soon as one of them went down, Rigan was out and crashing into the glass display case, not even considering the bottleneck of people around it. There were gasps, shock, awe, but before anyone could call for more help, a sword was in Rigan's hand. He threw it, and it landed in Da Vinci's grasp with grace.

One of the grunts plowed toward Rigan. Rigan thought quick and grabbed a second sword and slung the harpoon over his shoulder. But before the grunt could flail himself, Demeter stepped in and grabbed Rigan from behind.

To make matters worse, her minions picked up the few spare swords from the broken case, as well. Rigan was cornered. Quickly, he thrashed, spun, and got one swing against Demeter. She retaliated by slamming her fist straight into his face. She hit with the strength of a freight train, then picked a blade from the glass remnants of the case, and like that, they were belaying and clashing swords until finally, through sheer luck, Rigan found himself back to back again with Da Vinci.

"It was smart thinking, but we're outnumbered," Da Vinci mused. "Feel like going a second round?"

"Am I supposed to answer that?" Rigan continued, attempting to thwart their enemy.

Da Vinci dropped his voice low. "So the man on your right has a limp. We both got him pretty good. So, when they get close, get him down, and we'll bolt for the door."

"And go where?" Rigan shot back. "I can't navigate us off a moving ship."

"We'll jump."

"And ruin all of our mission materials?" Rigan snapped.

"And save our lives!" Da Vinci wailed back, his voice rising above the gathered crowd and army of grunts.

"Okay."

Before the grunts could take another step closer, the two of them charged like wild banshees, plowing right over the goon and storming out of the side banquet doors. The ship's deck was packed, but their adversaries were quick to find them in the crowd.

"Kid, we gotta jump now if we wanna make it out of here." Da Vinci had one hand firmly holding on to the ship's guardrail and another out in front of him.

"How about we just wait for Dresden to get here?" Rigan looked over the deck and could see the third member of their team coming closer, a small boat with an incredible engine gaining on the distance between them.

"What?" Da Vinci spun around like his prayers had been answered. Tim came over on the horizon. "He must've seen the liner take off." He sighed with obvious relief. "All right. Let's buy us some time."

Da Vinci and Rigan both turned and punched the nearest random bystanders. Those bystanders swung wildly, hitting yet more bystanders, and before anyone could get even remotely close to Rigan and Da Vinci, the deck broke out into a frenzy. Fists were flying, pins were torn from hats and jabbed in shoulders, lifesavers were thrown like lassos, swords still swung wildly in the air, diplomats were punching mob bosses, and mob bosses were punching CEOs. The only calm, collected people on the boat were Rigan, Da Vinci, and a closing-in Demeter, harpoon gun in hand.

She approached them, slow and sultry amongst the chaos. "Not everyone is so quickly distracted." She was beautiful and very much ready to strike.

"Do you really want to give the CIA another reason to blacklist you?" Da Vinci had his fists out again, ready to fight.

Demeter rolled her eyes. Rather than answer, she charged.

"We gotta jump now," Da Vinci screamed, pushed Rigan over the edge, and jumped of his own accord. They hit the water with a loud smack. The screams from the liner were still audible even under the water. Da Vinci and Rigan recovered. They broke the water's surface, gasping for air. Tim was standing over them in the boat, his expression still, his hair controlled, and his skin pale.

"Did we get the file?" He offered his hand.

Da Vinci took it and pulled himself into the boat, and then Tim and Da Vinci turned to help Rigan over the lip of the boat. "We're fine. It was a rough mission, but we're fine." Da Vinci gasped for air as he collapsed onto the floor of the boat.

Rigan looked up to see Demeter's peaceful eyes staring back at them. "We've got to get going, though, or we'll be fa—" Rigan was cut off by the sound of the engine starting up and a harpoon whizzing just over their heads and scraping the front of their ship. Tim revved the engine, and they pulled away as Demeter reloaded. They narrowly escaped a second harpoon. Like that, in the gentle winds of the sea, in the light of the setting sun, they were off, as *The Albatross* got smaller in the distance.

*

"Okay, now, that is the most ridiculous thing *I* have ever heard." Da Vinci cackled. He, Diana, and Tim had joined Rigan and Ruby in the fort shortly toward the beginning of their story, but rather than interrupt or correct, they'd listened. It was only once Rigan was done that Da Vinci broke out in laughter.

"I don't know. That seemed right up Demeter's alley," Diana joked.

"What, again? Rigan!" Ruby was snorting from laughing so hard. "Goddammit! Stop lying. Do you understand how boring my real life is? I live for these stories."

"I was there for the whole thing," Tim muttered under his breath.

"What really happened did *not* make for a good story," Rigan whispered to Ruby. The agents were still laughing when Ruby took a glance down at her watch.

"You got a shift coming up?" Rigan asked.

She shrugged. "I do, but it's not the end of the world if I miss it. It's rare I get to see the whole posse in the same space."

"No worries. Tim'll do something offensive in a hot minute and we'll disperse," Rigan assured her.

Diana lost it at that. A smile blossomed on her perfect and cracked face. "Go on, sweetheart. We will still be here when you get back."

"I'll be right back. I'm going to go walk her down." Rigan brushed off his torn shorts and stood but was stopped.

"Wait, wait." Da Vinci's words bubbled with laughter. "The entire reason I came in here was to get you to help with some lumber. Do that and then you can come back and take a walk."

"All right, all right." Rigan stood and helped Da Vinci up off the damp grass. They exited the fort and headed for the woods.

Ruby wrapped herself up: jacket, scarf, gloves, scarf, hat, scarf. When she was appropriately bundled, she, Tim, and Diana sat in comfortable silence. Diana had regained her stone-cold composure. Tim had the same blank stare he always did. When she had first met them, Ruby felt compelled to fill the silence between the two, but now she knew. Silence was just their nature. And besides, if she waited long enough, she knew they'd fill it for her.

"We ask because we care," Diana cooed, her attention shifting from the flames of the fire to Ruby and her cocoon of misprinted fabrics.

"Ask what?" Ruby replied curiously.

"About your work. We ask because we worry what will happen to you when we're gone. When we escape, you need a life to go back to."

"After this?" Tim cut in. "Her life has already changed forever." He dismissed even the slight possibility that Ruby would return to waiting in a diner.

Ruby looked around uncomfortably, not wanting to watch their eruption of passive-aggressive remarks and dirty looks. Lucky for her, Rigan was quick to pop back in.

"Let's get going," Rigan said. Ruby fled, leaving Tim and Diana to bicker amongst themselves.

"So how long did Tim make it before doing something to upset Diana?" Rigan teased.

"I'd say maybe five minutes, possibly six if I was distracted by something else." She let her head roll back and the sun hit her face. It was cold out, but the sky was bright. "They tried to tell me you ask so much about work because you care, or something like that." She winked as they left camp and entered the barren, white woods.

"Pfffft," Rigan scoffed and redirected the conversation. "Maybe they're going back in the business, but if Adams ever comes and we ever get out of here, I'm out for good. Those junkies can't get enough of the danger, but I've have. I never thought I'd miss going to the grocery store so much. I crave the mundanity of weekly sales. If I live, we can hang out every goddamn weekend if you want."

"If you live?" Ruby was surprised by the concept that there was a chance he *wouldn't* survive. "You're so dramatic. You'll be fine. And trust me, it's not all that great. I usually just end up in the canned goods aisle going 'If I get this, will Rigan find some way to give me grief about it?' I've never felt so awful about bringing someone canned pears before."

"You know I'm just teasing you."

"I don't know. You were *vicious* about bringing books for Tim."

"That's because it's Tim," he grumbled, shoving his webbed hands into his pockets.

Ruby shrugged. "Tim's got some redeeming qualities. Hopefully one day, he'll confide in me how he gets his hair so perfect."

"Apathy and complete disregard for others." Rigan clicked his tongue. "It's all you need for the perfect hair."

"Now, that's not true." Ruby nudged his arm with hers. "Tim doesn't have complete disregard for Da Vinci."

Rigan slowed to a stop, which worried Ruby. He seemed deep in thought all of a sudden. That's when he said it.

"I think I could have loved you."

Ruby reeled from the sudden declaration. She slipped on the partially muddy, partially icy path they were walking on. She stopped herself just short of falling by grabbing onto a thin tree trunk. "What?"

He seemed hesitant for a moment, anxious, but after letting it sit for a moment, he shrugged. "You see the best in people. Even people like Tim. I love that about you."

Things were never going to be the same, right? Ruby was still processing the words when the faint sound of screaming came in the background. "What was that?"

Rigan was silent. His face grew tense as he focused. And then all of a sudden, the expression on his face terrified her and she didn't know what to expect next.

"It's Da Vinci." Rigan seemed to be holding his breath.

In that moment, she found herself more scared than she'd ever been. Rigan had her arm before she could ask what to do next. "Come on." He pulled her off their makeshift path and into the woods. "Stay down and stay close."

Da Vinci's voice was still too far off to be heard correctly, but there was obvious distress. As Ruby grabbed onto Rigan's hand and squeezed tightly, there was an absolute shift in how she viewed the woods. Comfort and familiarity were now null and void, instead, providing her more reasons to fear since she knew exactly how many different places someone could be hiding. She pulled her mace from her coat pocket and brought her breathing down as low as it could get. Her words were caught in her throat, and her desperation to talk to Rigan was outweighed by her desperation not to be found.

Da Vinci's voice was becoming clearer now. "Run! Rigan, run! Nikola's here!" His voice was hoarse from screaming as loud as he could. Rigan could just barely make out his shouts from down the mountain.

"Nikola?" Ruby couldn't bring herself to move. "Who is that?"

"She's a KGB agent. She's dangerous." Rigan scanned the wasteland around them. "You've got to make sure she doesn't see you." Rigan began the trek back toward the camp. "Come with me. We'll meet with the others and regroup."

"Rigan! Rigan?" Da Vinci's voice was still echoing through the maze of trees.

Ruby froze. "Rigan." She felt out of breath, yet they had barely moved since Da Vinci's first cry to them.

"Ruby." Rigan spun around and took her face in his webbed hands for a moment. "We need to—" Rigan's voice dropped the second Nikola came into view. She was dressed in red and walking up to them casually, as though there was no urgency to the situation.

"Run." Rigan grabbed Ruby's arms and shifted her behind him. "Go. Now, Ruby."

Her heart seemed to have stopped beating. Ruby was fixated on Nikola.

"You've got to go, now!" Rigan shouted.

The Soviet moved like film, one shutter she was close, the next, closer. It didn't take a genius to figure out she'd been enhanced just like the rest of them.

Rigan must've figured it out too. His tone was grave. "Shit. Ruby, run."

"Run with me." Ruby took Rigan's hand and tugged back toward camp.

"There's no time." He twisted back around and shoved Ruby, pushing her as far back as he could before Nikola collided with him. He and the Soviet fell and crashed into the hardened, icy ground.

"Kids!" Da Vinci cried out. His voice echoed in the mountains. He'd be there any minute.

Nikola scratched at Rigan, her claw bearing down on his scaly and now-scarred face. He threw his elbow up. It smacked into her cheek. She took it like it was nothing, then pinned him. He bore down on her hand with his teeth and blood squirted out from the impact. She yanked her arm back, sprinkling the snow with blood.

Ruby panicked and charged at her. "Get away from him!" She jumped at Nikola, only to be deflected.

RUBY FLEW BACK yards and crashed against a tree trunk, then ricocheted to the ground, where her head slammed into a rock, making her forehead bleed.

In the time Nikola spent handling the girl, Rigan threw a punch and it landed. She fell off him and he hopped back to his feet. She was ready to retaliate when he started speaking.

"Let me go, Nikola. You know that as soon as you get rid of us, the KGB will kill you, too. Escape with us rather than fight against us," he pleaded with her. The boy was desperate, even if he was trying to keep some sliver of dignity about him.

"Please, I am a Soviet sweetheart." She gave a soft, closemouthed laugh, tilting her head gently to the left. "This could have been you, Marco...Or should I say Rigan? That's your real name, right? It took some digging, but we found out everything. About you, the old man, Ruby." She pushed her hair back, a smile still on her face.

"And this could have been you," Rigan spat back, his body full of green scales and his jagged teeth hanging over his bottom lip, stained with drying blood, his nails overgrown and dangerously sharp. He seemed to want to display his deformity. "I was a freelancer, by the way. I had no allegiance to break. Just a contact."

Nikola gave a halfhearted *hmph*. "Funny how that works, but I've grown bored with our little scrap." Her heart raced, not with nerves but excitement. She was going in for the kill. She could hear footsteps now, coming closer, closer. Soon, the whole team would be there.

Rigan looked ready to strike, so when she charged at him, she didn't let them collide. Instead, she used her running start to jump. She leapt over him, gliding through the air, her spine contorting and allowing her to land feet-first behind him.

He spun around, swinging. But it was too late. Nikola's reflexes were faster. She struck and landed, her claws digging into the damp, scaly flesh of Rigan's chest. He froze. She squeezed tighter and dug her nails deep into the soft tissue underneath his tough exterior. She stayed silent as his body folded in. His arms twitched and his eyes welled with tears. A quiet whimper escaped his lips before he went limp.

Nikola withdrew her bloody fingernails and turned to Ruby's battered and unconscious body. Ruby bled from her temple and her body heaved with each slow labored breath. Nikola gently ran her hand along Ruby's face, Rigan's blood smearing across her forehead. Nikola loosened the girl's scarves. Da Vinci's screams grew louder. There was no time.

Nikola gripped the girl's shoulder and drew her hand back, preparing to slice open Ruby Starr's throat. "They shouldn't have dragged you into this." She swiped down with the intent to kill, only to be thrown away from her at the last moment.

Nikola felt like she'd been hit by a goddamn freight train. It was Diana. She didn't need to see her to know it was her. They both ricocheted through the snow and over a small bluff.

"Get away from her," Diana growled, her body shaking and hands balled into fists.

Nikola raised a single brow. She watched Diana carefully. "Surprising."

"You have five seconds," Diana whispered, although there was no chance of anyone hearing over Da Vinci's screaming. "Don't give me the pleasure of ripping your spine out of your back."

"Five Seconds? Guess that's more than last time."

Diana loosened her fists and reached out to grab Nikola, but the Soviet jumped from the bluff.

"NO!" DA VINCI screamed as Rigan's body came into view. He couldn't catch his breath. They'd been barreling down the side of the mountain, and now they were there, too late. "No." He fell to the ground before he could even make it to Rigan's body. "No! No! No!" He grabbed at his hair, noticing for the first time that his bandana had gotten lost on the run.

"Da Vinci." Diana's honeyed voice sounded by his ear, but he didn't look for her. He fumbled over to Rigan's body, crawling most of the way and letting out a weak cry when he arrived.

"Rigan, no." After the steroid, Rigan had been cold. His body temperature never reaching much above sixty, but as Da Vinci held him now, Rigan felt even colder than he had before. His face was torn open and his heart long stopped. Da Vinci took the boy's webbed hands. "No, no, no," Da Vinci cried, tears running down his dirt-stained face. His words were choked out in between heavy sobs. "No. I was supposed to stop this. I was going to stop this."

Da Vinci closed his eyes; the tears kept coming. He reopened them only to find that Rigan was still dead. He held him closer. "I should have known sooner. I should have known sooner."

"Dammit." Tim was there now. Somewhere behind him.

As he sat there, Rigan in his arms, Diana wrapped an arm around Da Vinci and kneeled next to him.

"My boy," Da Vinci whispered. "Oh, Rigan." He placed his palm to Rigan's ship tattoo, feeling the lack of heartbeat beneath it.

Ruby began to stir, not speaking words but letting out a low, pained groan. Da Vinci wasn't equipped to handle it. He'd been ready to ask for help when Diana took the lead and signaled for Tim to take care of her.

"She's going to need us," Diana whispered. She brushed the back of Da Vinci's hair down.

Tim crouched beside her, giving her space so he'd not spook her when she came to and had to face that Rigan was gone forever.

Lost River

DECEMBER 12, 1963

Deep in the mountains, surrounded by pine and the skeletons of dying oak trees, Da Vinci kneeled in the snow and the mud, clinging to the body of his boy. Diana had her arms wrapped around him, encasing him in a hug, her chin resting on his shoulder. Ruby was still crying somewhere in the background of Da Vinci's white-noise world. The moment felt suspended in time, always existing and never moving forward or back. After what felt like an eternity, Da Vinci moved his chapped lips and said, "We need to bury him."

"What?" Diana let go of him, a sense of concern in her voice.

"We need to bury him," Da Vinci repeated. "We can't just leave his body out here like this. They could find him again. A forest ranger could find him. We've got to get rid of his body."

"Da Vinci, we've already lost so much time. We need to get moving." Diana reached out to him, and for the first time ever, he flinched away.

"We've got to bury him." Da Vinci shook his head. "We can't go until we do."

"The KGB will take care of that, Da Vinci. I am certain." Tim guided a sniffling and hoarse Ruby closer to them.

"I don't want that." Da Vinci pressed his lips together and took a long inhale, never wanting to let it go.

"Even if we had the time, Da Vinci, we can't. We've got no way to." Diana took his hand and squeezed it firmly.

For a second, there was silence but no tension, just the acceptance that she was right. Short of burying him under loose leaves and snow, they had no means of covering the body. It wasn't about where the KGB was and when they'd come back. It was about the fact that they didn't have a shovel to spare—that was until Ruby spoke.

"I-I know a place," Ruby said quietly. Da Vinci looked to her for answers. "There's a waterfall close by. People drown in 'em all the time.

They get pulled under by that current and never resurface. Happens every couple years." For the first time, perhaps ever, Ruby spoke with no enthusiasm, no fear, no emotion but a dry tolerance. It broke his heart that this broke her.

Da Vinci looked at Ruby as though she were a savior. He slid his arms under Rigan's body before Diana could stop him.

"We've got this." She looked up to Tim, who quickly helped Da Vinci to his feet.

"Okay, all right." Da Vinci found Ruby had joined him at his side. Her knees still shaking, her forehead poorly bandaged with one of her scarves. "You've got to show us the way, kid." Da Vinci tried to muster up a smile, but couldn't bring himself to it. Tim nudged Ruby forward and she started walking.

Ruby was at least a few feet ahead of them when Diana spoke, creating the illusion of privacy. Her words were well-intended. "Keep your eyes on the tree line, Tim."

They navigated through the cold, frosted mountains. Ruby was a blur of color in the muddy, icy terrain. As they came closer to the waterfall, the wind picked up and the tiniest specks of snow could be seen in the air. There was no sign of the KGB. As they reached the end of the woods, Ruby froze just a few steps before the falls. Her eyes welled with tears again.

"Come on, sweetheart." Diana kept her distance from Ruby, likely not wanting to bring the body closer. Ruby continued to sob, her chest rattling and heaving. Da Vinci knew that at any moment her knees would buckle. But before she could fall, before she could cry any louder, Da Vinci was there for her, his arm around her. He helped her stand straight.

"We'll go together." Da Vinci swallowed hard, and he met Ruby's gaze for the first time since the attack.

A wail started in Ruby's throat, but she stifled it with her hand. She collapsed against Da Vinci, her head on his shoulder and his support being the only thing that seemed to keep her upright. They moved forward through the trees and into the clearing. Despite the weather, despite the cold, the waterfall still ran, dumping gallons of water a minute into a large pool. Da Vinci turned his attention back to Diana.

Just a second, he mouthed as he led Ruby to the river. He could trust Diana and Tim to watch over Rigan one last time.

He and Ruby stood over the pool of water, the lapping of the waterfall drowning out Ruby and Da Vinci's voices.

"This is why you wanted me to go. That first night we met and then again when I came back." Ruby sounded distant. "If I hadn't come back, would things have been different?"

"Don't torture yourself like that," Da Vinci replied. "He would have died without you."

"Doesn't change that he still died." Although Ruby was growing hoarser, the tears kept coming.

Tim interrupted their vigil. "We need to get moving soon. We are exposed out here. Are you two ready?" He placed a hand on Da Vinci's shoulder.

Da Vinci nodded and Ruby let out a low whimper. Diana walked over, Rigan's body still cradled in her arms. She paused as she came to the riverbank.

"It should be you, Da Vinci." She turned to him and it took him a second to register what had been said. He was consumed with how small Rigan looked in Diana's arms. Finally, he took the body from her.

Da Vinci laid him down in the water with a tender kindness. For a moment, Rigan remained visible, but then quickly vanished, pinned under the current of the waterfall. Ruby dabbed her wet cheeks with one of her scarves.

"Not one word, not one gesture of yours shall I, could I, ever forget, old friend..." Tim murmured.

Da Vinci wiped his face clean with a spare bandana he'd had in his back pocket. "Yeah. That sounds about right."

"We need to move." Diana spoke softly but firmly.

There was a quiet between them that no one seemed to want to break. No one knew what came next. But, never being one to wait around, Diana spoke again. "Where do we go from here?"

"I say we get Ruby down the mountain." Tim shoved his hands in the pockets of his pants and turned to face Ruby. "She's saved us. Least we could do is save her."

Diana's face lit with an indescribable surprise, like she hadn't expected him to be so forward about wanting to die.

"If we can get to my van, you could all fit. We've got nowhere to go, but it could help," Ruby suggested timidly.

Tim shook his head. "The point is to get you away from the danger, not keep you in the middle of it."

Da Vinci didn't like the sound of anything, but this suggestion was the only one that felt morally right. "I want to get Ruby down the mountain." Da Vinci's sad gaze drifted up and locked with Diana's. "But you both know what it means if we do. You both know the prices you pay."

"What are you talking about?" They could see the gears turning in Ruby's mind as she put two and two together. "This is it." Ruby wobbled again, a hand raised to her stomach. "This is why I shouldn't have come back. It's all because I came back. We're not all going to make it down the mountain, are we?"

Da Vinci's throat tightened, the words unable to leave. Before he could find the strength, Diana did it for him.

"Oh, sweetheart." Diana hushed her. "What's to come will be taxing, but it will not be fatal."

"She's right, Ruby." Tim smiled at Diana with no sincerity in his expression. Da Vinci couldn't watch their petty witticisms. He focused in on Ruby. Diana and Tim lying wasn't enough. Ruby apparently needed to hear it from him, to know that Da Vinci had seen the future and things were going to be okay. Otherwise, she'd fight them tooth and nail on taking her down the mountain, but before Da Vinci could make any empty promises, gunfire cracked and echoed against the tall walls of the mountains.

"Get down." Diana grabbed Da Vinci and pulled him close. Tim covered Ruby, but there was no bullet erupting dust and no shrapnel beating against the rocks behind them. No screaming out in pain, no bleeding, the bullet wasn't meant for them. There were no KGB agents in the clearing, or the treetops, or the field. It was a false alarm.

Ruby spoke breathlessly. "It must've been-a bear."

"Or friendly fire," Diana said. "Come on. Let's move." She pushed Ruby gently on the shoulders, starting their descent. Da Vinci followed her in a daze, leaving Rigan behind for good.

"You're sure about this?" Diana whispered, but not low enough for it to be unheard by Da Vinci.

"Are you?" Tim asked.

They crept cautiously. Everyone was doing their part, keeping their gazes shifting and their stance fluid. Every breeze that rustled the naked limbs sent the four of them into a moment of panic as they made their way down the mountain, racing against the setting sun.

"You will have to be quick once you get out there," Tim said. "There is no knowing what will be waiting on the other side of the tree line."

Diana shook her head in disagreement with Tim. "They're here for us. They might not even connect Ruby with us if she comes out looking enough like a hiker."

"True," Tim agreed. "Ruby, once you get out, you know not to come back, right? No matter what?"

"Yeah." Ruby was nodding mindlessly. "We're about sixty minutes out from the van. We've got sixty minutes left of this." They had to stay like this, back to back, white-knuckled, and scared. But then Nikola stepped out from just beyond the tree line, gun in hand.

"No." Da Vinci's word came out as a whisper.

Nikola moved like a lioness, walking over with such prowess and lack of fear. She struck terror into their hearts. Her hair feathered in the light breeze. Her lackeys were nowhere to be seen. She smirked.

"You want to play nice?" she asked.

"Turn around, sweetheart." Diana shook her head. "You don't want this fight."

Nikola laughed coolly. "I've waited my whole life for this fight."

Diana tilted her head and stepped past her partners. "You think a gun and some flashy abilities are going to save you?" Diana grimaced. "You've got to remember. We're still the better fighters, Nikola."

"I think more than anything it's the poison that'll do you in." Nikola tsk'd.

"What do—" Diana's words were cut off by a loud commotion behind her. Da Vinci had dived at Tim, sending Tim crashing into the ground just seconds before a bullet flew through the air and cut right where Tim had previously been. Da Vinci was quick to spot Roderick and Sergei coming out from the woods. They stood talking amongst themselves as though this mission was no big deal.

"Run." Tim pushed Da Vinci off him and stood, his fists already up.

Nikola quickly took aim at him, only to be struck by Diana.

"Ruby, come on." Da Vinci took her hand and tried leading her away, but she stood frozen, as though possessed by the erupting violence. She wouldn't budge until the second crack of gunfire. Then, they all ran.

They moved like animals. Diana to the left, Da Vinci to the right, Tim straight ahead. When they'd moved forty-five degrees opposite, they circled back. It was their signature split-up plan, but somehow, in all the madness and the rushing and the panic, they lost Ruby.

"No one managed to grab her?" Tim was livid.

Da Vinci looked ready to puke.

"This is how we die," Diana said to herself. "We had it. We just needed to make it a bit farther." She picked at her skin, visibly frustrated.

"We cannot stay here," Tim cut in. "We are sitting ducks. We need to make a plan and get moving." Tim dove into the band of his pants and pulled out a gun.

"*What?*" Da Vinci gawked at the weapon in Tim's hands.

A smirk lit up Diana's entire face. "The finest goddamn thief I have ever had the pleasure of working with."

"It's the negotiator's, Gulliver. I rushed him when we broke. I am assuming it has the poison Nikola spoke of." Carefully, Tim removed the clip, peering at the oddly colored and encrusted bullets. "These are special made, all right."

"So you're saying we go for the negotiator first?" Diana's eyes danced with a dangerous excitement.

"This isn't *The Most Dangerous Game*. This is us saving Ruby." Tim put the clip back in.

"Of course." Diana's regained her composure. "Are you all right, Da Vinci?"

Da Vinci shook his head. "I don't know. I don't know how we're going to get there, but by the time this is all over, you'll both be dead."

"Haven't you changed the future before?" Diana cooed.

"Sentence order, meal decisions, clothing, the future changes only in the most minor of ways." Da Vinci rubbed his hands together. It was getting colder.

"Then perhaps consider that this can be changed, too." Tim placed his hand on Da Vinci's shoulders. "You are often the one with hope, Da Vinci, but for now, we will have enough for the three of us. Now come on." Tim shifted his weight and started back toward the clearing. "We'll likely be able to follow her footsteps."

"If they don't find her first." Da Vinci shut his eyes for a moment and let out one long, deep breath.

"They won't." Diana wrapped her arm around him and pulled him along as the three returned to find Ruby Starr.

Forward

DECEMBER 12, 1963

Nikola appeared to be in full hysteria. She stood strong. It was enviable, her ability to remain calm in the throw of things. He and Sergei approached from behind.

"What's the plan, boss?" Sergei asked.

"We've got five minutes at the most until they catch up and reconvene. We gotta get this done fast. Check your guns." Nikola's gun was still in her hand.

Roderick and Sergei both felt for their weapons. Sergei pulled out a standard handgun. Roderick, however, came up empty-handed.

"Bollocks." Roderick felt around his back holster again. "There is the possibility that I just forgot it."

"No." Nikola shook her head, already pulling one of her own guns from her holster. "That thief has it, fucker. That means she has it. The real question is, was it loaded with the poison?"

Sergei could die. Nikola could die. He could die. The weight of what this meant hit Roderick hard. "Yes."

"Here." Nikola placed her hand on his shoulder and offered one of her guns. "Take this, cover each other, and don't let it happen again. They've got...three to five bullets left at best. We'll have to bait them." Sergei and Roderick nodded in confirmation. "You two take the negotiator's tracks. I'll take the thief's. Hera has likely covered hers. Good luck, comrades."

"Good luck." Sergei cocked his gun and turned toward Da Vinci's exit point. He and Ruby had gone to the right.

Roderick and Sergei moved back to back, both with their guns out and ready to fire at any moment. Nikola's gun felt so foreign in Roderick's hands. She had been using hers much longer than Roderick had been using his. They followed the pair's tracks for a while, right up until they diverged.

"She went the wrong way." Roderick stood over the hiking boot tracks that led far off from the negotiator's swift and calculated steps. He bent down, and picked up a yellow elephant-print scarf, and ran his thumb over it, feeling snags in the linen from constant wear. "Let's go find her." Roderick looked over Da Vinci's path. "It doesn't look like he came back. What if she's hurt?"

"Those weren't the orders." Sergei always said things like this when he didn't want to give a clear answer. It was leaving the decision up to Roderick, and he was immensely grateful for this.

"To hell with the orders." Roderick looked around the vast, white wasteland. "They've got one of our guns. This mission just got more dangerous than any other. Let's run. Together."

This was not the first time Roderick had suggested running. In fact, this was not the first time in the past week that he'd suggested running. Sergei would reply as he always did.

"I can't just leave Nikola, but you may go."

Roderick sighed and then bowed his head. "I'm not going." He wrapped the scarf around his knuckles. "But I'm also not leaving this civilian out in the open. Help me at least clean up her mess." Upon examining her footprints, he discovered a trail of scarves and mittens leading deeper into the forest. Roderick loved to save civilians. He had no problem icing an agent, but people on the streets? It was too much for him. He suspected it was one of the things Sergei loved about him.

"We need to make it quick." Sergei moved past Roderick, heading toward the next misplaced piece of clothing. "We can't let Nikola get caught out. She's our best bet for getting out of here."

"I don't know. She feels off. She's more intense than usual, if that's even possible." Roderick snorted, stuffing a paisley-print scarf in his jacket.

"Well, you know what the goddess did to her, don't you?" Sergei handed off a jacket to Roderick.

"No."

"You must have her tell it to you sometime. It is a good story, a sad one, but a good one."

"Why don't you tell me? We've got time to kill." Roderick approached the edge of the bluff, curious as to where she'd gone from this point.

"It is not mine to tell." Sergei shook his head, and in that split second, the ledge under Roderick gave way and he slipped, surviving only because Sergei was quick enough to catch him. "You must be careful."

Roderick's heart had jumped to his throat. As he slipped, he saw something he could never unsee, the corner of Ruby's skirt hanging off the ledge below them.

"Oh, no." Roderick curled inward, closer to Sergei. "She's down there."

"What?" Sergei craned his neck over the ledge. "Ah, I see. She will be fine."

Roderick looked around the woods for a moment, no other spies in sight. "I'm going down." He slid off his heavy Kevlar and handed it to Sergei.

"Roderick, we do not have time. Nikola will notice our absence if we don't hurry."

Sergei's words went unacknowledged as Roderick stared down the icy ravine, eventually dropping down just a few feet and landing on the very same ledge as Ruby Starr.

"Don't scream. I'm here to help." Just looking at her, Roderick could tell she'd gotten into more trouble than she ever bargained for. Her shoulder was dislocated and her leg was bent and bleeding. She'd need a tourniquet. He crouched down, careful not to slide farther into the ravine. "I'm going to tie up your leg. It'll help stop the bleeding."

He took one of her scarves and began to tie the fabric above her knee. "If I've got time, I'm also going to set your shoulder. I want you to stay here, though. Nikola is still out there, and if she finds you, she will kill you without hesitation, all right?"

"She killed Rigan." Ruby barely moved her lips while speaking, her eyes bloodshot and her face tearstained.

Roderick went to tap her leg and found her tender to the touch. She recoiled away from him. "Ah, he was the navigator, right?" Roderick tried to keep her distracted. "Your friends are in a dangerous profession... What's your name?"

"You son of a bitch," Ruby groaned, thrashing forward and swinging. She missed miserably.

"Going to be like that." Roderick tsk'd, tying the knot tighter around her leg.

"You kidnapped all of them. They had a dangerous profession, but this isn't something they got themselves into, so don't act like it." Ruby winced at even Roderick's delicate touch. He covered her in her jackets. "Are they all dead?"

"I don't know. I came straight to you." Roderick placed his hand under her back and lifted her. "Are you going to let me set your shoulder?"

Ruby inspected him for a moment. "Why are you helping me if you think so little of my friends?"

"Because I do not think little of you." Roderick placed one arm on her back and the other on her arm. "If you yell, you could attract Nikola, okay? On three—One...two..." Roderick shoved her arm back into place and she let out a quiet but pain-filled yelp.

"What happened to three?" she hissed.

"It's always better when you don't see it coming." He smoothed her hair back before standing again. "I've stopped your bleeding for now. Stay out of trouble. I'll be back for you if I make it."

"You're leaving?" Although the idea of her safety hinging on her friends' death was upsetting, Roderick could clearly see she did not want to be alone. "Don't go, please."

It was then that there was a large crackle of static from the walkie-talkie at Roderick's hip. It was her voice.

"Boys, you see anything? Over." Nikola's voice buzzed.

Roderick picked up his radio cautiously, making eye contact with Ruby as he spoke. "All clear, over."

"Kal? Over," Nikola asked.

Roderick held his breath. Sergei would never betray him, but every time they had to lie for one another, he found himself getting a little light-headed.

"All clear," Sergei said. "Over."

Hearing Sergei's voice over the radio sent a wave of calmness over Roderick. "I won't be gone long." He grabbed onto an exposed rock and hoisted himself back up the bluff, then climbed until he met Sergei at the top.

Sergei helped him back over the ledge. "Are we done?"

"We're done." Roderick slid his Kevlar back on, feeling confident in his decision to help. "Once this is all over, I'll come back for her. You get Nikola to the van and I'll meet you both there."

Sergei nodded. For them, this was routine procedure. "Back it." They moved carefully, neither of them wanting to end up at the bottom of the ravine.

"You think Nikola found anything?" Roderick asked as they came back to Da Vinci's footprints.

"No, she would have at least let on about it on the radio."

"Unless she's hostage," Roderick gasped.

Sergei paused and looked Roderick dead in the face. They stared at one another for only a few seconds before laughing, loudly, seemingly proud.

"I didn't think so, either, but could you imagine?" Roderick then heard a rustle that sent chills up his spine. Someone was close.

"Shhhhhh." Sergei pulled Roderick back. The two of them quickly dipped farther into the brush. They listened. Whoever they heard was running down the mountain and quick. Sergei and Roderick both drew their guns, careful and quiet. "If you've got a shot at her," Sergei whispered, "take it."

Roderick nodded. They kept their attention wherever the sounds led them. Eventually, they came. It was Da Vinci and Diana tearing down the mountainside like banshees.

"I've got the shot." Roderick cocked his gun, readied his aim, and then smacked into the ground. Sergei had shoved him. He was just about ready to shout when the sound of gunfire cracked through the valley.

Two bullets ripped through Sergei's face.

"No!" Roderick's heart bottomed out as Sergei smacked the ground with a loud, crashing thud. He scrambled over to Sergei, who lay there, limp already, blood pouring out of his neck like a poolside tear. "Sergei. Sergei." Roderick strained his voice as he let out a broken cry. He clasped his hand around the side of Sergei's neck, pressurizing the wound.

It didn't matter, though. The poison was already pulsing through his veins. Sergei was clearly gone before he'd even hit the ground. It must've been the third teammate. Da Vinci and Diana had just been distractions. Odds are, Roderick was next if he stayed there by Sergei's body. At this point, he didn't care what happened next. He only lived because Nikola lunged down at him from a tree overhead.

"We've gotta move," she shouted.

Roderick latched on to Sergei and was moved only when Nikola yanked him off at full strength, the two of them just barely escaping another shot. They ran deeper into the woods. Roderick was frantic, but Nikola moved with laser precision, ducking and swaying until they were at the opposite edge of the bluff, far enough away that Roderick could scream. He collapsed into Nikola, hugging her bony body.

"I'm sorry, Roderick." Nikola's heart pounded hard enough that he could feel it.

"It's-it's—" Roderick's voice cleared up for a moment, his sobbing coming to a stop. "You-How—How do you know my name?"

"Sergei told me."

"He what?" Of course, she'd known. Roderick flushed with embarrassment, only to instantly let up into more sobbing. "He's gone. Oh, my god, Nikola. He's gone."

"He is." Nikola swallowed hard and hugged Roderick tighter.

"We were so much more than partners, Nikola."

"I know, I know." She pulled away, brushing a tear from his face.

ACROSS THE WOODS, the group reconvened. Tim joined Diana and Da Vinci in the clearing.

"She's fast." Diana crept toward the corpse cautiously, stepping through dead rhododendrons. She prodded Sergei's body with her foot a few times before swooping down and searching gear. He was unbreakable underneath all that skin. He'd been invincible like her. But the poison worked. "They got his weapon before they took off." She brushed off her skirt before stepping back over the brush and meeting up with Da Vinci and Tim again. "We're on the upside of this." Diana placed a hand on Da Vinci's back, slowly rubbing between his shoulder blades. "We outnumber them in strength alone now, all right?"

"All right," Da Vinci turned to her, and she gave him a smile. For a moment, she'd created serenity. It was then that she hit him over the head.

"What?" Tim shouted. "Don't worry. We outnumber them? And then you knock out our third member?" Tim balled his hands into fists, as though he was about to pummel Diana.

"Quiet down," she hissed. "You really want him running around when this goes down? When has he ever been anything less than trouble in combat?" She knew she made a good point. "We've got this, Tim. We have got this. And when it is all over, we will come back for him and find Ruby."

There was a moment where it seemed it would all explode, but Tim quickly simmered down. "You're right. It'll be easier without him."

Diana bent down and scooped Da Vinci up in her arms. "Now, let's hurry and hide him."

Backward

DECEMBER 12, 1963

Nikola's suitcase rolled methodically along the tile floor of the hall. She knew it was only a matter of time before she heard the familiar click of high heels, and right on time, they came.

"Nikola." Diana's voice cut across the hallway, but Nikola kept walking.

"You can't change my mind," Nikola called behind her.

"The hell I can't. Why didn't you tell me sooner?" Diana started toward Nikola. "You're just going to throw this away? All of this?" Diana demanded attention, her voice laced with such strong authority that for one tiny second Nikola hesitated in making her next step. Diana hurried behind her and grabbed her by the arm. Nikola spun around.

"What?" Nikola growled. "What could you possibly need from me? I am on my way out. Now let me go in peace."

"You're acting crazy, Wesley. Pull yourself together," Diana scolded. "Come with me. It'll take some string pulling, but I can sort this out with Adams."

There was that old name, *Wesley*. It made Nikola's skin feel like it was on fire. Wesley was dead. "There's nothing to talk about with Adams. I already talked to him. I've got my discharge papers. I'm going into a placement program, and I'm getting the hell out of here." Nikola yanked her arm away. "This isn't my line of work. It's yours." She tried reading Diana's soft, delicate face. She was looking for acceptance but couldn't find an ounce of it in her.

"Stop," Diana pleaded. "You don't want to do this. Not to yourself, not to the CIA, and not to me. You love this work."

"*You* love this work," Nikola snapped back, angrier than she'd expected. "You love lying and manipulating and killing. I may be good at this work, I may be goddamn excellent at it, but I do not love it." She turned away from Diana, only to find her arm grabbed again. "What?"

"I'm sorry." Diana frowned, reaching out to touch Nikola's face.

Nikola cringed away, contemplating whether or not beating the CIA's best agent into a pulp would be worth a lifetime on the run. "You're sorry? Yeah. All right. Sure. No, you're not."

"I love you, Wesley," Diana cooed. Her gaze cast to the ground and her doll-like face flushed red. "Please, think about me before you leave."

Any expression of cockiness vanished from Nikola's face. A stoic stone-like scowl replaced it. "I love the way you make me feel, Diana, but I don't love you. You're just another reason to leave." Nikola took Diana's hand from her arm and held it, using this intimate gesture only as an excuse to free herself from Diana's grip. "I've told you this a hundred times, but I will repeat myself again in hopes that it gets through to you. We are over, Diana. We have been over for months. You need to get off my back and leave me alone." Nikola pulled away from Diana and then pushed her suitcase out.

"Please, don't go, Wesley, for me. Just give me a few more days. I know I can convince you to stay."

"You can have anyone in the world, Diana. You don't need me." Nikola turned, her suitcase smoothly rolling again.

Diana still called out after her, "Listen, please."

Diana's voice was at a near whisper, causing Nikola to slow just a tad in order to hear the last of what she had to say.

"When I'm with you, my cheeks hurt from smiling so much," Diana pleaded. "When I'm with you, I'm excited about something. That's the only time I'm ever excited about anything. Everything else is so one-note. Everything is just gray, except when I'm with you, Wesley. Please, just turn around."

Nikola stopped. The click of Diana's heels still echoed in the hall. She turned slowly, her heart still hardened.

"You are the last humanity I have left. If you go, there'll be nothing. I'll be nothing." More than love, more than passion, desperation etched Diana's every word.

Nikola laughed and took a pause before she spoke. "Honey, there wasn't anything left when I got here. There sure as hell won't be anything left once I'm gone. Get over yourself." She resumed walking.

She was nearly scot-free when the first few shots rang out. Diana must have already had the pistol loaded. First, she shot out the cameras at the ends of the hall.

"What the hell are you—" In the time it took Nikola to swing around, Diana had already shot herself. "Hey!" Nikola dropped her bag and rushed over to her, catching her as she fell. "Jesus fucking Christ, you crazyass—" Nikola looked for where the blood was coming from. It was then that she saw it was just a simple shot through the skin on her non-dominate arm. "Of course, you wouldn't *really* hurt yourself."

"It got you over here, though, right? Don't be so cold, sweetheart."

Footsteps approached from the distance. A slew of grunts ran toward the source of the gunfire. There'd been four shots already. Why wouldn't they come?

"You can tourniquet yourself." Nikola let go of Diana and stood. As she rose, two security agents entered the end of the hall. "Hera's throwing another goddamn tantru—" Nikola's voice dropped off as two more shots were fired. Both bullets buried themselves deep into the skulls of the security agents. Nikola whipped around. "What the hell are you doing?"

Diana stood straight up. Her arm bled onto the ground, drops of red blotting the tile. She turned away from Nikola, a firearm locked in her hands. More security agents entered the hall and she fired again.

"Diana!" Nikola's voice was a guttural scream. She rushed over and then grabbed Diana from behind, spinning her around. The gun was now pointed at her. Nikola smiled and laughed. "You wanna shoot me? Go right on ahead."

Diana held the gun in line with Nikola's head, only to move it inches to the left and take out another group of security agents who were entering the hall. Her eyes looked vacant. She went to spin again like a machine, but Nikola stopped Diana. They struggled over the gun. Nikola dove for it and knocked Diana down. Diana shoved at her, firing at another couple agents entering the scene as she crashed against the floor. Nikola smacked against the ground, a wave of pain seizing her body, her ears rang from the gunfire and impact and the metallic smell of blood tinged the air. By the time Nikola managed to sit up, Diana was back on her feet, firing at another four agents, shooting them down like target practice. Twenty security agents to a floor and Diana had managed to kill them all.

"What's your game?" Nikola snarled, crawling back to her feet.

"Who do you think they'll blame?" Diana asked, her eyes glazing over as she pulled her luscious lips into a smile. "When they find us, who will they blame?"

"You." Nikola didn't miss a beat. "You've got a self-inflicted wound and a hell of a temper. Besides, they all know I don't have that kind of shot." Nikola's gaze was fixed on the pile of bodies at the right end of the hall.

"Will they, though? Pin it on me? Let's think." The tile under them was slick, saturated with blood. "Floor five. Administrative. Adams's floor. So, I ask again. Will they blame it on me?"

"He may love you, but he's not stupid." Nikola snorted. "How did you think this could work?"

"I don't think it will. I know it will. No video footage. No witnesses but us. The CIA's top female agent. Some semi-pro agent who was mysteriously leaving with little to no reason. I've got influence, Wesley, and I'm committed to the cause. You're the easier scapegoat. Admit it. What's harder to tell a widow, KIA or friendly fire?"

Nikola's heart sunk into her stomach. As much as she wanted to tell Diana she was wrong, she was right. Nikola could feel the floor giving way underneath her. Diana was right. All the evidence in the world didn't matter now.

"You bitch." Nikola covered her mouth with her hand. She could even feel her eyes tearing up just a hint. "I was supposed to get out," Nikola screeched, her voice echoing down the hall. "What the hell did you do?" Nikola took short, sharp inhales. "What the hell did you do?" Nikola swung at her and knocked her to the ground. She was quick to straddle her. Diana didn't put up a fight as her face broke with new cuts and bruises. Five minutes later, Adams found them, with Nikola still trying to kill Diana.

*

The snow began to fall right as the sun went down. Diana and Tim pushed through the woods, both listening closely, checking and rechecking the tree line, waiting for the time when their hearts would collectively jump and they were face to face with the enemy. The gun's cool metal was welcome in Diana's hands. Tim had taken out the last target, now it was her turn. They had four bullets left in the clip. There was no room to let them go to waste. And although with most other missions, there would be nothing wrong with the simple act of waiting, the last few months had made Tim and Diana more personal than clinical in their objectives. So, when Tim talked, Diana was not too surprised.

"Do you think we'll find Ruby when all is said and done?" Tim moved with his back to Diana.

"We will find her. I only hope she's still alive."

"I don't think he'll make it if we find her de—" Tim dropped silent for a moment at a rustling in the distance. He grabbed onto Diana, not saying a word but alerting her to the situation. She turned mechanically and rested her extended arms on his shoulder, the gun just beyond them. They stood there as one unit, their breath held, their hearts stopped, the wind just blowing enough to tousle their hair. They waited for a lost Roderick or a limping Ruby, but instead, a black bear crossed their path—there one second and gone the next.

"Nothing," Diana whispered, withdrawing her arms and returning to her position in front. They were walking only for a few seconds before Tim began to speak again.

"You seem tense."

Diana scoffed, rolling her eyes but not responding.

"Do you feel confident that you can kill her?"

"If I can't, you sure as hell can't." Diana drew her hair back and out of her face.

"I was not commenting on skill." Tim shrugged.

Diana paused, then turned toward him with her head at a slight angle. "What are you talking about?"

"You two have a history. The whole CIA knows it. Then, when we were on the mountain, right after you peeled her off Ruby—" Tim relaxed his stance, he seemed comfortable, as though he was asking her about something as simple as laundry. "—you both took a spill down a ravine and were down there more than long enough to fight, but you chose not to. There was not so much as the sound of a scuffle. You came back unharmed. She did, too. So, what happened?"

"You're out of line. You have no authority asking me about my tactics and decision-making. Resume your post," Diana chided.

"Wow," Tim huffed. "Diana, we have been out of the ranks a long time now. I am asking a simple question. There's no harm if you want me to kill her for you."

Diana stood her ground, glaring.

"I'm just saying. If you can't kill her, I won't be surprised. I would love to be the one to pull the trigger, honestly. She w—" Tim's voice dropped as two of their shared bullets sliced through his abdomen, stopping his words and his heart. He looked at Diana, devoid of anything but shock and an overwhelming rage. "Y-You." Tim fell forward, collapsing.

Diana took him into her arms.

"Y-You bitch." Tim panted in between his body seizing.

Diana's next words were precisely chosen, knowing that Tim had only seconds left before the poison took him. "You are a man of many despicable acts, Tim, but what I always hated the most was the way you'd pretend to read over my shoulder, just to get a whiff of my hairspray." Diana didn't hesitate to drop him to the ground. His body thudded as it hit. He weakly reached for her ankles like a wounded animal. Diana stayed and spoke over him, providing one last romantic gesture before she departed. "Whatever our fate is or may be, we have made it and do not complain of it."

And it was there she left him, crumpled upon the ground, dead. She was confident in her own skills to get her, Da Vinci, and Ruby out of the woods alive.

RODERICK GASPED AND Nikola was quick to cover his mouth as the two of them watched Diana murder her partner from the top of the mountain. Since their initial engagement, Roderick hadn't stopped shaking. His pulse pounded against her arm where it lay on the side of his neck. After what felt like forever, he pulled away.

"You were right," Roderick whispered, his eyes filling with tears again.

Nikola nodded, turning away from their view of the clearing.

"Why would she do that? She's got nothing to gain from being a man down." Roderick followed Nikola into the maze of pines that concealed them.

"She doesn't need him," Nikola replied. "In her mind, she's competent enough to handle the two of us. Whether we get that gun away from her or not, it doesn't matter. You know that, right?"

"Right," Roderick said. "We're not like they are. The steroid didn't take to us in that way. We're...still destroyable. Still warm-blooded."

"Good." Nikola cocked her gun and handed it off to Roderick. "Keeping that in mind, I want to offer you a chance to run. I won't report on it for at least another few hours. I don't feel confident enough in my ability to protect you from her, not without Sergei. You may be a hell of a shot, but if she gets even one swing at you, that could be it."

Roderick gulped. He seemed to be taking his time in choosing his next words. "Come with me. We'll go back, report, come back with more agents."

Nikola shook her head. "I've got unfinished business with her. I'm not going anywhere."

Roderick took her hand for a moment and squeezed it gently. "You won't hate me for this?"

"I'd think you're an idiot if you didn't run," Nikola answered truthfully, beaming the same skeptical but confident look she always did.

"Thank you," he said. "For everything."

"Go before I change my mind."

And like that, Roderick ran, leaving Nikola to her vices and the goddess.

WHEN NIKOLA FINALLY came down the mountain, Diana found herself at a loss for words for the first time in a long time. Since the day Nikola brought Rigan to them, Diana had run through this moment. She knew it'd come, but here she was, still stunned by the Nikola's beauty, something no amount of preparation could have accounted for. Before Diana had much of a chance to think, her head gently tilted to the side in admiration. Diana laughed that same low, closemouthed laugh.

"Sweetheart, how long it's been."

Nikola raised her brow skeptically. "I'm here to kill you, Diana. We're a long way past *sweetheart*."

Nikola's words sent a wave of cold through Diana. "So quick to speak, Wesley. Are you sure you don't want to rethink that?"

"Wesley?" Nikola laughed, her head thrown back and her mouth open in a smile. "Oh, Diana, you don't get to call me that anymore." Nikola tilted her head and mimicked Diana, her neck craning forward and bringing their faces to a near touch.

"Why's that?" Diana cooed.

"You killed her." Nikola laughed again, her nose brushing against Diana's right before she swung. Diana's skin cracked underneath Nikola's fist and chips of flesh drifted to the snow. Diana was quick to retaliate, reaching to grab Nikola's arm before she had a chance to retract, but she failed. Nikola moved faster than expected. Nikola swung again but was caught this time. Diana twisted her arm, ready for it to break. Pieces of her own skin chipped off from the intensity with which she yanked, but Nikola slid right out of it, her body and bones flexing.

"Fine, we'll play it that way." Diana raised her gun and fired. Nikola shifted to the right and the bullet whizzed past her. Nikola swung again and missed Diana as she ducked and dove, then wrapped her arms around Nikola's waist and brought them both to the ground. Diana kept her arms locked around her as they landed, squeezing as hard as she could, pieces of her shoulder cracking and rehealing as she crushed Nikola.

Thrashing, Nikola landed a few ineffective kicks. "So," Nikola huffed, trying to free one of her arms. "Three bullets shot in battle, two bullets to kill Kal, two bullets for your friend." Nikola wormed one of her arms out of Diana's grip. "One you missed. So what? That leaves you with...one?"

Nikola's bones bowed under the pressure of Diana's grip. "You saw that?"

"You killing another partner?" Nikola took a sharp breath, then extended her claws and dug her free hand deep into Diana's arms. Diana lurched away. Nikola sprang out of her grip and bounced back onto her feet with a loud, rasping groan. "I wouldn't miss it for the world."

Diana stared at her arm, watching as Nikola's claw marks failed to heal over. She bled. "Like you didn't just kill yours. Too selfish to let the twit in on the fight?" Diana rose back to her feet. She could feel the hate radiating from Nikola. She'd been warm to the touch. "You should reconsider. Even if the bullets run out, something tells me, I don't need them to kill you. You didn't need poison to claw the life out of that poor boy back in the woods."

"You've killed more than a few poor boys," Nikola said before rushing Diana. She plowed into her stomach and sent her spiraling backward.

Diana went airborne from the force of Nikola's hit, but skimmed the ground with one hand and took control of the momentum with a flip.

Nikola drew her gun and fired. Diana narrowly escaped the poisoned fate with a dive and roll to the right. Nikola took a few steps closer, bettering her aim. She closed one eye and looked down the front sight, only to stop short of placing her finger on the trigger.

"Second thoughts?" Diana steadied herself and took a few steps closer to Nikola.

"I'm just wondering. Being out here in the woods and all, has anyone had the guts to tell you how goddamn hideous you look?" Nikola fired the gun. What she hadn't accounted for was Diana charging at her so quickly.

They hit. Nikola and Diana both sprawled on the ground. Diana reached to grab Nikola's neck, but Nikola snatched her wrists seconds before she could break her neck. Diana yanked her arm back with enough strength that it pulled Nikola's arm from the socket. Nikola gasped and gritted her teeth from the pain. Quickly, Nikola let go of Diana's arm and slashed with her free arm. She dragged her claws across Diana's face, then rolled over onto Diana's opposite side. She jumped to her feet, her dislocated arm hanging there limp.

Covering the open wound on her face, Diana pushed herself off the ground and back to her feet.

"You sure you want to keep this fight going, sweetheart? Seems like you need a minute." Diana let out a sickeningly sweet laugh, and Nikola pounced at her. She charged, then propelled herself up off Diana's knee and wrapped her legs around her former love's neck. They smashed into the ground, and before Diana could throw a fist, Nikola had one of her arms in a tight grip and her throat surrounded by two tight, crushing calves.

Diana laughed loudly, unafraid. "You'd think it would work," Diana coughed, wrapping one arm around Nikola's calf and another around her thigh. "But I spent an entire fucking day in the bottom of a lake. Breathing's optional, sweetheart." And like that, Diana shoved her arms in opposite directions and Nikola's leg snapped in two.

Nikola screamed, her eyes welling with tears. "Oh, god," She struggled to move.

Diana sat up from in between Nikola's legs nonchalantly and pushed herself free with grace. "You knew better than this, Wesley. I made you."

Nikola let out one loud, curt laugh. "You don't create. You destroy."

Diana grabbed the nearest rock and slammed it across Nikola's face.

Nikola gagged as blood filled her mouth. She gurgled something, something she wanted Diana to hear, but Diana was already looking away, thinking through how she'd rescue Ruby and Da Vinci.

Nikola grabbed at her wrist in desperation. "Y-You." Nikola coughed, blood spattering the snow and mud.

"What was that?" Diana teased, tilting her head and leaning forward just a bit.

Nikola spoke again, her words coming out in a soft whisper. "Honey." Nikola's grip lessened as her words dropped down to nearly inaudible.

Diana leaned farther and smoothed her hair. "Honey? I thought we were past cute nicknames."

"Honey." Blood speckled Nikola's face. "At least...put me..." Nikola took labored breaths. "Put me out...of my fucking misery."

"That's not a terribly nice way of asking." Diana hadn't meant to, but she laughed, more pleased with herself than anything else.

"Please."

Diana smiled, allowing just a hint of teeth to show between her deep purple lips. She slid her hands up Nikola's neck and rested one hand underneath her chin. Before she twisted, she smiled, leaned forward, and dipped her face closer to Nikola's.

"I have always loved you." Diana wouldn't be able to live with herself if she hadn't said it. She wanted Nikola to know that even at the very end, it could have all been avoided.

Nikola looked up at her. Her face was neutral, hard to read. Diana couldn't expect much from someone dying. Finally, Nikola said, "I haven't."

And like that, Nikola's gun went off and Diana felt the sharp, cool rush of poison surging through her veins. Her arms went limp first, and then her vision started to tunnel. It happened so quickly. It happened all at once. She let out a low yelp and slumped over, her body curling in on itself.

"And you said seduction wasn't my bag." Nikola laughed again, her teeth bloodied and grinding. This was it. This was the last thing she'd ever see.

Who I Was

DECEMBER 12, 1963

When looking up, there was nothing to see but stars and snow. Da Vinci felt the cold on his face and deep in the bones of his hands. Everything dawned on him at once. He jolted up as his stomach bottomed out. It was done. It had to be. He hadn't even had a chance to try to stop what he knew would come. A stabbing pain pulsated on the right side of his skull. They'd knocked him out. It was likely the only reason he'd lived.

He stood now. He had to find them. He had to move what was left of them. There couldn't be any bodies to find. First, Da Vinci went to where they'd killed Sergei, but the body was already gone. He then searched for the others. He found Tim first, who was crumpled over on himself and stiff. Da Vinci shut his partner's eyes before dragging him to the waterfall and burying him along with Rigan. It was funny to think their bodies would be down there together forever, given the problems they'd had in life.

Da Vinci continued searching until he found the second KGB agent. Nikola was on the ground, curled up on just a few hundred yards away from the clearing where she and Diana fought. Blood stained the snow around her and a makeshift tourniquet was tied tightly on her broken leg. Her mouth hung open post-mortem and her lips were drained of any color.

Da Vinci stood over her for a second. He wanted to blame her for what happened, give himself a faceless villain to hate, but he couldn't bring himself to despise her. She'd meant too much to Diana to be hated. He closed her eyes, too, feeling the coarseness of her skin on his fingertips. He brushed a hand over her face, then stood and pulled her along the same path he'd taken Tim. He dropped her in the river, as well. Rigan and his killer would be buried together. Da Vinci could feel his heart pounding and his system draining, but he had one more body to dispose of, one more tithe to pay.

He found Diana faceup, not too far from the ledge of a bluff. She'd been shot. Just like Da Vinci had seen it play out hundreds of times. Everything he'd been trying to stop led up to this moment. But when it came down to the wire, he was still alive and she was still dead. It was while standing over her that Da Vinci realized he'd been crying. He could feel the wetness of his face with his hands, but could not feel the tears as they ran over his cheeks. He slumped down and sat, then took her head in his lap. He closed her eyes and smoothed her hair. His breath shook. He'd seen this play out countless times. That moment when he'd find Diana dead, but in no scenario did it hurt this much. In no scenario did she look this dead. In no vision did he foresee his own will to live dying off with her. He collapsed, certain he'd rest there only for a few minutes.

He didn't move till the sun was starting to rise and Roderick wrapped his hand around his shoulders. "Come on, mate. It's time to go."

In his hours sitting there, he had seen the fall of nations, the wrath of man, and of course the death of his own son. A vision that revisited him as often as he revisited it.

His gaze left Diana's body for the first time in hours. "You lived."

"Surprisingly."

A silence fell over the two of them. In the break of dawn, they watched each other. "We don't kill each other," Da Vinci finally said. "Not now, not later."

"She's asking for you." Roderick ignored Da Vinci's proclamation. "She doesn't know the others didn't make it."

Da Vinci glanced back to Diana's corpse. He was once again being taken by visions of her healthy on the night they first kissed.

"I moved my partner's body. The river is a smart choice."

Da Vinci raised his brow in surprise. "How did you know?"

"We saw you bury the boy, but we waited till you were done to attack."

Da Vinci closed his eyes and lingered in the dark. "I'm sorry about your friends."

"I'm sorry about yours."

Swallowing hard, Da Vinci stood and then grabbed Diana's wrists. He went to drag her when Roderick stopped him.

"Here." Roderick took her ankles and helped lift.

As they walked, Da Vinci talked. "How did they go out? I know they were both shot, but I never saw who pulled the trigger."

"Huh," Roderick grunted as the two maneuvered down a steep slope. "I thought you of all people would know. Hera killed Dresden. I'm assuming Nikola killed Hera. I wasn't actually there to see it."

Da Vinci stopped in his tracks. His palms sweated despite the intense chill in the air. "Hera killed Dresden?"

"I'm sorry." Roderick and Da Vinci briefly traveled together until they came to the lip of the river at the bottom on where their allies now resided. They moved her body over the bank and released her. Diana vanished under the waves.

"I think I'll be going now." Roderick's morale seemed to fall apart with the last of the bodies gone. "I'll file a false-success report. That should buy you and the girl a few days. I'll be gone by the time they realize what's happened. It's about time I leave this business."

Da Vinci let out one short, sudden laugh. It was loud and filled with just a subtle suggestion of happiness that felt out of place next to a mass grave. "I wouldn't count on it."

"What?" Roderick paused, giving Da Vinci a confused expression. Somewhere along the line, it must have dawned on him that Da Vinci saw all. Da Vinci knew all. "Ha. Guess not. That's very typical of me."

"Until we meet again, Roderick." Da Vinci pulled his jacket in closer and then tightened his bandana. He wiped away the grime on his face with the back of his hands.

"You know my name. Guess it's only fair. Right, Da Vinci?" Roderick laughed again, louder this time. "Guess I shouldn't be too surprised. Until then." Roderick walked opposite Da Vinci, heading back to the west side of the mountain.

WHEN HE ARRIVED, Da Vinci could hear Ruby arguing with hospital staff from behind the doors of the elevator.

"Don't call them yet," Ruby shrieked.

The doctor was halfway through ordering a nurse to restrain her when Da Vinci knocked on the doorframe.

"What is going on in here?" Da Vinci would have shouted it, but his energy was zapped.

"You must be the girl's father." The doctor hurried over to him and began rattling off medical jargon and recommendations.

Da Vinci was quick to stop it. "If I could please just have a couple minutes alone with her?"

"As you see fit, Mr. Harrison." The doctor stuffed his hands in his pockets. "Please alert the nurses' station when you're ready to talk."

The door clicked behind the staff.

"Ms. Robin Harrison," Da Vinci started. "That's something I never thought I'd hear. You gave your real name."

"I wanted my folks to know if I was dead." There was something so hollow about the way she said these things. "How do you know it's my real name, anyway?"

"Keeping secrets was not one of Rigan's strengths." Da Vinci pulled up a chair next to the bed where Ruby lay, her leg propped up in a sling.

"The others..."

Da Vinci shook his head. "They knew they weren't going to make it out of there. This is what they wanted." He assured her with the little white lies he would tell himself on the harder nights.

"I'm happy you made it out okay."

"Me, too." Da Vinci patted the top of her hand before glancing at the clock above the doorframe. "We don't have much time. I have someone I need to go meet."

"The agent who saved me?"

"No." Da Vinci shook his head. "Someone else, but you have to believe me when I say that I will come back. Not soon, but I will."

"What?" Ruby widened her eyes and her heart rate spiked so quickly the monitor lagged behind it. "You're leaving me, too?"

"I have to. For you to be safe and be able to live a normal life, I have to, Ruby. It isn't safe for us to be in contact right now."

"Da Vinci, you can't." Her mouth hung just open, her breathing shallow. "I...I...What if something happens? What if more agents come?"

"They won't. I promise you they won't, but you have to let me go for now."

"Where are you going to go?"

"I'm going to see my son." It was such a pretty lie. "There's a war coming, a big one. Lots of people are going to die and he's going to be one of them."

"More death." Ruby stared at her lap. "I'm so sorry."

"I'll be all right, and so will you, okay?"

"I'm scared." She teared up.

"Here." Da Vinci took a pencil and notepad from the bedside table next to her. It was watermarked with the hospital's logo. "Take this address and write to me. You remember the cipher Diana taught you?"

Ruby nodded in confirmation.

"Use it." He then scribbled a number below it. "And call this number, but only in a serious emergency. Things are going to be rough at first, but you'll grow back into your old life. You have to. This dark, horrible world I'm in, that Rigan was in, it doesn't have to be yours, but you have to make that choice, Ruby. Contact me when you need me and know that I am looking out for you. We'll see each other in due time."

"I've spent nearly every day for the past three months with you all, and I'm just supposed to go on pretending nothing happened?"

Da Vinci smiled sadly. "For now. It's the only way to guarantee your safety."

She hesitated before speaking. "Do you know this because you've seen it? Or is this...uh...wishful thinking?"

Da Vinci moved his shoulders with exhausted exaggeration. "I know how you die, Ruby Starr, and it's got nothing to do with spies."

"Okay," Ruby said. "And you have to go...in order to make that happen?"

"Yes." A tear ran down Da Vinci's cheek. "You don't want to know how you die?"

"And torture myself like you? No, thanks." She smiled through the pain. What was done, was done.

"Before I go, I need you to promise me three things."

"Anything."

"First, you steer clear of drugs. There's a plague coming and I don't want you in the middle of it. Second, you stay in the hospital long enough for your parents to come visit you."

Ruby opened her mouth to protest, but Da Vinci quickly shut her down.

"I said come and visit. You don't have to move back in." He teased her with a melancholy kind of tone. "Give your folks some closure and peace of mind before you run off into the great beyond, kid."

Her face relaxed as she listened to his third stipulation.

"And last—" He dug into his back pocket and fished from it an old, beaten compass. "I want you to take this."

Ruby held it in her hands and ran her thumb across the scratched-up glass.

"It was mine, and then it was Rigan's, and now it is yours. Whenever you start to doubt if any of it *really* happened, I want you to hold onto this, all right? It was real. We were real. We mattered."

"I'm going to miss you, Da Vinci." Ruby nodded tentatively, likely not understanding the gravity of his words.

"I'm gonna miss you, kid." He leaned over the barricade of the bed and hugged her before standing. "I'm going to leave now, but I won't be gone too long, all right? Just long enough."

Ruby bit her lip and smiled, simple tears running down her face.

As Da Vinci left, he remembered the first time he'd seen all the day's deaths unfold some months ago in the basement of the KGB facility. Da Vinci revisited this memory all too often. It was the last time he'd spoken to her before he knew. The last time he saw her before he saw her death. There was a careless optimism about his former self that he envied. But his wallowing was cut short by the wailing of a steam engine and the reappearance of three familiar faces.

The tall always-graceful Minerva stepped off the train first. Sleek, swooning Geronimo followed her, and behind them was Adams. Da Vinci stopped them all midstride.

"Niccolò." Adams sounded surprised.

"You're alive." Geronimo smiled, wide. "Where are the others?"

Da Vinci maintained eye contact with Adams. "Top of the mountain by Hazel Creek. Nothing left but a remains recovery."

"Shit." Minerva balled her hands into fists.

Adams turned to his partners, then removed and cleaned his thin-framed glasses. "You two go. I'll be there shortly."

Geronimo turned and started off toward the end of the train terminal. Minerva stayed back only for a second before following.

"How'd she go?" Adams asked, then walked past Da Vinci and sat on a small, wooden bench close by.

"Nikola." Da Vinci joined him on the bench.

Adams had an expression on that showed little surprise but great sadness. "Always knew that one would come back to haunt her...Marco and Dresden?"

"Both killed by Nikola," Da Vinci assured him. "They died defending her."

"What about Nikola's team?"

"No team." Da Vinci shook his head. "She'd gone rogue."

They sat for a moment, staring out at the trains pulling away from the station, and the crowds of people hurrying by.

Eventually, Adams said, "I'm sorry about Marco."

"I'm sorry about Hera." Da Vinci ran his hands along his head, smoothing his bandana. "I don't think I can do this anymore, Adams."

"Give it time," Adams hushed him. "We'll go over your options later."

Da Vinci sat, knowing he had only one option. He'd spend the rest of his life protecting Ruby Starr. She'd get to live. She'd get to be happy. They'd all died for her. In due time, he'd die for her, too. Da Vinci stood and followed Adams out of the station, back to the woods where he knew no bodies would be found.

Epilogue

JULY 3, 1965

Ruby rested her elbow on the diner counter, she had a Coke in her hand and a straw pressed between her plump lips. Her hair was beautiful and wild, curls in every direction. She had not only a compass dangling on a chain around her neck, but also the attention of all the patrons at the diner's counter.

"So, I'm running as fast as I can, and my feet are slipping and sliding on the ice of the mountain, and for a second there, I think I'm going to go over the edge of this cliff. When all of a sudden...*Wham!*" Ruby slammed her hand on the diner's counter and the girls listening all jumped in their seats. "A yeti bigger than my van comes tearing out of a cave and runs right past me." She spread her arms as wide as they'd go, showing just how large the yeti had been. "I catch my balance and narrowly escape with my life. I was this close." Ruby held up her hand and pressed her thumb and index finger close together. "To death and the yeti, come to think of it."

"Bull!" A tall, dark-skinned girl cocked her head to the side and jumped down from her seat at the counter, pulling Ruby's attention away from the flock of listeners and centering it on herself. "I can believe the one about aliens in Greece. I can even believe the one with the groovy harpoon death on an ocean liner, but Ruby Starr, I cannot—*cannot* believe that a North American yeti would reveal itself so easily. That just don't make sense."

"Misty, girl, you are always bringing me down." Ruby sighed, looking to her friend Bruno for support. "Bruno, do *you* get me?"

"Mission control, I hear you loud and clear." He laughed, wrinkling his forehead.

"But are you receiving?" Misty pulled off Bruno's hat and placed it on her head. "Come on. Let's blow out of here. We've still got a couple hours left before dark. I bet we can make it even closer than last time."

Ruby picked up her bag from the counter and left a few spare bills as a tip. "You two are always tag-teaming me." She pouted.

As they stepped outside, the desert heat hit her. They were in for a long day and an even longer night. Ready to roll, she slid on a pair of sunglasses and dug her keys out of her purse. She paused only when the sound of a motorbike echoing off in the distance caught her attention. For a moment, her heart broke and overwhelming sadness took her, followed by overwhelming happiness.

Acknowledgements

Many thanks to my parents for their immeasurable love and support.

Thank you to my partner Pedro for encouraging me to follow my dreams when I was ready to give up.

Unyielding thanks to the team over at Nine Star Press for picking me out of hundreds of twitter pitches and helping improve both the manuscript and myself.

A grand bow to Sara Gay, Brett Hill, Alec Schaeffer, and Andrea Stimpson for reading the book in its earliest draft −I speak for all of us when I say *yikes*.

And a special shout out to Susan Halle Hays and the rangers over at the Smokey Mountain National Park visitor's center for always ensuring my love of history was strong and fiercely fact checked.

About the Author

Hannah Carmack is a writer and spends most of her time connecting reluctant readers and bookworms alike to the world of literature and science. Although living with an auto-immune disease is difficult, she finds power in using her writing as a way to convey the world that people with disabilities live in to people who may not fully comprehend it.

Website: www.hannahcarmack.com

Facebook: www.facebook.com/HannahCarmackAuthor

Twitter: @manlyhamm

Instagram: www.instagram.com/manlyhamm

Also Available from NineStar Press

Connect with NineStar Press

www.ninestarpress.com

www.facebook.com/ninestarpress

www.facebook.com/groups/NineStarNiche

www.twitter.com/ninestarpress

www.tumblr.com/blog/ninestarpress